HENRY TREECE was born in the West Midlands in December 1911. Educated at Wednesbury High School he won a scholarship to Birmingham University where he graduated in 1933. War-time service as an intelligence officer with R.A.F. Bomber Command interrupted a very fine teaching career. His literary career began as a poet; Messrs Faber published four volumes. Contact with George Orwell helped him enter the world of radio broadcasting of verse plays, short stories and schools programmes. In 1952 came Treece's first historical novel, *The Dark Island,* and during the years until his death in June 1966 he wrote a succession of Celtic novels for adults, including *The Great Captains, The Golden Strangers* and *Red Queen, White Queen,* as well as the Greek novels *Electra, Jason* and *Oedipus. The Green Man* in 1966 was the last adult work. His work also included criticism and a number of co-edited anthologies *War-Time Harvest, Transformation* and others. Among the many historical novels for children are the Roman books *Legions of the Eagle* and *The Eagles Have Flown;* the trilogy *Viking's Dawn, The Road to Miklagard* and *Viking's Sunset; Man with a Sword* (Hereward the Wake); and the much praised posthumously published *The Dream Time.* Mary Treece, his widow, lives in Abingdon, in Oxfordshire.

# Henry Treece

# THE
# GOLDEN STRANGERS

**Introduced by Michael Moorcock**
**Illustrated by James Cawthorn**

## SAVOY BOOKS
in association with
### NEW ENGLISH LIBRARY
TIMES MIRROR

First paperback edition
Savoy Books Ltd 1980

First published by
John Lane The Bodley Head Ltd 1956

Copyright Henry Treece 1956

Cover artwork: Michael Heslop

Published by Savoy Books Ltd,
279 Deansgate, Manchester M3 4EW

Printed by Hazell Watson & Viney Ltd.,
Aylesbury, Bucks.

ISBN 0 86130 018 1

The chapter "Notes on Vision and Perception"
which appears at the end of this book is taken
from *The Bodley Head Monograph on Henry
Treece, Ed by Margery Fisher,* and is printed
by kind permission of Mary Treece.

The short introduction to this chapter was
written by Margery Fisher and appears by
permission of The Bodley Head.

# Introduction

*I step from a land no eye has seen*
*To a land no hand may ever hold;*
*My name with the sea's cold tears is green,*
*My words are the wind's words graved in gold.*

That first verse from the first poem in Henry Treece's first published book of poems (*Invitation and Warning*, 1943) is probably as good a statement as any of Henry Treece's outlook. A Romantic who followed a form of anarchism (he received encouragement in the thirties from Sir Herbert Read), he was a leading light in the movement which called itself the New Apocalypse and his early fame was as a poet. His earlier novels (of which this is one) show more of this spirit, in my view, than do the later ones. He was always at his best on territory he 'felt' and I suspect he 'felt' Britain more than he did the Hellenic world of his later books (*Jason, Electra, Oedipus*). Even his anarchism was typically British. He came from more or less the same part of the world as J.R.R. Tolkien and his romanticism has something in common with Tolkien's, though his prose, his imagination, his eye on the world, are all far tougher than anything Tolkien or any other Bagginseer could come up with.

Even those of us now jaded by too many stones, too many mysterious ravens, too many Old Ones, too many portents, dooms, Celtic twilights and Saxon dawns, will find a freshness in Treece's tales of Ancient Britain: perhaps because he was the first to imagine with clarity and realism what human beings were like and what their attitude to Corn Men, Green Men and even Chalk Men was likely to be in actuality: for his characters are not the romanticised adolescents of generic Stone books. Unless they are described as adolescents, they are usually mature men and women who know the score. They do not necessarily have the information, but they certainly have the experience. They might see things in magical terms, but they are rational. They are of their own time.

Fundamentally what we are reading in *The Golden Strangers* is the story of one race's fight for survival against a more powerful race equipped with a superior technology. This is the story of the centuries and it is a story which has yet to see a conclusion. It is set in a past which was in some ways simpler; but the issues are the same. The actions of the Great Powers in the Third World are not so very different from those of the Cattle Lords in the land of the People of the Hills, except the Cattle Lords are a little less hypocritical. It is worth remembering, that Indians are still being poisoned in Brazil according to semi-official policy, because their land is in demand. One can read Treece, if one wishes, in this light: for an insight into the issues and the methods employed when one race embarks on the conquest of another. At least the Cattle Lords had no ethic to justify their actions, no sense of the future to rationalise their genocide.

In this book equilibrium is achieved, if only for a while. The story continues. It continues in books which chronologically follow this one — *The Dark Island, Red Queen, White Queen* and *The Great Captains*. It continues in Britain to this day.

Michael Moorcock
Ladbroke Grove
May 1979

# Barley Dream

A T LAST the ice withdrew over the edge of the world and now, wherever willow did not grow, the wide plains swarmed with creatures, reindeer and buffalo, so that the masked Hunters forgot the thin days when they had dug deep in the ground for frozen roots and grubs. Now they had but to cast a spear to eat meat for a week.

Then as darkness fled and sun smiled warmly on the land, the rains began to fall. Trees planted themselves wherever they could find a footing—birch and pine, oak and elm, hazel and indomitable alder.

So the hunting grounds became fewer, for the trees' great army had occupied the land, and at last men looked towards the sea for food, forgetting the sweet taste of deer and giant ox.

At length, majestic, sea roared down the tree-hung valley, and one golden morning an island stood separate, new-born, afraid with loneliness. Those who came now must cross in boats, must dare death in the valley, among the blackened oaks.

This was the way the dark folk came, the little ones who brought the barley seeds.

The hungry hawk, poised high above the hills, at last looked down on a land that shaped itself into something it had not been before, an island that had made up its dark mind to live, in its fashion, to give home to men, to such men as were brave enough to help in the remaking of a world.

And this hawk saw the roads these men trod for themselves, white snail-tracks, high above the dusky woods, running the length of the land wherever ridges were; saw the great stones pointing, stark fingers to the sky, from hill-top to hill-top, guiding the dark ones down their spider's webs; saw the brown villages, clustered hives, grabbed in a hedge of thorn, whose fires must never be allowed to die; saw the strange barley-fields, set round with lumps of chalk.

Kaleidoscopic eye swept over hill-top corral where the short-horned cattle lowed; swept down the slope to where a shepherd lad leaned with his back against an ancient tomb, dreaming of barley-cakes and honeyed milk, leaving his dogs to watch the thin-legged flock.

The hawk's keen eye followed the flax-field down, down past the clustered bracken in the wood. There by a fallen oak a blind man lay, happy in sunlight, grunting to his herd.

The hawk's red eye tasted the jostling swine, picked out the farrowing sow who struggled from the crowd into the sheltering patch of willow herb, swollen with time.

"Now! Now!" the buzzard's cold heart urged.

"Now! Now!" called beak and talons back.

The hawk's stone eye saw feast below it laid, red meat among the fern—and stooped to strike.

Then stone to stone, flint arrow-head struck deep, and plummet to the earth the buzzard fell, grey feathers scattered careless on the herd, among the squeaking new-born farrowlings.

Archer, smiling in his dark-eyed way, watched tired sow take up the staring hawk, watched those gold eyes ringed round with blood's bright hue, stare fearless down the glistening dark maw.

So hawk was paid. He'd known the best, the worst.

The Archer watched the sow crunch up the bird. More hawk than swine, regretting the quick loss of that dear arrowhead, he walked up to the village, wondering.

The land was born. Yet with its birth had come another thing that made men fear the force that gave them life.

'A payment must be made,' they said, 'for nothing comes of nothing.'

They said, 'The bread we eat calls out for blood. Out of the belly of the earth it comes. Into that belly we must pour our blood if we would prosper. Nothing is given for nothing, barley asks for blood.'

So grew the Barley Dream, out of men's fear, and so the Earth, as though anxious to please her new children, created signs for them to follow, granting their wayward hearts permission to shed blood in the furrows every year.

# PART ONE

---

## Dark Folk

---

# 1: Strangers

TWO-FINGERS stood on the bare chalk hill-top, black as a stone against the red sun. He was quite still. Even the clay beads on the thong round his neck had stopped clinking against each other. He was listening, his thin dark face screwed up like an otter's, his broad nostrils opening and shutting as though he might find the scent he wanted, wanted and feared, if only he tried hard enough.

Then it came to him like a harsh slap in the face, and he knew. 'Hair! Hair!' he said to himself, for in his village below the hill no man must ever name a wolf. That would be the quickest way to bring them howling round the stockade at night.

He reached down to his cow-hide belt for the polished green-stone axe with his right hand. Then he remembered and dragged the axe out with his left. His right hand was only a finger and a thumb, barely healed yet, and they would not hold an axe. It had happened only recently, the adder-bite, when he was gathering red berries, and did not see the coiling creature till it had bitten him. He was not used to it yet, just a thumb and a finger.

As he grasped the axe, he recalled the Old Man curing him of the bite. His arm was swollen and red in long streaks when they found him. The Old Man made them hold him down while he did what had to be done with his keen black-flint knife. Two-fingers did not remember it all. But he remembered someone screaming, and then he was home again, in his mother's house under the stockade. The Old Man made a paste with the three fingers and tied it to his swollen arm with strips of flax cloth. Two-fingers was able to walk and talk again when three moons had come and gone. He was grateful to the Old Man. That must have been strong magic. Now he must repay the Old Man and tell him quickly about Hair.

Below him the little sheep nibbled at the short wiry grass. They had smelled nothing. Nor had the two young dogs who lay beside them. Two-fingers was angry with the dogs for not smelling Hair. He thought of hitting them on their heads, just hard enough, with the axe, but then he remembered they were little more than puppies and did not know much as yet. The Old Man had asked for their mother, the trained bitch, at the time of fires, before snow-falling. She went into the big fire, with the other animals. There was a baby in the same fire, one from a young man's house, too poor yet to own animals. Two-fingers thought how lucky that man was, not to lose a trained sheepdog, as he had done. Yet the fire was a success, for the snows came and went quickly, and the Old Man was right. He had guided his people through the dark-year once more and into the light.

Two-fingers drew out a little bone whistle, carved with bulls and stags. It was very old—older than the People of the Hill. His father had found it deep in the dank moss of the oak forest that swirled below the hill, about the river. Two-fingers only used it on special occasions like this, for he was afraid to waste its magic by blowing through it too often. It was made by the early folk, he knew, and they were powerful spirits. Now he blew it gently and the two dogs sprang silently into action, as though wakened from sleep, jostling the puzzled sheep down the hill.

Two-fingers followed, looking fearfully over his shoulder from time to time, lest Hair was behind him. He wondered whether to drive the sheep over the hill's shoulder to the next one, where the village had its great earthwork corral, protected with rampart and ditch. But perhaps there would not be time. He hurried on, turning his head away from the Long House that suddenly loomed out of the dusk, a fearsome hunchbacked thing. This was the place of long silence, where the most important of the People of the Hill went, back into the womb of Earth Mother, to lie in their rows, painted with bright red ochre to represent the blood of birth. Its stone entrance seemed to yawn at him and he struck himself hard on the temple with the antler shaft of the axe, as a gesture to Earth Mother. She let him pass on safely down the hill, so he knew that she was not too angry with him.

An owl started from a gorse bush and Two-fingers was almost sick with fright. At first he thought it was the man they had put at the bottom of the mine-shaft when they sank the new cutting for flint. His bones were still there and each miner touched them when he climbed down the notched tree-trunk in the morning on his way to work. That ensured a good day in the curving, treacherous galleries where the hard keen flints were dug with the antler-picks. Two-fingers barely remembered the man being put down there to bring luck, but he was always afraid of the place.

Then his quick steps brought him to the last slope before the stockade. In his haste he almost passed the great, leaning stone, which they called 'The Old Woman' because of the two lumps which stuck out from it. He shuddered to think what might happen if he ever did forget, and ran back to bruise his jaw against the hard mossy surface before passing on. That was the law; all villagers must do that by night and by morning. Only the sick did not do it and they soon died, which was a proof of its importance.

'Forgive me, Mother,' he said, and then ran after the little sheep, who were already rubbing themselves against the oaken stockade.

He had expected everyone to be excited when he shouted 'Hair!' as they swung the heavy gate wide for him to enter. But they only smiled in their dark slow way, and nodded as though it happened every day. Some of the women, the younger ones, even tapped their foreheads and then shrugged their shoulders.

Two-fingers felt hurt. One of the men he spoke to shared a field with him. They had worked together, breaking that hard land with their pointed sticks and singing the Barley Song that would bring good crops:

'Spring quickly, Barley Woman,
There is blood in the furrows to feed you!'

But this man only shrugged his shoulders like the women and stood aside.

Puzzled, Two-fingers almost ran towards the Old Man's warren. It was a cluster of huts, set about a bigger central one, connected to it by dry-stone passages through which a man might crawl on all-fours. The roofs reached high about a central king-post, roughly thatched and pointed. Two-fingers ran towards the biggest one, where light from the fat-lamps glowed.

The chief's proud young son Garroch, met him at the curving doorway, pushing him hard against the windbreak and sticking a sharp flint knife against his throat.

'There are strangers,' he said. 'Old Man must have quiet.'

But Two-fingers would not be silent.

'Hair! Hair is on the hill!' he yelled.

The talking in the house died down, then there was a little scurry of laughter. The Old Man had three proud wives who always made fun of the tribesmen like that.

A deep voice said, 'Come in, Two-fingers, and tell us about Hair then.'

The shepherd broke free and ran into the great circular room. The light from the chalkstone lamps with their rush wicks was dim and the smoke from the fat-oil sent whorls of greasy blackness into the air. But Two-fingers saw, all the same, that strangers had come. He counted seven of them, squatting on their haunches before the Old Man. He could not wait to inspect them then, but ran forward and knocked his forehead before the Old Man, who sat serenely, draped with his cere-monial robe of deer-hide and wearing his thick black hair, that must never be cut, piled upon his head with bone pins, on the slate stool that had been fetched so far from the sunset for him.

Two-fingers pretended to ignore the women who squatted behind the chief, giggling at him and shaking their jet ear-rings and bone-bracelets as they pointed derisively, but he saw their plump pale breasts moving as they laughed.

'Hair is here on the hill, Old Man!' he began.

The Old Man smiled and shook his head. 'Perhaps Hair can wait, Two-fingers,' he said, taking the man's wrists in his strong hands so that the power flowed into him and made him silent. 'We must show our visitors something else than Hair.'

The Old Man called to a slave girl who stood waiting with a wicker basket full of barley-bread for the guests. She flung a barley cake on to the earthen floor beside Two-fingers. The Old Man leaned forward and swiftly drew a circle about the little loaf with the point of the black flint knife, the one Two-fingers knew so well, the magic knife.

'Take up the cake, friend,' he said to the shepherd. 'Eat with us now.'

Two-fingers felt proud that the Chief should invite him and tried to take the cake. But something always seemed to push against his hand, something soft and furry, forcing it away from the bread and back over the circle. Behind him he heard a faint laugh.

'I cannot reach it, Old Man,' he said at last.

The Old Man smiled and smoothed out the circle with his foot. Two-fingers grabbed out for the cake again. The furry thing had gone. It was easy now and he sat with the cake in his mouth, looking wide-eyed at the strangers, inspecting them for the first time.

They were all big men, much bigger than any he had ever seen, even the Hunters. But only two of them frightened him. One wore the horns of a stag and horses' hide about his thin body. His face was thickly daubed with white clay, but his eyes were big and blue. Two-fingers had never seen blue eyes before, nor such a necklace of little skulls, of birds and weasels and even of the cat. The other man was broad-shouldered and fat. His belly hung over his belt. His hair was golden and spread about his back. On his head he wore a round shiny thing that gleamed almost red in the lamplight. His thick body was clothed in linen, which Two-fingers knew, but coloured red and green in little squares. He had not seen that before. Nor had he seen such a knife as this man wore on his coral-studded bullhide belt. It glistened like a dull fire as he moved. Two-fingers would have liked to touch it, but dared not.

Then the Old Man said to the strangers, 'You have seen some of my magic. Now let me show you more.'

He took Two-fingers by the nape of the neck and bent him forward, poking among his thick black hair. The Old Man's fingers hurt, but Two-fingers kept still, proud to be shown off like this.

'Feel here, and here,' the Old Man said. 'Here are the places where I let out a demon from his head many moons ago. Which of you could do that?'

Two-fingers felt their unbelieving fingers exploring the old wounds where the chief had scraped holes in the bone. He began to whimper for the pain was still there if anyone touched them, ever so gently. Sometimes it even came when he was asleep, then he cried in his dreams.

After they had felt his holes, they flung him backwards and he lay at the Old Man's feet. The one wearing the horns said, 'We who have come here in our boats have magic stronger than that. Your magic is weak. It is nothing.'

Two-fingers was surprised to find that he could understand the words this one spoke, though they were said differently, as though the man had a stone in his mouth.

The other in the coloured linen clothes nodded and said, 'See this knife! It is so sharp that it will cut through this little man's arm with one slash.'

He drew out the red knife and swung his arm upwards. Two-fingers shrank back, his eyes closed. But the blow did not fall. The Old Man was staring into the blue eyes of the visitor and he was smiling, his strange dark smile, the one he made when he drew his circles, or when he gave the chosen animals to the fire. He was thinking of Earth Mother, Two-fingers knew, and she was helping him, putting her magic in his eyes. The knife slowly fell.

Then the Old Man signed to one of the women. She hurried forward with the cow's horns and the pot of barley beer. The strangers drank, afraid to anger this strange old man. And one by one they sank down on to the floor of the hut, sighing deeply and clutching at their bellies, a strange froth gathering about their lips, speechless.

Two-fingers smiled for he knew that they had drunk the foxglove poison without a murmur, so they couldn't be very clever. Even he knew that trick.

Only the big one, their leader with the red knife, still sat upright, glaring silently at the Old Man, who was staring back at him, almost pleasantly. They waited for a while looking at each other like two hawks locked in a death-grip, but the man did not fall down like the others.

The Old Man said, 'This is a strong one. Earth Mother would accept such a man. He would make good crops with this body.'

He whistled sharply and his sons came running in. It took six of the small dark ones to drag this great visitor through the stockade to the leaning stone, he was so heavy. But they bound him with strong thongs and the villagers stood in a circle, beating their foreheads, gravely, while the Old Man made the deep cut down his body and drew out the steaming heart for all to see.

The man's helmet fell off his head as he jerked back with the cut, and the copper knife clattered on to the ground. No one seemed very interested in these things, except Two-fingers, who snatched up the little blade eagerly and not understanding its sharpness, sliced himself deep into the palm in his hurry.

The big golden man died quickly after that for the Old Man knew how it should go. But before he had suffered the big cut, this stranger man had groaned, 'My brothers are coming in their boats. They bring horses and great hounds on their rafts. Their spears will pin you to the earth like foxes. They will come tomorrow, never fear.' Then the blood came out of his mouth and he died.

The Old Man had laughed hoarsely and the villagers had imitated him, as was proper. Then they went back to the village.

Only Two-fingers, who was a little strange in the head, stayed by the Old Woman's stone, wondering, the metal knife still in his hand. He already saw pictures of these golden men, the hill black with them, all with sharp knives and coloured clothes, and big booming voices, like the dead one on the stone.

He did not hear the Old Man call out, 'Come, friend Two-fingers, now tell me about old Hair on the hill!'

He was thinking that these golden men might be more frightening than Hair. He wondered if he would be the first to see them, and shuddered.

Then he did not have time to think about them any more. Old Hair crept softly on him when the noisy villagers had gone away, and with a sudden scurrying rush took him by the soft throat in an almost unbreakable grip of hunger.

But Two-fingers had time to use the copper knife on Old Hair's belly, and so two offerings lay on or about the stone, for Earth Mother to take her pick, before the moon went down. Two-fingers stayed bleeding on the ground until dawn. Then he crawled back to tell the Old Man all about it. But first he dropped the little copper knife down a deep fissure in the chalk as an offering to Earth Mother who had helped him so much that night.

So the golden strangers and the metal knife came and went, and were soon forgotten, like the death of a dog, or the splintering at last of an antler pick. There were other, harsher things to remember each year, as season created season in this dark island, famine and fire-times, visits from the hungry wolves or the savage Hunters from the dim woods. Death never moved too far away from the hill; the rank smell of his breath came to the villagers, even in their sleep.

# 2: Hunters

THE BLACK-HAIRED little girl looked up just in time to see the tuft of painted feathers rising above the holly bush, twenty paces nearer the wood. She gave a sharp yelp and dropped the green lizard she had just decided to keep as a pet. Then she began to run. That is what the women had always taught her: 'Run as fast as you can, if ever you see the Hunters. They will put a stake up through you and toast you for supper over a slow wood fire if you don't! They are a cruel folk—not like us. Their Gods are different—bad Gods! They are a bad old folk!'

Brach heard heavy footsteps behind her and the jangling of bracelets. Then a new smell, different from that which hung about her own folk. She did not wait. Her heart thumped hard against her new linen tunic, urging her on. A nasty-edged little throwing-axe glanced off a stone before her and swung round, a-straddle, between her legs. She stumbled, chin forward and fingers out like a frog, but somehow she kept on running, her dark eyes wide with fear and the whites showing all round the irises.

Then she began to cry as she ran, sorry now that she had passed by the Old Woman that morning without making *the little sacrifice,* as they called it. She was really very frightened. This was the first time she had ever been chased by one of the ancient enemy from the dark oak forests.

'Earth Mother! Earth Mother! Help me now!' she panted.

A flint struck her in the middle of the back. At first she thought it was an arrow and wondered why it didn't hurt unbearably. The warriors at Craig Dun boasting about the fires, had always said how much an arrow hurt—more than a knife or an axe. Expecially a tanged arrow, the leaf-shaped ones weren't so bad, for it often dragged things out with it when it was pulled, the wet things that screamed in the light. But this didn't hurt as bad as that, not anywhere near.

All the same, Brach decided not to take any chances. Earth Mother must be asleep that evening, thinking about the Barley in her womb.

'Old Man! Old Man! Help me now!' she sobbed—picturing her grandfather, lolling by the dry stone wall of his roundhouse, scratching circles on the floor with his long horny thumbnail or the black flint knife—if he could remember where he had put it, for he was becoming very forgetful lately. She hoped he would hear her in his magic dreams and send a spell to help her.

Almost as she said the words the runner behind her gave a high laugh. She felt hands on her shoulders, in her hair, on her arms. His breath was hot on her neck. She would have bitten but her gasping mouth was open and would not obey her in its terror. So she kicked backwards with her hard heels. Once, twice, five times! As many as the fingers on one hand.

She heard the man give a deep grunt. There was a very painful tug at her hair—then she was free again and running like the wind. And now it was as though she could run for ever. And the feet no longer thumped along behind her.

An ordinary girl might have rested then or have let her heart sing a victory song. That is what they did—and then they were caught! Brach had heard about things like that before.

But she was not an ordinary girl. Her grandfather was the Old

Man who had once outwitted even the Strangers, in Craig Dun.
Her father was the 'fighting-chief', Garroch, the Old Man's
son, who would be the Old Man himself one day, when the
time came to put her grandfather in the Long House, with the
clay thick in his eye-sockets and his limbs tied with hide
strips.

So Brach did not do as ordinary girls might have done.
Instead she recited the names of the trees: oak, ash, holly,
birch . . . And then the names of the creatures: bear, badger,
eagle, stoat, hawk, lynx. Only the wolf would she not name.
When she came to him she called him 'Hair'—just as old Two-
fingers the Fool had done fifteen corn-growings before. She
thought of old Two-fingers who had gone to Earth Mother on
the leaning stone when Brach was six corn-years old. Brach
recalled him as she ran. He had lain quietly there as though on a
sheepskin bed, without howling. Her grandfather had stroked
his hair and had gently felt the holes in his head where the skin
was thin. The Old Man was proud of that bit of surgery.
Two-fingers had grinned and said: 'Old Man, can the dogs
come with me?'

The dogs he meant were not those that had chased the sheep
down the chalk hillside when first the Strangers came. They
were their great-grandchildren but like them in grey shagginess
and obstinacy when a task was to be completed quickly.

The Old Man smiled back at Two-fingers and said: 'Yes,
in a case like this a wish must be granted.'

The two dogs were fetched from Two-fingers' mud hovel. The
shepherd was unbound for long enough to caress them and then
the whole affair went quietly and more easily than was the rule.

Brach thought of all this as she ran. It was surprising how it
passed the time. The oaken stockade was ramming into her
chest almost before she knew it. She was giving the village
warning howl and the gates were opening just as by magic.
Then she was inside being sick and the gates were closed again.

'The Hunters are here!' she gulped as the women tried to
find out what troubled her.

A dark-skinned warrior, his face streaked with the blue
war-juice, smacked her back as she bent.

'How many, my pretty?' he asked. 'We have enough men
to kill a handful but no more. Garroch your father has taken
our warriors to get food from the Fisherfolk.'

He was an old man, six hands old, skilled, but cautious. Another one whose age could be counted on four hands pushed for-

ward and said, 'Let us go out and chop them, master! They must
be tired after the long snow when the creatures died in the forests and would not feed them. Let us go out and chop them!'

But the warrior turned sharply and struck him across the
mouth with the flat of his green-stone axe. The young one
was silent, licking his teeth.

They led sobbing Brach to the Old Man. She was still sick
from eating berries and running. He stroked her and said, 'If
your father, Garroch, was only here he would kill them all.
But he has gone away to get food for us till the Barley springs.'

In the gorsebushes, an arrow's flight from the stockade, a
red-headed young Hunter sat rubbing his groin and showing his
teeth. 'Garroch's girl can kick like a horse,' he said. 'She for my
wife one day.' Then laughing at the fright he had given her he
hobbled back towards the forest where his tribe were waiting
for news about the defences of the village under the hill.

# 3: Fishers

A LONG raw wind howled up the estuary from the grey
sea over the broad green-slimed mudflats, until it reached the
sand where the dugout boats were drawn up, black under a low
and leaden sky. The gaunt dog-toothed rocks which fringed
the inlet stood a dirty white with the droppings of countless
generations of seabirds, whose cracked cries echoed and re-
echoed from side to side of the gloomy place.

This was the spring settlement of the Fisherfolk to whom
Garroch of the Hill had come, a princely beggar for food to
keep his father's people alive until the little barley shoots of
Craig Dun had grown full enough for harvesting.

Garroch stood erect on a flat stone, trying to be proud,
though the sand was hurting his eyes and the thick stench of
rotting fish that came with the wind from the village middens
made him screw up his nostrils. He was talking earnestly but
with dignity, in the simple common language of the tribes,
stressing his points as he made them with the white 'talking
stick,' a long spatula of deer-horn, the holding of which insured
that the speaker would not be interrupted until he had finished

and had passed the thing to the man who held up his forefinger as sign that he also had something to say.

'My folk are waiting, Kraka,' he said, sweeping the stick round behind him, where a score of men, as small and dark as their prince, squatted on a long ridge, their eyes never leaving their leader, though they were too far away from him to hear his words.

'They have brought their baskets, four hands of them, for your shell-fish. The Old Man of Craig Dun asks for it to keep his folk alive, Kraka.'

As he spoke Garroch's eyes swept over the scene in contempt. He saw the miserable sheds that leaned against the ordured rocks, black with damp and rottenness, their Chief's hovel perched on tottering wood-piles above the slime; and everywhere the broken shells and decaying fish-guts that fouled the air about this enclosed place.

Somewhere among the huts women were burning a great heap of seaweed. The stuff spurted and crackled, sending up its brown smoke to join the already overladen atmosphere.

Kraka the Fisher Chief lolled before Garroch, negligently, against the side of his great black dug-out boat, picking his yellow teeth with a thorn. His red-rimmed eyes never left the thin dark face of the visitor. His lips seemed perpetually to be twisted in a sneer. After all, it was Garroch who was begging for food, not Kraka! Garroch did not like Kraka's smell. It was like that of a creature he did not know. Behind their chief, the Fisherfolk sat in the damp sand, their salt-cracked and blackened hands hanging down loosely over their knees, watching Garroch's eyes and mouth for signs of fear; judging the worth of the boar's tooth necklace at his throat; envying the brown bearskin cloak which covered his shoulders, the thick flax-linen tunic that shielded his body from their bitter wind.

At last Kraka held out his hand for the talking-stick. Garroch tossed it to him proudly, without a smile. For a moment Kraka grinned and scratched himself with it, in the middle of the back where the fingers will not reach. The men behind him laughed, proud of their Chieftain's wit. The women, burning seaweed, halted in their task to wonder what made the men laugh so loudly. There was usually little enough to laugh about.

Kraka said, 'What do you bring for my beautiful shellfish, Garroch of Craig Dun? Surely it is worth something?'

Garroch took back the bone stick, but as though he did not relish the idea of touching it. Kraka observed this and for a moment the confidence left his mouth.

Garroch said, 'We bring you a basket of arrow-heads. One basket of arrow-heads for twenty of shellfish. A good price, Kraka of the Shore.'

Kraka half turned to the men behind him, smiling so that Garroch could not see his face. Then he said, 'We do not shoot fish with arrows here, Garroch of Craig Dun. Take your arrows to the Hunters. They use arrows and will give you goods for them, no doubt.'

He saw the hot blood rise in Garroch's cheeks and knew that his taunt had pierced where he had wanted it to. He knew that for the lives of four men Craig Dun had gone in fear of the Hunters from the low valley forests.

Then Garroch shifted a little on the flat audience-stone, as though he was about to signal to the warriors who waited on the ridge. Kraka knew well enough that it would be an easy thing to knock Garroch's legs from under him and run him through with a fish spear. But the watchers on the hillock carried bows and his own men, sitting defencelessly in the mud, would die before they could reach the shelter of the rocks.

Kraka spoke quickly before Garroch should make the sign. 'Arrows are not good medicine in this village. They would offend the Fish Woman. She would give no more fish. Then we too would die.' He gestured sideways, to where the shrivelled carcase of a basking shark swung from hide-thongs at the head of a salt-encrusted post. This was the Totem of the Fisherfolk.

Garroch bowed his head in respect to the stinking thing. He knew that Kraka would not be able to go back on his word of refusal after mentioning the Fish Woman, for she heard all that was said along the bleak estuary.

Garroch said at last, though the words were hard to speak, 'Give us the fish, Kraka, then when barley comes, three baskets of the grain shall be yours.'

Kraka said, 'Three baskets for twenty, is that good exchange? Besides, you are offering nothing for something. How do you know that your barley will ever come out of the ground? Perhaps it has deserted Craig Dun and gone away for ever. Perhaps Earth Mother has eaten it!'

Garroch gave a choked cry and leapt down from the stone, his dark eyes wide with anger. He did not take the talking-stick, in his haste.

'Don't say that!' he shouted. 'No man must talk of the barley like that. If you make her leave us with such words we shall come back here and take the heads of all your people!'

He was standing before Kraka, his white teeth bared, clutching at his own broad belt to keep himself from grappling with the Fisher Chief.

Kraka was leaning back over the dug-out boat, his red face no longer smiling, the vein throbbing in his neck.

A hunchbacked man who wore the skin of an otter about his waist rose quietly from the mud and began to edge his way towards the dugout, a broad flint dagger hidden in his great hand. This was Kraka's 'killing-man', a slave from a tribe along the coast, whose only work among the Fishers was to protect the Chief.

Garroch shouted, 'Kraka swine! Kraka dung-eater! Worm in your mouth!'

Then his sudden fury wore itself out. He stood still trembling. Had he been at home among his family he would have let the tears come then as they wished to, but here he knew that he must keep them back or the Fishers would risk the arrows in their frenzy to fling him down and cut the man from him. He had been there once when it had happened to one of their own folk who had howled like a woman when he had slipped in the green mud beneath the clumsy dugout boat they were dragging in, heavily-laden. 'Weep like woman; then *be* woman!' they had screamed, clustering round the wretch.

Garroch held himself straight and made his mouth smile. Then slowly he bent and took up the talking-stick, keeping his eyes fixed on Kraka all the time.

'*Four* baskets of barley, Fisher Chief,' he said.

Kraka was leaning against the boat, smiling again in his old way, though the thumping of his heart had not yet quietened nor the smell of blood left his nostrils. He observed that the boar's teeth in Garroch's necklace were trembling and knew that he too was still unsure of the situation. He would see how far he might go.

'Dog's blood! Dog's blood!' said Kraka. 'Is the worm still in my mouth?'

Garroch thought of the baskets of shellfish and of his father's folk waiting for food under the chalk hill. If this had not been so and he had been there for his own amusement, he would have plunged forward then and have ripped his black-flint knife up the man's belly. He controlled his itching hand.

'Spit now, Kraka,' he said, 'and the worm will fall from your mouth.'

Kraka made his sneering smile and bending away from them all spat into the mud. Among all the casts and small fish entrails it was impossible to see which of them was the worm.

When he turned again he smiled at Garroch differently.

'You shall have the fish, Garroch of Craig Dun,' he said, 'and we will all pray that your barley comes so that we shall get our dues.'

Garroch opened his mouth to speak, but the Fisher Chief held up the talking-stick for silence.

'You have a good bargain, Garroch,' he said, 'better than you know. And there is still more to come, as you shall see.'

He turned to the men behind him and two of them ran forward, pushing another figure between them, one muffled in a long cloak of many worn and greasy skins. Kraka tore off the covering and a girl stood before Garroch, staring him in the eye.

Kraka said, 'This is a mouth I have fed which now you must feed; Rua, my daughter. She goes with the shell-fish to be your woman. Then one day both our peoples may live under One Old Man, if you can make her lie still underneath you.'

Garroch stared at the dark greasy hair, the flat nose, and the big teeth that showed between the panting of her thick lips. She smiled at him and he wanted to turn away. But he forced himself to go through the ritual action and putting his hand inside the old robe, he ran it up and down her body as she stood for him. Her skin was cold and rough to the touch and she reeked of shell-fish.

Garroch stood away from her, shaking his head and trying to smile.

'I have other wives, Kraka,' he said. 'They would not give place to her. They would do things to her which might offend you. A warrior does not need so many women. I cannot take her.'

The men squatting on the shore sucked in the air through their worn teeth with surprise. This young fool from the hill didn't know what he was turning away, they thought, digging their elbows into each other. Such a woman would make a man forget whether she was beautiful or not. Some of them, the youngest ones, even felt a sort of regret that Garroch should be such a fool. They wanted him to know too. But the older ones were secretly glad that Rua would not be taken away from them. She comforted even the old ones, when Kraka was away fishing.

After the whispering had died, Kraka said, 'If your pride will not let you take her, it can hardly let you take our baskets of shellfish, man of the little white hill.'

Garroch bowed his head a little and said, 'Then we must eat small birds and tree-bark until our barley comes to us. We have done it before and we can do it again. But have no doubt, we shall come here again, Kraka!'

Now the girl fell at Garroch's feet and clasped him by the ankles. Her hands were strong and warm. She looked up at him, her brown eyes fixed on his, begging to be taken, but forbidden by the ancient laws to speak.

Kraka watched her for a while and then said, 'Yes, you may eat small birds and tree-bark and you may live, but this woman will not live. Among our folk a woman does not wish to live when she is refused by the man she has chosen.'

Garroch shuffled his feet, trying to disengage her hands. She held him even more tightly. He knew that her hands were very strong.

'That is your law,' he said, 'not mine. It does not concern me, Kraka of the Fishers. A man may do as he wills with his own flesh.'

Kraka bent down and dragged the last covering from the girl's shivering body. Garroch saw the faint white marks of the rod across her broad thin back and for an instant his heart felt a little pity for her. Yet he knew that folk must die, must suffer and die, one way or another. They were doing it all the time and there was nothing very unusual about it. He shook his head again, in spite of the little wave of pity.

Kraka said, 'Then at least take her body with you in one of the baskets and put it with dignity in your long house of silence on the hill. So her ghost will be satisfied when you join her at last. I give her to you!'

As he spoke the last words, he bent over the girl and raised his broad bladed axe above her head, taking careful aim so that the spilling might be made at one blow.

But Rua suddenly kicked out as the man leaned forward, wriggling sideways away from the falling axe. Kraka gave a grunt and sprawled on his face in the mud, trying to find the axe. But the girl was on his back, her naked body covering him, writhing as he writhed.

Men ran forward but did not touch her as she pressed her skinning-knife under his skull, once, twice, three times, carefully. Kraka's outstretched fingers clasped and unclasped, his thin legs flailed, and then his body gave a great heave which sent the girl sprawling into the red that now puddled round his head.

Then he was quite still, with his mouth open in the red mud.

Rua bent over him and then touched her cheeks and forehead and breasts, leaving the sacred marks on them in thin streaks.

The old men of the Fishers kneeled before her now for she had dared Sea Mother's wrath to make herself more powerful than her Chief.

She stared past them in contempt, her gaze only for Garroch. 'The shellfish is yours, Lord,' she said.

He looked down at the still body of Kraka, then he bowed his head to Rua of the Fishers, in ritual respect.

'I shall keep my side of the bargain,' he said. 'I shall come back with the barley.'

Rua stooped and snatched up the fouled skin garment, swinging it about her cold body. She went to Garroch and let her cold breasts and thighs touch his in token of submission.

'You need not come back,' she said. 'I shall come with you and eat the barley in your house.'

Garroch would have struck her then but the young men of the Fishers were all about him, snuffling like otters and he knew that they would kill him if he refused Rua this time in her pride.

So the men of Craig Dun carried away twenty baskets of shellfish over the windy ridge on their journey from the shore.

Rua walked with Garroch, silent and shuddering now. When they were out of sight of the village smoke, he turned on her in his sudden anger and struck her with his clenched hand again and again on the face.

But she did not weep at this and when he walked on quickly after his laden men, she got up and ran as fast as she could to catch him up, like a dog with only one master.

# 4: Craig Dun

THE GREAT chalk hill stood above the village. At the Spring festival, with the grey-fleeced sheep grazing on its slopes, it seemed kind and smiling. But when the dark time came, after the burning of the straw to keep away the snow, the hill seemed to glower down, asking for sacrifice. Then it was not kind. It was a hunched monster that held the frightened village in its hand. Then the folk of Craig Dun cowered over the hearth-place, shivering in the smoke, speaking the charms against evil that they had learned from their fathers and their fathers before them, hoping to drive away the horrors of the hill.

There were forty houses under the hill. Their walls of stout flint, brought up from the flint-shaft in the hill's bowels, their roofs of ashwood and thatch. Go down the three sacred steps of flint into the circular room and you were safe from cold. Pull down the staghide door curtain on to its pegs and you were safe from the wolves. At least, almost safe—for once when the snow had lain on the hill for three moons they had braved the skin doors and the axes behind them and had brought death into the village before the ancient Hunters had come from their caves in the wood and driven them away. In Craig Dun no man said 'Wolf' now. That was the law.

The forty houses clustered about the great steading of Marrag. He was the Old Man of the folk and made their laws. His palace housed twelve people and three cows, whose milk fed the children. When the ewes dropped their lambs in the village, they were brought into Marrag's steading too. Then, the air that was already thick with the smoke of peat and heather, vibrated to the sound of calves calling out for food, lambs bleating with their new voices, men and women arguing or singing, and children shouting. For Marrag's son, Garroch had three wives, Gwraig, Mona and Garreg-wen, though he loved none of them. There seemed to be children everywhere. The women cuffed them away incessantly, for there were too many tasks to perform—food to prepare, flax to spin and weave, hides to scrape, fuel to gather. Some of these tasks went to Brach, Garroch's eldest daughter. She was eight yet could already clean an oxhide with her little flint scraper so evenly that it fell in perfect folds to make a cloak for her grandfather, Marrag, or her fine young father, Garroch.

Brach's mother was proud of her daughter, with her great doe's eyes and her long black hair that must never be cut. But the other women were cruel to her when Garroch was away and the Old Man was asleep, as he often was now, because he was so old.

His last remaining wife, the Old Woman of the folk, Wraich, was dead. She had died two winters before when food had been so hard to get as it was this year.

'Do not put me on the hill,' she had said in her thin voice. 'I do not want the hairy folk to break my bones and tear my liver out while I am watching them. I want to be with you all, to hear you talking. Then I shall feel comfortable in my own home.'

So they had dug her a place under the floor of the hut and had put her there, with a comfortable scooped stone to sit on. They put her clothes down there with her, the best fur cape and the flax skirt that she had always liked, dyed blue and yellow with the herb-juices. They gave her a flint knife and a clay beaker, though they could spare little food to go into the jar.

Then they laid many boughs and beams across the hole and placed the clay over them, stamping it flat. On that they built their fire, hoping that the warmth would go down to her and comfort her. She heard them walking above her for three days and sometimes heard the sounds of children's voices, the high-pitched ones. Then she went to sleep. The wolves would have hurt much more.

Now the hut was a sacred one. She watched over it. Sometimes when the villagers were in difficulties, they came to Marrag's house and asked permission to speak to the Old Woman. They shouted their questions into the fire hole and then put their ear to the floor and waited. Old Marrag would smile and tell them what she said. They would go away believing. Brach, who had sharp eyes despite their softness, sometimes noticed that there was a still smile about the old man's face when he interpreted the message of his dead wife, Wraich. But she said nothing, for she loved her grandfather almost as much as she loved her father, Garroch, who had gone to get food from the Fisherfolk.

One day they would take the Old Woman's bones out from under the floor and paint them and place them in the Long House of Sleep, at the other side of the hill, among the bones of all the great ones who had ever died in that village. Then she would rest without murmuring in the quiet summer nights when it was too hot for anyone to sleep in the stuffy hut. But it took time for a body to become bones, and so they waited impatiently; the wolves did it all more quickly, up there on the hill.

This winter had truly been a long one. Many of the ewes had died in the snow and even the cows had been eaten. The Hunters, the ancient ones, who lived in the caves of Coidun, down in the oak forest by the river, and were clever enough to hit a hawk at fifty paces with their little leaf-shaped arrows, had almost starved too. They were hardy men, into the bargain, with great jaws and red hair, the few that were left of them.

They did not know how to weave or to grow the beautiful little barley shoots that made the hearts of the villagers rejoice as they pushed up their pretty heads in the fields outside Craig Dun. The Hunters boasted that they were the first folk; that they had always been there with the reindeer and the buffalo, and had not come in boats like the villagers. They were friendly, up to a point unless they were hungry, but they did not like being teased because of their fur jackets and their difficulty in speaking the language of the dark barley-growers.

But this year, even the Hunters had found that it was a hard one. Many of them had starved in their caves, unable any longer to draw those pictures on the walls in red and black and deep yellow that would bring the deer into their nets or the wild pigs within range of their flint arrows.

In the village there was sadness too. Garroch, the son of the Old Man, was away, trying to buy food from the Fishers on the seashore, five days off. Marrag was alone in the hut, with the wives and their children. He slept long now, with age and hunger. When he didn't sleep, he muttered to himself or drew signs on the clay floor of the hut and brooded over them. His long hair was almost white. He no longer bothered to coil it about his head, in the proper manner, and keep it in position with the bone pins which were his by right of rank. He would not have bothered even if someone cut his hair off in the night as he slept. Often he did not know where his flint knife and axe were. When a man has come to that state, his power must be doubted, even by his family.

As the Old Man dozed in the one ray of wintry sunlight that filtered down the steps on to the hard-trodden clay floor, he saw the pictures of his life. He saw himself as a young one again, taking over the task of ruling the folk of Craig Dun from his own father after the Harvest Feast. He recalled how his father had placed the black bearskin on him, its pelt covering his shoulders and back, its grinning mask falling over his own black head. Then the women placed the necklace of bear-claws round his throat and the amber bracelets round his wrists. He remembered how heavy his father's great axe and oxhide shield had seemed before, and how light they suddenly became when the bearskin fell into position on his shoulders.

'Old Man, Old Man!' the people had shouted, though he was younger then than many of them. He smiled at them and made the high prancing dance that the Old Man must do. They beat their hands and shouted out again, 'Old Man! Old Man!'

Then with the blood still bouncing in his head, he noticed his old father, who seemed so small now and afraid. The bearskin and the axe and the shield became heavy again, burdens not pleasures. His father was waiting for something, something that he did not want to happen yet knew to be inevitable. Marrag went to the man and whispered, 'Do not fear, father, I shall not put you out on the hill. The hairy grey ones shall not mock at your bones while I am strong.'

His father came closer to him then and tried to smile like a little child again. Marrag placed his arm over the old man's shoulders and led him back to the Chief's house. The folk of Craig Dun followed at a distance muttering and discontented, for this was to break the old law and disaster would surely come. Some of the youngest ones even waved their axes and flint knives about wildly and whispered hoarsely that they should take the deposed Chief, whether or not, and put him on the chalk hill with the stones tied to his hands and feet so that he could not run away from the grey folk.

But at the door of the house, when his father had gone down into safety, Marrag had turned on them and made his swarthy face look as grim as the bear's above it. He had waved his own long-bladed axe viciously in their faces. 'Who dares question the Old Man now?' he asked. And the younger ones had looked on the ground, their hands by their sides, afraid that he would choose one of them for a sacrifice if the barley did not push through the thin soil next year.

In the dimness of the hut, with only the little clay lamp flickering, his father had said, 'I have brought suffering on the people, my son. I should have gone to the hill as they wished. It always has been so. Now the crops will fail and the ewes bear no lambs.'

But Marrag had put off the bearskin and laid down the axe and shield. Now for a moment he was the son again and not the Old Man. He put his flint-scarred hand on his father's thin thigh.

'If sorrow comes to the people,' he said, 'it will be my bargain to settle, not yours. I must deal with Earth Mother now, not you. A year ago, when I went south to trade with the Fisherfolk, I broke Earth Mother's law for the first time. On a hill such as ours, set above a village such as ours, I came on an Old Man such as you, the great flints at his wrists and feet, the crows already settling about him. He looked at me with such sad eyes that I did not pass him by as the law says I must do. Instead, I took out my bear knife and went towards him. His eyes told me that he welcomed my knife but it was not my place to do what he wished. I only cut the thongs that held him.'

Marrag's father had sucked in his breath sharply at these words. 'Aiee! Aiee!' he said. 'To let loose a man on the hill! Yes, you have broken the law twice indeed, Marrag. What did the Old Man do then?'

Marrag had said smiling bitterly, 'He followed me begging me to tie the thongs again for it was the law. But I walked faster and faster so that I could not hear his words. When I looked back he was standing on the hill slope, crying and calling to the villagers to come out again and set him where the old law demanded.'

So the Old Man of Craig Dun remembered the past, the faults of his life, the strange echoing in the vaults of the House of Sleep when the new guests were laid there upon each other after a famine or a battle against the Hunters. Leaning against the clay wall of the hut these things came back to him again and again as they do in a sickly dream. Then it seemed to him that he stood before the sacred stone that leaned over the village, at the place where the woods ended and the fields began. It had been roughly carved beyond man's memory so that a gravid belly and two swelling breasts emerged from the stone. This was 'The Old Woman'. Marrag in the hut dreamed he was standing in the sunlight before 'The Old Woman', when a voice came from her, a frightening voice like the shrill barking of the vixen on the frosty hill at night-time. 'The Old Woman' said, 'Your time has come at last, Marrag. You have at least two debts to pay. Go up on to the hill and make ready for the House of Sleep. Your place is waiting for you. Hasten, hasten, Marrag!'

Then Marrag woke out of his dream with a start. He was relieved at first to find that he was still in the house, leaning against the cold clay wall. But when he looked towards the smoking fire in the centre of the floor he was afraid again. Garroch's three women crouched there hungry, their eyes red with smoke, their fingers pointing. They did not smile at him as once they used. As Marrag's mind came out of the caverns of sleep, he heard Gwraig say, 'There is hardly enough for the little ones. He has eaten his belly full for years now. It is time for him to make way for the children.'

Then Garreg-wen, Garroch's youngest woman had said, 'Gwraig speaks true words, the Old Man eats as much as any of us. Yet if we put him on the hill before Garroch returns from the Fishers, he will be angry with us, for he loves Marrag.'

Marrag was astounded that they were speaking words which he could understand, and not in the Woman's Tongue, which was kept a deadly secret from the menfolk.

Gwraig spat into the glowing embers and said, 'That should trouble no one. Once this old man is on the hill, I shall be the Old Woman here, being Garroch's eldest wife. My word will be as true as his, my anger as great, my power with Earth Mother as strong. She will listen to me before Garroch even. She loves women, not men, if the truth be told.'

The other women bowed to her and then the three rose to go. As they reached the steps, Gwraig said again, 'If Garroch does not return before night, we will get the men of the village to put the stones on his wrists and ankles. Then it will be done, whatever Garroch says!'

They laughed and went up into the light. Marrag shook his head, thinking how right they were, and then he went to sleep again. This time he dreamed about the cave where Kaa Fox, the Chief of the Hunters, lived. On the walls were great bulls and stags, their colouring glorious with red and yellow ochre, the outlines swift and clear with lamp-black, making the bulls seem to bellow again, the stags to leap out of the past. In his dream Marrag longed to make such pictures though he knew that his people, the small dark ones, were not meant by Earth Mother to do such things. Only the first folk, the ugly red ones who lived by killing beasts and not by tilling the fields, had ever been able to draw and paint like that.

Marrag wept in his sleep with longing to draw beautiful bulls and stags and men shooting their flint arrows deep into the savage flanks. Then he woke again. Now the shaft of sunlight had ceased to come through the doorway and the fire had burned down, leaving white ashes within the circular hearth-stones. Someone was shaking him by the shoulder. It was a little hand. Marrag looked up into the great dark eyes of the girl, Brach. She was not afraid of him like the others of the village because he was the Old Man. She had always spoken to him as though he was eight, too.

'Quick! Quick!' she whispered, 'The men are waiting for Earth Mother to put on her cloak of darkness then they will come to tie the stones on you and carry you on to the hill. Quick! Come with me.'

Marrag began to draw on the clay floor with his long finger nail. He made a circle then placed four straight lines across it like the spokes of a wheel. He seemed very interested in what he was doing. Brach became impatient. She shook him again, and even slapped him lightly on the back of the hand to make him see reason.

'Silly, old grandad,' she said, 'I am telling you what we must do. You don't want to go out on the hill and have the grey folk hurting you, do you? Do you, then?'

Marrag shuddered but made himself smile. Her face was so serious, her voice so urgent and commanding, for a little child. He patted her cheek and said, 'What can we do? If they have decided I am no longer the Old Man then I must go on the hill. That is the law.'

The little girl thumped him quite hard on the shoulder. Now she was angry. 'Silly, silly man,' she said. 'If you come with me they will not find you and then they can't put you on the hill. When Garroch returns with the fish they will forget about putting you on the hill and you can be the Old Man again.'

Marrag smiled and stroked her long black hair that must never be cut. It was so shiny and beautiful. He wished he had a ring of blue stones to put round her forehead, to show that she was a princess. She was so beautiful. He said, 'There, there, Brach, I am still the Old Man and I know magic. Look, my drawing is not silly. It makes me safe, this circle. While it is here they will not touch me. They dare not for I have often told them it is a magic thing.'

Brach listened then turned to him with a little smile of sadness, 'I can hear them coming,' she said. 'They are saying things which tell me that they will not be afraid of the circle now. Come with me, quickly, Old Man.'

Marrag tried to stand in the hut. He too heard the excited voices and their tones sent a strange shivering through his body. He knew, only too well from the sacrifice stone, how men sounded when blood was in their nostrils. He remembered the proud Stranger who once came, and even poor silly Twofingers. The girl dragged him towards the door. Then she stopped and said, 'I am the daughter of Garroch, who is the son of Marrag. I have magic in me too, grandad. Look, I will show you a stronger magic than your circle, perhaps, if it will work for me.'

Quickly she ran to the beds of straw in the shadows of the hut and taking up a great bundle twisted it and set it against the clay wall where the old man had been sitting. Then she flung a sheepskin over it and bending until her forehead touched the floor she said, 'Earth Mother, make me a straw man to be like Marrag! One, two, three! A bracelet for you, Earth Mother! Make me a man like Marrag.'

Marrag looked back through the gloom of the hut and seemed to see himself sitting there, asleep in the dusk, a tired old man.

Brach tugged at his arm and said, 'They will wait until the straw man wakes, and that will give us time.'

Marrag gazed at her in astonishment and said nothing. He had never seen anything like it and he had been the Old Man for many years.

But even as they turned to go from the steading, there came a sudden savage pattering of feet towards the door, and then, as they looked up in fear, they saw the shaggy black hair, the wild eyes that gazed down on them. The killers had come to take the Old Man to the hill. One of them carried the binding-thongs; others, the sacred stones that must be lashed to his neck and limbs. Their leader, a man who had always hated Marrag since that sacrifice when his first-born child had gone into the flames with the animals of the village, stood before them all, holding his long-bladed axe out and saying, 'If you do not wish to go on the hill, Old Man, all you have to do is to run up the steps and try to escape us. I will put a quick end to your waiting then.'

Then the others laughed, even the wives of Garroch, who stood at the back of the crowd, anxious for it to end as soon as it could before Garroch could return.

Brach looked at her grandfather. He stood like a man in a trance, his thin arms hanging low down by his sides, his back bent and his head thrust forward. He was nodding to the man and saying, 'Yes, yes, I know it is my time at last. I shall come with you to the hill, do not fear. The Old Woman has been calling to me from under the floor telling me of this. I am ready.'

He began to walk forward. The man was secretly disappointed that Marrag had not tried to push past him up the narrow steps. The antler shaft of his axe itched in his hand.

Then Brach cried out, 'No, no, Old Man! You must not go. Garroch my father will be angry if they put you on the hill and he is not here.'

She scampered before the old man and stood in his path so that he should not go up to them. Marrag smiled at her in his silly tired way now, and tried gently to push her aside. But she stood firm and would not move, her eyes full of tears and her long hair hanging half over her face with the effort she was making.

Then the man with the axe gave an exclamation of impatience and grasped her by the shoulder, meaning to fling her aside. She turned on him suddenly and taking his wrist in both of her hard hands, bit deeply into his forearm. He howled with the pain and dropping his axe tried to shake her away, but Brach bit and bit and would not let go. The others now tried to drag her off in the narrow doorway, but could not get at her properly.

The Old Man stood back, staring at this sudden struggle with eyes that hardly understood its significance.

And then, beyond the stockade, Garroch's bull-horns began to moan.

Brach heard them and let go the man's arm. He fell back, rubbing it, the tears heavy in his eyes.

'My father!' she said. 'Now you will know what it is to lay your swine's hands on me and to threaten the Old One.'

The man fell before her, begging for his life, but she kicked him in the mouth as she ran forward to greet Garroch.

Inside the gate, Garroch stood proudly, letting the folk crowd round the wicker fish-baskets, praising him for his skill in bargaining. Brach ran full tilt into him and clasped her arms about his middle, her heart beating wildly and the tears running down her soiled cheeks.

Garroch stroked her thick black hair and tangled it with his tired fingers. He loved her more dearly than any other women he knew. His other children were younger than Brach, and came from his other wives. They were a sullen lot who always seemed afraid of him and would not speak to him or dare to play with him like Brach.

'What is it, my Queen?' he asked at last.

The little girl pointed back at the terrified group about Marrag's steading.

'They were going to put the Old One out on the hill for Hair,' she said, gulping. 'Kill them, Garroch! Knock out their teeth and let them wander on the hill and see how *they* fare.'

Garroch passed his thin dark hand across his brow in exhaustion, for they had walked five days back from the coast, eating only a little of the shell-fish on the way and drinking from the sour salt water of the marshland.

'Later, Queen,' he said. 'We will find a time later. Let me take this fish to Marrag for he is the Old Man who must share it out in the village.'

Brach stood back from him, disappointed that her warrior father had not gone straightway and chopped the man who had bruised her shoulder. She had pictured him doing it, and the man's head falling sideways with that funny look they always had in their eyes, as though they were very surprised and offended.

Then looking up, she saw that someone else stood behind Garroch, a woman she had never seen before. Rua, thin and dispirited by the cruel treatment she had had on the journey from the shores, pulled her tattered robes round her body and tried to outstare this hostile little girl.

'Who is that cow?' asked Brach, drawing back her lips and pointing at Rua with her tongue.

Garroch did not answer, but strode forward between the people to where Marag now stood in the doorway of his house, his hand pressed against his breast, breathing hard with the effort of climbing the three steep steps.

'One of you, who is that bitch?' asked Brach again of the warriors who carried the fish-baskets.

Rua still stood as proudly as her weary body would let her.

One of the warriors pushed past Brach with his load, saying, 'That is Rua, who killed her father in the mud. She is a stinking fish. Anyone could tell that by her smell.'

The folk of Craig Dun clustering round her laughed at this and decided that this should be her name, Stinking Fish, from then on.

But though her eyes were suddenly flooded with bitter water, Rua still tried to look noble as befitted the daughter of a chief. And though there was a great pain in her breast now, she vowed to avenge herself on these folk, and especially this savage little girl, one day, before long perhaps.

# 5: Rua Fish

SO THE folk of Craig Dun did not die that year. The fish kept them just alive, half-rotten though it was before they finished it, until the ewes had dropped their lambs and the badgers their kittens. The folk had been in a dangerous state;

the Old Man, speaking now through his son, had not dared to call for a sacrifice.

In the darkness of his hut, with a trusted guard at the door, he had told Garroch: 'I have known times like these before, on one hand's fingers. Then we begged Earth Mother to help us. She was kind. She turned the old men and women into hogs and the young babies into sucking-pigs and we ate them to keep strength in our bodies.'

Garroch nodded. 'It would be wasteful now to sacrifice them. Old Man. I understand you,' he said.

Brach lay in a dark corner of the hut, her eyes shining out of the blackness of her hair with excitement at what she might see, might eat. She was a privileged one: the only Other who was allowed to be there when the Old Man spoke to his son, who would one day be the Old Man himself.

But she did not see *it*, eat *it*. The famine passed and the Hunters did not pad round the thorn fence at night any longer. The People of the Hill ate well on berries and lamb and badger meat. And the barley thrust up through the light soil as though glad to meet the sun and then to nourish the bodies of her worshippers.

Garroch went out every day, acting as Marrag's eyes, to watch the tender green shoots growing, becoming stronger in the new sun that the Old Man had persuaded Earth Mother to let them have. Brach went with him, careful not to tread on his lengthening shadow. She showed her young father great respect when other eyes could see them, however foolish they were together in the warm privacy of their house. And when Garroch kneeled, praying and caressing the green barley, she kneeled too and knocked her forehead gently and rhythmically on the rain-softened earth below and the great chalk hill.

Always on these mornings, even when Garroch's wives and the village folk had gone back to their tasks, away from the stones which marked the white stone boundaries of the various fields, they had a third companion.

She always stood at a distance, wrapped in her greasy cloak, watching them hungrily. The smell of cockles had gradually left her body and now only the most unkind of the folk called her Stinking Fish. Her name in the village was now simply Fish. She had heard this name often, even from the youngest children. So as the months passed she had forgotten that her name had once been Rua, and even heard herself called Fish in her dreams.

And every morning she would leave the draughty hut that Garroch allowed her, separated from his by a clay wall, and wait until he went with Brach to stroke the barley so lovingly.

Fish always wept and asked her Shark Goddess why she couldn't become a barley woman, so that the prince's dark fingers might stroke her and feel so tenderly into the joining-places, the secret warm places of growth and renewal.

But the Shark Goddess seemed to have forgotten her since that horrid day on the shore when she had pressed her flint under Kraka's head-bone. Fish felt neglected of all creation and wept in the darkness of her hovel more often than she smiled in the sunlight, even though the good Spring was dancing on to the warm Summer.

True, she had much to be unhappy about. The folk of Craig Dun would not speak to her, for they were afraid of Garroch who was already the Old Man in their minds and might become angry at any moment and call for a sacrifice or a cutting. And a cutting was worse than a sacrifice. For a sacrifice was quick and perhaps without pain, if the Old Man chose so and knew his trade. But the other was worse; husband might be chosen to cut wife, or wife husband, whenever, however, wherever the Old Man decided, as he had heard the Old Woman of the stone direct. There was fear in that treacherous cutting almost as sharp as the sudden agony. It was as though one body had turned on itself to make pain, not love. So the folk of Craig Dun feared to speak to Fish, who wandered alone about the high chalk hill, even braving Hair the wolf, anxious only that someone, something, should admit her right to be called a creature of flesh and blood, worth loving, worth tearing to bloody shreds and eating.

The other wives of Garroch had been cruel to Fish. They had grown used to the idea that they each shared something of his lithe dark body over the few years they had known him. They had each been children of the village, an element in the interlaced community of the Chalk Hill, where one blood flowed almost in the veins of all.

But to share him yet again, with a stranger, a salt-skinned fishy woman of an alien folk, that was unthinkable.

So, at first they ignored Fish, and merely did not reply when she spoke to them, respectfully, in her uncouth simple common-language, anxious to be friendly. They turned away from her later, in the presence of others, nodding their heads derisively, or pointing backwards with their thumbs over their shoulders at her to indicate their contempt.

Yet Fish stood it all and still spoke to them, the smile on her broad face becoming always more fixed, harder, more cruel in its turn.

And then at last, when they feared that they could not hurt this stupid creature in these ways, they met together at night and created ways in which they might humiliate her.

So, one night, they had burst in a sudden rush down the steps of her solitary hovel, cloaked—as though she had eyes that could pierce the blackness of a hut- and while two women lay on her, pinning her starved limbs to the clay floor, the other with frantic and inexpert fervour slashed with a flint skinning-knife at that which they all envied, her youth.

Even so, when she had found that they were too strong for her, falling on her in her uneasy sleep as they did, Fish had not screamed, as others would have done. She lay back, biting through her lip, silent and sweating as she had never been before, until the thing had finished. Then the weight had gone from her body and only the searing blind agony remained. She heard the rustle of bodies in the narrow passageway up the steps, and then she bled into an exhausted sleep which left no energy for speculation.

Garroch's wives had not treated Fish well. Yet she loved Garroch in spite of that, because she had killed her father for him. For a few baskets of cockles when these folk of Craig Dun were starving. So she followed him as her wounds healed, not daring to speak to him, but hoping that one day he might recall how she had driven in the little flint, how she had covered his body with hers to keep his open mouth in the mud, how she had pressed herself to him in offering.

She followed Garroch to the barley fields and hated black-haired Brach for being always there with him, walking so carefully, so as not to defile that almost-sacred shadow.

And this particular morning it happened that when Garroch had gone from the barley field to take back his message to Old Marrag, Brach stayed behind, singing to herself as she sat on one of the big stones that marked the boundaries of her father's field. She rocked herself as she sang, for every bit as though she did not know anyone else was there. And as she watched the girl in her contentment, Rua's anger was so great that she picked up an edged flint as big as her hand and came up behind Brach. She did not know quite what she was going to do, but she thought that if Brach was out of the way Garroch might let her walk in the barley fields with him every morning. When the harvest was in, then perhaps he would not want her any more, she thought, but at least she would have known what it was to walk with him alone. Besides, Brach's mother was one of those who had cut her in the dark.

But even as the woman raised the flint above the black head, Brach said in the Women's Tongue, without turning, 'I know you are behind me, Rua Fish. I know what you have in your hand. Put the stone down, Rua Fish, or your eyes will turn to pebbles and your heart will be a flint.'

Rua's anger left her. She felt attracted to this little girl because of her courage. She knew there was no magic about this: Brach had seen her shadow, out of the corner of her eye, for the sun was behind them both.

She said, speaking the same secret language of Women, 'I could have killed you, Garroch's girl, but I didn't. Perhaps I shall kill you another time.'

She sat on the stone next to Brach for she was anxious to have someone to talk to, even if it was only this child, whom she both hated and liked curiously at the same time.

And as she sat down, the otterskin robe fell from her shoulders leaving the upper part of her body uncovered. She saw Brach staring at the long and curling white ritual scars round her breast and down her body into the place which the robe covered.

'Only the daughter of a Chief may wear these,' said Rua, tracing the circular scars with her finger. 'That is the custom of my folk. You may touch them.'

She leaned forward and held Brach's finger to the puckered marks. The girl felt a strange thrill run through her.

'Are you magic?' she said, a little afraid now and yet strangely attracted to this foreign woman who was so different from her dark fat-bodied little mother who always spoke in a high angry voice because there was so much to do, skins to scrape, flax to beat, babies to feed.

Rua lowered her eyelids and smiled. 'I can make the voices of the gull and the gannet,' she said, 'and they come when I call.'

She looked up; the child did not seem very impressed.

'I am a seal-woman at the time of full moon,' said Rua, looking Brach straight in the eye. 'I slip into the water and this'—she smoothed her hands down her flanks—'this becomes all furry.'

Brach sucked in her breath with excitement. 'Do it now,' she said. 'I will not say that you have shown me.'

Rua's thick lips drew back from her big teeth in a smile. 'It is daylight,' she said, 'and there is no water here. If you will come with me to the sea tonight, I will show you. Will you come?'

Brach was suddenly afraid of this strange woman. She was trying to take her away. The little girl got up from the rock and was about to run back to the safe village; but Rua Fish beckoned her, staring all the time into her eyes. Brach felt that she must go to her, to the seal-woman with the white cuts about her breasts.

'What do you want, seal-woman?' she said, frightened.

Rua took her by the wrists and drew her close to her body as she sat on the stone. She waited a while until her own spirit might have entered into the little girl's body. Then she whispered hoarsely in Brach's ear, 'I want Garroch, your father. By the spilling of blood he is mine. I want Garroch.'

Brach began to shudder, feeling the little waves of excited fear running up and down her body, from her belly to her throat and back again. She tried to speak, once, twice, but her tongue stuck in her mouth and she made sounds like a fool.

'I want Garroch,' said Rua. 'He is my body and blood now. You must tell him to come to me tonight. He loves you and will do what you say. Will you promise to tell him to come to me?'

Brach was suddenly aware that this mad woman was pinching her wrists most painfully in her hard hands. She nodded, the tears falling from her eyes as her head moved.

'Yes, yes, I promise,' she said.

The woman pulled her hard against her body again.

'May the worm live in your mouth and the snake go inside you in the dark if you break your word! Promise again!'

Brach burst into tears and shook her head blindly. 'Yes, yes, I promise,' she said.

Then, breaking away, she ran towards the village. At the farthest boundary stones she dared to turn and look back. Rua was still sitting there, the cloak fallen from her body, her hands out as though she held someone, her eyes shut and her broad lips moving as though she spoke to one she loved.

# 6: Little Death

INSIDE THE gates of the village, Brach ran into a man she hated. It was the one who had tried to put Marrag on the hill when her father was away. He was a sullen man who bore a grudge against all who seemed to do better than he; those who could find kindling in the cold times; those whose flints snapped off sharply to form an arrow edge at the first stroke; those whose skinning-knife slid over the pelt, shearing away fat and gristle without going through on to the hairy side and making a hole. He hated other men and women to do these things. When he saw them happen, his head bobbed up and down and his eyes went red, and he muttered angrily. Then he would go away and punch his clenched fist at the wall of a hut until the blood came. He was a violent strong man, who dreamed each night that he was a great warrior chieftain. Yet so uncertain was his temper and his courage, that Garroch had never yet asked him to carry axe and shield. And this also was a bitter burden to his mind.

So, when Brach ran into him, full-tilt, he caught hold of her since no one was in the compound, and remembered how she had kicked him in the mouth when he begged for mercy once.

His senses left him for a moment and he put his hand over her mouth and tried to drag her to a place he knew, under the stockade where kindling was stacked and it was dark and unvisited.

Brach bit his palm hard, but not too hard, only hard enough to make him let go. She knew this man and suddenly she saw that he could help her. She did not want to lose her father to the seal-woman; nor did she want this man to drag her among the damp wood and furze and hurt her.

'Warrior,' she gasped, calling him by a name which she knew he would like, 'Warrior, you would be a fool to hurt me. I can tell you a secret.'

The man stopped rubbing his bitten palm angrily on his backside and changed his grip on her, so that she could talk but not run away.

'Speak quickly,' he said, 'for I have two scores to settle with you.'

Brach's words flowed from her in her fear. 'Men have been unkind to you, warrior,' she said. 'They have not praised you as they should.'

He nodded: this child has sense, he thought, although she had treated him badly herself.

'Tell me,' he said, 'or I will break your thumbs.'

She did not need his inducement. 'Since you deserve a chieftain's pleasures, I tell you,' she said. 'My father means to visit Rua Fish tonight. It seems she is greater than we thought. If you will let me go, I will see to it that Garroch my father does not go. And then you can go in his place, into her house, into her bed. What of that?'

The man thought for a moment and then his thin face wrinkled with a sour and bitter smile.

'That is good,' he said, 'to despoil a chieftain! Yes, that is good.'

'Can I go now?' said Brach.

He loosed one of her hands. 'Do you swear that Garroch will not find me there?' he asked.

Brach said, 'May the worm live in my mouth and the snake come inside me in the dark!'

'That is good enough for me,' said the man, letting go of her other hand. 'I shall go there tonight.'

Brach stood some paces away from him.

'Let her think you are Garroch,' she said, suddenly remembering her oath to the frightening seal-woman. 'If you do not do that, she will swallow you whole and spit out the bones at the next barley sowing.'

Then she ran swiftly to her mother's house, half-afraid, half-laughing.

So that night, Rua did not sleep alone on her sheepskins. She heard the hands and knees along the dark tunnel and put out the fat-lamp so that Garroch should not feel ashamed at having to come to her and surrender at last.

She placed herself for him, holding her breath with fearful expectation, and was momentarily astonished at the roughness of this prince. Not even the most savage of her father's fishers had been like this.

And then she ceased to compare critically in the urgency of the repeated occasions. Life was short, she thought, as she lay on her side for a moment before the next wave thundered to her shore. There is always pain while life lasts, she thought. But there are differences in pain, she thought. And then her speculations were interupted yet again.

The cattle were already lowing outside when they both knew that this night must end for them.

'Garroch,' she said, burying her hands in his hair and pulling at him in farewell.

He broke away laughing, leaving his hair. He was some time finding the way out of her house. She heard his smothered laughter as he crawled away from her along the low tunnel, and she wondered what could have been amusing in that night.

Yet, when she lit the fat lamp again, she partly understood. The strands of hair in her fingers were grey and short, not like his hair, long and as black as the night sky.

Weeping as bitterly as a child whose clay doll has been broken by a laughing boy, Rua curled up on the hard floor and slept into yet another vision of revenge.

So Rua suffered: but before she woke again, she knew what she must do. Earth Mother had come to her in the dream, a shapeless hairy thing, all glistening with dark dew, and had told her, seeming to gloat as she spoke, in her thick furry voice that was somehow as hard as a stone.

# 7: Hair Wolf!

AT THE time of village gathering, when the folk assembled in the compound to await the Old Man, who always said the charm which helped them in their work—fuel-getting, flint-knapping, weaving or herding—Rua Fish came quickly out of her house and stood in the only place they allowed her, near to the stockade gate by the midden ditch.

Already the sun's heat, which shone alike upon barley and refuse, was growing and the stench from the open middens made Rua feel sick. She began to wish that the Old Man would come soon, not that she wanted to see him. It was Garroch she waited for, and she knew that he would come out of the hut and walk across the beaten earth compound with his ailing father, whose eyes and ears and voice he had become since the return from the Fisherfolk.

Rua still trembled with fury at the thought of the trick they had played on her, Brach and her father. They had sent a stranger to her, to use her in laughter, like some worthless thing. She glanced round at the older men as they stood waiting,

wondering which one of them had lain with her so savagely.
But it was impossible to tell: there were so many whose hair,
like that she had clutched in her fingers, was greying. In this
village men seemed to grow old very quickly, she thought.
And all the women seemed to have their broods of children
when they were little more than children themselves. Then
they grew very fat and shapeless and waddled about screaming,
with their greasy black hair always escaping its bone pins and
falling about their shoulders.

Then the bull's horn sounded and the hum of voices was
stilled. Marrag came up the steps, leaning on a thick white staff.
He was pale and kept talking back over his shoulder queru-
lously at his son, who walked behind him, his dark and noble
head bowed.

When they reached the thickest of the folk, Marrag stopped
and looked round at his people absently, as though he wondered
who they were and what they were doing, staring and nodding
to him like that.

Garroch whispered in the Old Man's ear and then gently
slid out the Chieftain's sacred black flint knife to make the
blessing sign. With a quick stroke, he drew a circle in the air
and cut across it three times, as Marrag used to do.

'Go your ways in peace,' he said, in a loud clear voice, 'for
Earth Mother smiles on you today.'

Rua felt the blood beat in her head. She flung back her chin
and throwing the robe from her with a wild movement of her
arms shouted, 'This Garroch is a liar! What does he know of
Earth Mother's face?'

There was a sudden horrified gasp from the People of the
Hill. They turned to stare at her in fear, almost expecting something hunched and shambling to come out of the midden pit
behind her and drag her down red and screaming.

Garroch's face had turned white and ghastly, the knife
trembling in his hand now. Marrag was shaking his white head
petulantly and turning from side to side. 'What is it?' he was
saying. 'Who spoke then! I cannot see.'

Only that rebellious man who had lain with Rua in the night
seemed to find any delight in this awful occasion. He called out
derisively, 'Let the Fish Woman say what she knows. Perhaps
Earth Mother has been to her in the night, who can tell?'

Rua ignored him and spoke out in a loud voice:

'Earth Mother sends Garroch a challenge. Garroch has
grown too proud, she says. Let Garroch go out and prove to

the People of the Hill that he is fit to be the voice of the Old Man, Marrag.'

Like a man in a trance, Garroch made a pace forward, towards her.

'I am afraid of nothing,' he said. 'Earth Mother knows that.'

Rua laughed harshly. Then she pointed her long finger at him, between the eyes.

'Yes, Garroch is afraid of one thing,' she said. 'He is afraid of Hair Wolf!'

And Garroch started and bit his lip for the woman was speaking the truth. Of all the creatures and the men, of hill and forest and shore, Hair Wolf was the only one he feared, though he had never told his fear to any man.

Rua's quick eyes told her that she had found the mark. Her heart rejoiced.

'Go out today, Garroch the Chief's son,' she cried, 'and show Earth Mother that you are fit to be the voice of Marrag. Bring back Hair Wolf and lay him by her stone, then we shall believe you!'

Now, by the muttering about him, Garroch knew that he must do as she said if he was ever to lead the People of the Hill. He raised his head and stared Rua in the eye. She looked back at him without flinching, so great was her vengeance towards him. 'I will go,' he said, 'but we have a law here that only the Old Man or his voice must speak the messages of Earth Mother. So, in judgment on you now, I tell you that when I come down the hill again tonight, with Hair across my shoulders, you too must join him on the great stone. That is the law.'

He turned and walked back to Marrag, leading him to the house. Garroch must make ready for the hunt.

As they dragged Rua away to set her under guard until Garroch returned with his kill, she shouted after the young Chieftain, 'Take witnesses to see that you do not bring back a wolf that had died of old age!'

Garroch turned at the door of the house, his thin lips twisted grimly. 'I shall take a hunting party of six. They will be my witnesses. Under our law, if I do not kill my quarry, they must kill me. You may rest content, Fish Woman, until I return.'

They flung her into the darkness again. The one who had been with her the night before was set before her door, with his axe, as her guard. He called in to her that he must break her skull if she tried to come out again before they fetched her to lie on the Stone.

And something in his voice stirred a strange raw chord in

Rua's memory and suddenly she was sure that this was the man who had betrayed her and his Chieftain.

She groped among her few belongings and found the sharp bone needle. She felt its point carefully in the darkness. It was very keen. For a moment she almost thought of calling this man in to her: if she stood above the little tunnel, she could put the needle down through his neck or shoulders while he was still on his knees in the dark. But she changed her mind again. She would not use it on him unless he came into the hut of his own wishing. No one could blame her for that.

In Marrag's great house, Garroch prepared himself for the hunting of Hair Wolf. His shiny hair, that must never be cut, he pushed through a long hollow bone and knotted it, to keep it out of the way. Then he wrapped narrow strips of horsehide round and round his forearms, and a broader strip about his belly and up between his legs. He wore his bears' claw necklace and white bones through his ear lobes. His running shoes were of light calfskin. And when he was ready, Marrag painted the red streaks of ochre and the black streaks of charcoal across his face and lengthwise down his body and thighs.

He took up his long-bladed greenstone axe and light wicker shield and stood in the doorway, laughing now.

Soon the villagers watched the small dark men streaming along the hilltop, with the sun on their bodies. They ran lightly, like questing animals themselves, their axes held slightly forward. Their vicious shadows followed them, moving along the slope of the hill.

Brach was proud and afraid at the same time. When her father and his men had vanished over the hill, she ran swiftly to the Old Woman Stone, to beg her not to let Hair kill Garroch that day at least.

Old Marrag did not pray or weep: he slept, leaning against the clay-wall, dreaming of his youth.

# 8: Hunting

THROUGH THE heat of the day they ran, stopping only to lap water from the small streams that trickled down to the distant plain or to stand, hands over their searching eyes, sniffing the air like hounds.

They loped easily, hungrily, with little in their stomachs, as hunting-dogs should run. They would not eat until the sun went below the hill, for that was their habit until the full-belly time of the year when the rich barley had been baked and ground in the querns and made into cakes, and the full berries had come out on the bushes, and the cows could spare milk from their calves. Then there would be bread, and fruit and cheese in plenty for a while: and with good fortune, the meat of the red deer and the wild boar. But now they ran hungry and silent, their minds empty of everything but the death to come, whether of beast or man. It did not matter which, for whatever was to happen would be by the will of Earth Mother, and there was no going beyond that.

Yet, when the sun began to sink and they had scoured the country round as far as they dared, almost into the territory of the Dog Men on the next great hill from their own, they sat down panting in a little hollow, their long hands dangling over their painted knees.

And the oldest of men, a warrior who had taught Garroch much about hunting in his boyhood, sniffed the dry air again. He made the little barking sound in his throat that hunters must make to draw attention, but he did not speak, for now they were not men but beasts of prey. Garroch glanced at him and the man stared him in the eye and then shook his head, to mean that they would not find Hair Wolf that day.

The dark eyes of the hunters all stared at Garroch, where he sat in the middle of the circle. They were telling him wordlessly that he was a man in the shadow of death, for he had vowed to Earth Mother that he would bring her back the beast she asked for.

Garroch knew what their eyes were saying, these witnesses. He looked at them each in turn, then, throwing up a blade of grass to see which way the wind blew, he stood up and sniffed again and again, following his nose, trancelike, to the lip of the hollow.

The oldest man, whose task it was to kill him for Earth Mother should his hunting prove unsuccessful, rose swiftly, his axe ready, and followed him lest he should suddenly run away from them towards the country of the Dog Men. For if that happened, this hunter, whose title was The Watcher, must pay a life for a life and lie on the Stone himself before the day was out.

Garroch turned and saw him coming, and smiled his thin dark

smile, as though to tell him not to worry. Then he pointed to a little spinney that straggled over the rocks almost an arrowflight away. The older man sniffed and nodded, his eyes alight. He lowered his axe and beckoned to the others, who came sniffing and then smiling, their lips drawn back over their white teeth. They looked towards Garroch once more, waiting to be led.

When at last he plunged noiselessly forward they followed him closely, like his many shadows.

And even as he leapt out on the death run, Brach, lying below the Old Woman Stone, started as though a little thorn had been pushed suddenly into her heart. Without knowing, she knew what was to happen and though her mouth and throat were dry with the heat of this long day she struggled up again and clasped her hands as far as she could round the Stone Woman who had sent her father over the hill to look down into the dark stinking throat of death.

But in her dark prison, Rua knew no such stirrings. She slept from time to time, suffering thirst and hunger for they had not brought anything to her. When she slept, her dreams were troubled by wolves. They came close to her and opened their cavernous mouths, almost engulfing her. She saw the yellow fangs, the black and glistening throat, and she woke, again and again, sweating with fear, the stench of the man in her nostrils. Then for a while as she struggled not to scream, her hands at her mouth and throat, the heavy darkness of her hut was full of the rustling of clawed feet, the obscene padding round of the dream that would not wholly die even though she was awake.

At last, Rua would even have welcomed that grizzled man who had betrayed her and whom she had planned to kill if he crawled in to her this day. She listened for him, hoping that she would soon hear his hands and knees coming along the curving passageway. But he did not come: he lay sprawled and asleep in the late sunshine, tired by his watch, his axe a yard away from his outflung hand.

At the outskirts of the spinney, where the starved and dry-branched bushes struggled for life among the rocks, and the trees reached down, gnarled and twisted, to form a natural doorway, a great dog-wolf stood, his amber eyes on them, his tongue lolling from his mouth, as though he had long expected Garroch and was waiting to welcome him.

When Garroch saw this, he flung his light wicker shield before his breast and ran forward even faster, trying to smother the great fear that swept over him by the violence of his action.

Then the great wolf seemed to smile at him, as though he understood, and springing round, with a strangely abrupt sweep of his tail, he darted between the trees, towards a small and rock-strewn glade, where the sparse grass grew among the dry-barked bushes.

Garroch bayed like a hunting hound and plunged after him. The other men ran now at their leisure, unafraid, but ready with their axes should the wolf turn on them. Their task was to defend themselves, not to kill the creature, and to form a ring of witnesses about the struggle when it should come.

Yet it came so suddenly that they were unprepared for it. They saw Garroch running forward, towards a darker part of the little wood, and then they saw the great wolf appear on a boulder above him, to his right.

They did not warn their prince, for in a case like this they were sworn to give him no aid. But what they did not do the wolf's own growl of triumph did for Garroch. Even as the great beast plunged down upon him, Garroch swayed towards him and under him, his feet planted firm among the rocks and pebbles. The wolf swept over the man's back, missed his stroke by a hand's breadth, and as he fell clumsily to Garroch's left side, the long-bladed greenstone axe struck down, once, twice, on that sharp backbone just above the haunches. Then the prince leapt sideways, an arm's breadth. The creature screamed and for a moment became a hairy jerking thing, whose jaws in their agony snapped with the sound of black flint being chipped with a hammer.

Garroch stood taunting Hair Wolf, walking round him and smiling, snuffling like a pleased hunting-hound, always just out of reach as the creature turned round and round, its hind-quarters dragging, the bloody foam dripping from his clacking jaws.

Then, when even Garroch had enjoyed this to his fill, he shouted 'Earth Mother!' in a great voice and brought the greenstone axe down on the suffering beast's skull.

The wolf's eyes seemed to glow in savage gratitude towards him for a moment before it rolled over, twitching among the dry boughs.

The hunters ran forward and swung the warm beast on to their shoulders, ignoring the blood and ordure that came from him. He should be Garroch's to carry only when they reached the village. Now he must rest.

But Earth Mother was not ready to let him go yet. As he

stalked on, ahead of his followers, the power and the pride of his victory showing in his upflung head and high-held breast, he suddenly halted and pointing to his right, barked again like a hound.

Ten paces from him, a bitch-wolf stood sniffing the air, as though she knew her mate was dead. As Garroch turned towards her, his eyes burning again in proud ecstasy, she scuttled round in terror and tried to leap to safety into a crevice between two great boulders.

But the prince had moved forward, swift as the night breeze, dropping his axe and grasping her by the shaggy hind-legs even as she struggled to hide from him.

Now the other hunters ran forward, their axes ready, for Garroch's duty had been done already and this wolf was any man's to kill.

But as he wrenched the bitch from between the rocks, Garroch shouted at them in his high Chieftain's voice, commanding them to stand clear so that he could improve his offering to Earth Mother without the interference of any other.

At one moment, they saw the heavy creature hanging down, her muzzle almost scraping the rocky ground, screaming with rage and terror. Then, as Garroch swung her round, meaning to dash her head against the rock, she seemed to curl upwards in an arc-like thrusting movement and the hunters saw that she had fastened on Garroch's throat, savagely and with deathly hate.

Now, as their prince fell backwards, they stood helpless, unable to strike at the wolf, for the two were rolling over and over on the ground, leaving a trail of red wherever their bodies rested.

And the wondering hunters saw Garroch's long thumbs dig deeply into the bitch-wolf's eyes. They heard her high unearthly yell of agony as she broke from him, shaking her helpless head and spattering them as they closed in. Then Garroch was lying across the wolf's belly, his hands clenching her long jaws together, his dark face nuzzling in among the grey hair of her throat.

And at last, as the muscles of his back hunched again and again with his great effort, her body began to thresh uncontrollably, almost flinging him from her, and when his hands unclasped about her jaws she made no effort to bite him any longer, but whimpered for a short while and then straightened her body abruptly, as a gout of dark blood spurted from her and she began to stiffen.

Garroch rose to his knees and looked up at his hunters. There was bloody hair in his mouth and his teeth that had been white now showed red as he grinned in his pain. Now the fear of Old Hair the Wolf had gone from him and he knew in the deepest part of his belly that he was more wolf than they.

On his knees, trembling suddenly with exhaustion and shock, he began to sing his triumph song, openly naming himself Wolf, not using the tabu word, 'Hair'.

The tribesmen stared at him in horror but then, when they smelled his pride and power, they sensed him as something greater than themselves and kneeled about him, touching the stony ground with their foreheads in respect.

And when at last he fell silent and rolled over on to his back, his eyes closed, they took him up as though he was already sacredly painted and ready to go into the chilly room that awaited him in the Long House of Sleep.

They carried the two wolves back, together with their prince. At the gates, the folk of the hill bowed their heads and sucked in their breath with admiring respect.

Then one of them ran to set Rua free, for now she could not be put on the Stone since Garroch's words had been, 'When I come down the hill again, with Hair upon my shoulders,' and it had not happened like that. He had come down on a litter made of broken boughs, with the two wolves lying beside him and not upon his shoulders.

But when they dragged Rua struggling out of the darkness and told her her good fortune, she stared at them wildly as though she had never seen men before, and bared her teeth at them savagely. They could not understand the sounds she made.

They saw too that she had scratched at her throat until it bled in the dark terrors of that day.


# 9 : Barley Warning


A SHUDDER seemed to pass across the land. As each warm day was followed by a night of gentle rain, making green the stalks and full the ears of barley, it was as though a new life, a realisation, an awareness came into the hearts of the crops, so that on every hillside and in every unwooded valley, the barley stirred and whispered, anxious for what was soon to come, the fulfilment.

And the dark folk of all the chalk hills, wherever they were, heard this living whisper, through their ears and their mouths, in the palms of their flint-scarred hands and across the hard soles of their feet. And most of all they heard it and felt its shuddering, this life, in the deep pit of the belly; and they did not know whether to laugh for joy, or to hide away in darkness for what might come to happen.

'Hark, hark!' they whispered, themselves, turning about like blind ones, holding their hands to their ears in the sunlight. 'She is stirring! Earth Mother is turning over, stretching her arms and legs. Soon it will happen now! Soon . . . soon . . . Aiee!'

And the children, playing *touch wood* just outside the safe stockades, or in and out of the midden-ditches, chipping at their little flints or rocking their clay dolls, stared wide-eyed at each other, knowing without needing to be told, that soon *the thing* was going to happen again. *It* was going to happen.

They made the sacrificial gesture, passing finger across throat and then across heart and spitting to signify blood. 'Cross heart and throat,' they said, '*It* will happen soon!'

And now men and women began to have bad dreams again: the sort they had everywhere just before sowing-time, but worse. Before sowing-time, it was always the same one, where you rolled on the broken earth with the red on your throat and thighs until the earth accepted you and wrapped herself round you, taking you down into her, among the roots and the worms, to feed the tender little seeds that had been so carefully saved in their clay beakers since last time, in the warmest parts of the huts.

These things were not easy to understand; unless the Old Man got the folk together and explained them. Then it brought comfort, if only to hear that all men shared the same dreams, that these were no private terrors.

He would say, 'Since the beginning of things it has been so. When Earth Mother took pity on man and gave him her wheat and barley to keep the life beating on inside him, it has been so. Earth Mother makes a bargain with her children. At sowing-time she calls for a little drink, a little blood, so that her seed-children shall grow inside her. That is a good bargain—one throat goes short so that a hundred throats be fed. Earth Mother is good to us!'

And all would beat their breasts or foreheads with blunt flints, rocking on their hams, and nodding at the Old Man's words.

Then he would smile and say, 'Earth Mother tells you that in your sleep, tells you that you may be the Chosen One to make the corn grow. She tells you this in the pictures you see. She tells you every night until the sowing is over and the little seeds are covered warm, for she wants you to be ready if she should point at you. She wants you to know, so that you will not scream and try to run away when I speak her voice and touch you on the neck. She wants you to lie still then so that I can do my part. That is why she shows you all this as you sleep. Earth Mother is good: she knows the weakness of her children and teaches them gently what is needed if we are to live.'

That was easy, when the Old Man had spoken, so patiently, even showing them gently how he drew the flint knife this way across, then that—just like the little children, when they said, 'Cross heart and throat.' Then they spat. Only what the Chief was showing them was not spitting. It was the real thing, that you didn't like to talk about, to think about, but which had to be faced, sooner or later, if you were unlucky.

But at the cutting-time of barley, it was different. The dreams then were nameless, many of them. And the Chief would not talk about them because now he had them too, especially if the crop came up thin, or with the worm in it; or if it did not dry out but rotted in downpours of rain before it could be stored. Then the Chief might have to offer himself to Earth Mother, to appease her anger. But this did not happen very often now: though each year it was done in a mime, with a knife of wood, to show Earth Mother that it was not forgotten.

But for most men, before the corn was safely gathered in and they had passed through the long low tunnel of fear into the light at the other end, the nights were hideous: milk turned sour on the tongue, flesh turned putrid at the knife's end, there were heavy paddings on the roof and furious snufflings below the door. Sometimes a child would wake, screaming, 'The worm is in my mouth! Ah, take it out!'

It was at this time of the year that thorn-bushes would lean outwards to strike a man through the eye. Or walking with his sheepdog beyond the hill at night, he would suddenly observe that it threw the shadow of a wolf upon the chalk. And women, squeezing the juices of berries to make their dyes would find that what trickled between their fingers was something else that did not flow inside a fruit. Then they would scream and scream again.

At this time of the year all suffered, until the corn was cut—and safely stored in the clay pots, in the warmest parts of the huts, away from cold and draughts that would freeze the hearts of the Barley Women and turn them green again and mildewed, making them hate the anxious people of the house.

Garroch could walk a little now. Before, he had lain day after day on the sheepskin bed, with the herbs tied to his throat, to the ragged wound that would not heal, where the wolf had ripped past the claw necklace to avenge her mate.

Old Marrag had mumbled all the charms he knew, and Brach had put fresh leaves into the long hole day after day. And at last the mouth of the wound ceased to grin so savagely; and then when it seemed time to do so, Garroch's women had gathered the webs of spiders and had spread them over the mouth to make it knit into whole flesh again. And this it had done at last, gradually, and leaving a jagged scar of red flesh where the wound had been.

Now Garroch could eat again, soft things like berries or the meat of small birds, and began to form his words so that they could understand what he meant at last.

Rua Fish had squatted outside his door for many days, smiling at everyone who passed in or out, making signs, trying to ask if Garroch was healed. Only Brach smiled back at her, in pity. The others threw stones and garbage at her, accusing her of Garroch's death.

Once at night Rua tried to push into the Old Man's house, but the guard at the door struck her a glancing blow at the side of the head with his axe. She fell down and could not rise again until the morning light had slanted across the village.

Then she got up and staggered away, through the stockade gates, crying, her face all bloody and her eyes black with pain.

It was the flint miners who next saw her, days afterwards. She was pale and shuddering with hunger as she stood at the head of the mine shaft, trying to peer into the galleries that spread out on either side of the great tree-trunk that stood up in the middle of the deep hole.

One of them, a broad-shouldered man with thick arms, leaned out and called up to her, laughing, 'You want food? You want food, little Rua Fish?'

She nodded down, pointing to her open mouth.

The man laughed again and whispered to his fellows, who clustered behind him in the gallery, in the dim light of the fat lamps, their antler picks in their hands. They were not warriors and could not afford to keep women of their own. Few women came their way, save at the feasting times.

'Come down, Rua Fish,' the man said. 'There is food here for you. Put your feet in the little notches and come down. We will catch you when you get down to us. You will be safe with us! We will not hurt you, like the others. Come down!'

He had to say it many times, and became impatient, before she could understand what he meant. Then she came down, halting and unsteady, talking to herself of the food they had promised her.

The big man leaned out of the low gallery and put his arms about her thin body. He drew her into the gallery and then, when he had his own balance again, flung her backwards into the sooty gloom viciously.

Not understanding, she cried out for the food they had promised, but they had nothing there. Laughing at her words, they used her again and again, promising her sheep meat and honey if she would be a good girl.

When they went back to the village, she lay at the end of the farthest gallery, among the rough flints, weeping in her exhausted sleep.

Garroch was now strong enough to walk outside again. The folk at the village stared at him in wonder, as at one who had come back from the dead. They bowed before him, some touching the livid scar across his neck, believing that this would save them from such a wound from Old Hair.

And when he could walk as far as the barley fields, he lay down among the tenderest ears of corn and thanked Earth Mother for dealing so generously with them. He lay there for a while, as though in the bride-bed, and then went back slowly to the Old Man's house.

His women were sitting about the fire, suckling their babies or scraping the fat from the skins of sheep and oxen. Gwraig, his eldest wife, wiped the sweat from her face with her hair and said, 'Wraich, the Old Woman, has spoken to us, up from under the floor. She says that you must be the Corn Man this harvest, for Marrag is too weak to do the dance along the hilltop. You are stronger now. You must be the one. Marrag would fall and then we should have to kill him. You must take his place.'

Garroch looked at her sternly, undecided whether to kick her in the mouth for such daring words. But she looked up at him so fiercely, the little scraper tightly clenched in her hand, that he decided not to treat her harshly.

He said to his father, 'Old Man, you hear what the woman says. Am I to be the Corn Man in your place this harvest?'

Marrag came back from a sunlit dream in which he was chasing a roebuck over the hill with the new greenstone axe in his hand, and peered at his son through the thick smoke.

'This is the time of the Corn Dance,' he said. 'The man who makes the dance must needs have strong legs for it lasts from dawn till the light goes down behind the hills.'

Garroch took the Old Man's thin hand in his own and said gently, 'Am I the Corn Man, Marrag?'

Marrag looked down at his son's hand as though he had never seen it before.

'This is a pretty bracelet,' he said. 'Who gave that to you, my son?'

Garroch stroked his hand and said, 'Wraich gave it to me, when we put her under the floor, Old Man.'

Marrag screwed up his eyes and seemed to listen for something. Then at last he said, 'Wraich says that you are the Corn Man, Garroch. Dance well, my son, so that the barley prospers in our fields.'

When the day came, the women mixed up the white clay in the pots with water that the Old Man had made, until it was a thick paint. Then they made Garroch lie down while they covered his body with the clay. And when it was dry on him, Marrag made lines of red ochre the length of his body. And between each line of red, he drew a line of black with the soot from the lamps.

Then they bound lengths of cowhide tightly about his arms and legs and belly, until his shape was different from that of ordinary men; and about his head and shoulders they wound the sheepskin that the Corn Man must always wear, with little holes cut in it for his eyes, and ram's horns tied to the sides of his head.

Brach came running in as Garroch stood upright, stiffly because of the thongs.

She stopped at the bottom step of the house and shrank back as he came towards her, his arms outstretched. Then she gave a little scream and fell before him, rubbing her face in the dust of the floor. And when Garroch turned to his wives, they too kneeled before him, crying with fear.

He walked up the steps into the village, his arms and legs

already crying out with the pain of the thongs. And everywhere he went, the folk fell to their knees, wailing and shuddering, until he had passed.

Then he felt a great power come up into his breast. They had never fallen before him like this before. When he was Garroch, they joked with him, slapped his back, and treated him almost like one of themselves. But now they were afraid of him. He could do anything he liked with them, he knew. For now, he was no longer Garroch—he was the Corn Man, the beloved of Earth Mother herself, the one who fertilised her, putting the Barley Women into her deep dark womb.

So great was his ecstasy then that he would have shouted out aloud, had the thick skin about his head allowed him, and the pain in his throat and limbs been gone.

At last, across the compound, the dawn sun struck. The villagers hurried out through the gates, their sickles in their hands, bowing their heads as they passed him. Before them danced three youths, their faces white with clay, their bodies decked with leaves—the lily-white boys, who would lead the reapers to a successful harvest, singing and playing on bone flutes.

Gwraig came to the door of the hut and whispered, 'Marrag gives you his spirit. You are Marrag now, Corn Man. Go up on to the hill and dance the corn dance.'

Garroch bowed his head towards her and went through the gates, taking the little path that led away from the fields, and up the far hillside, as the Corn Man must always do.

Brach watched him go, then she lay on the floor and began to sob. She felt she had lost her father that day and was afraid she might never find him again.

# 10: Barley Rape

AS THE folk worked their way across the slope in a long line, grasping the full ears of corn in one hand and slashing with the flint sickle in the other, the drums began to beat from behind the long House of Sleep. Its silence was broken now, the only time in the year unless a great Chief should go into its last darkness.

'Drm-Drm-Drm,' said the deep drums, the flat dark palms thudding down on the shiny sheepskin that was stretched so tight with its thong round the neck of the booming jar of clay.

'Drm-Drm-Drm!' said the drums again.

The folk went on working, hacking the long bodies of the Barley Women, as though they had suddenly become enemies, reaping them, raping them, the antler-shafts of sickles already sliding with sweat in their hands. Now backs were beginning to ache; muscles to twitch in the dark-skinned narrow backs. Sweat ran bitter into eyes. No one dared look up until the drums should speak again.

All each man could hear as he looked on the ground was the hiss of the reaper beside him, the hiss of the toothed flint against the shining barley stalk, the hiss of the wind over the high hill. And their hearts thudded in their throats as they waited, striking, inching onwards, wondering whether the third call on the drums would ever come and let the reaping go right.

Then suddenly a curlew started up with a thin scream across the broad fields.

'Drm-Drm-Drm-*Drm!*' roared the drums at last.

The long line of folk stopped in their slashing as though they had been one man. They looked up, half fearful, as though they had been one man. Then they smiled and nodded, and a sigh of relief shivered along the line of barley reapers. It would be a fortunate reaping after all!

Above them, along the sharp and sunlit ridge of the high chalk hill, the Corn King pranced on his way, Earth Mother's way, his head held high and jerking this way and that, his back arched so that his chest was flung out with arrogance, his thighs rising higher and higher with each toe-pointed step, one hand before him, one behind him, like some stiff-jointed doll from under the soil, from the womb of Earth Mother herself.

The drums began to speak faster, stuttering now in their relief.

'Drm-Drm-Drm-Drm-Drm!'

Garroch, hearing them quicken, quickened his reaping dance, the sharp flints cutting his naked feet, but proud and prouder so as not to make the reapers frightened again.

Under the heavy sheepskin shroud, that hung half-way down his back, his head and shoulders already sweated. He could hardly see through the little eye-hole cut in the skin. He felt the ram's horns rattling on each side of his head. He felt the tight thongs biting cruelly into his arms and belly and thighs. And he felt the cold morning wind about his legs and middle.

All was hot or cold, pleasure or pain, soft or sharp: there were no middle-ways. Life was sweet or bitter, light or dark: only that. Living or dying. Garroch gasped suddenly at the sharp agony of his half-healed throat, where Hair Wolf-bitch had ripped past his necklace. He almost fell down with the swift dagger of pain that clove up to his tongue's root. Under the stiff thick layer of white clay, his face suddenly went cold.

If he fell down now? he thought. They would stop reaping the corn: they would run away, back to the dark houses, to hide. They would think Earth Mother had called him away from them. He must not do that or they would starve: either that or come up the hill and kill him there and then, and choose another Corn King. He did not like to think of how they would do it, with the hooked sickles; how they would have to do it to keep the old law. He could feel the rough rasping of the things on his throat as he stumbled, and righted himself in the cruel sunlight, to carry on with his dance.

The drums echoed now among the hills. They were joined by the wailing of the long horn. That was the signal for the folk to bend once more and continue their cutting of the barley ears.

He was safe for a time. They might not see if he stumbled now. The sweat poured down his body, turning to cold water as it came from beneath the thick sheepskin and met the gusts of morning air on the hilltop.

He began to think of old Marrag, rocking himself back and forth in his dark hut, almost forgetful of what the season was, lost in his old dreams, a weak old man now, unable to perform the corn dance.

Garroch was doing this for the Old Man, risking death for him so that the Earth Mother should smile on the folk and let them get their harvest in once again.

Garroch pranced on along the hill ridge, until at last he came to the point where the folk could see him no longer because of a little hillock that reared itself from the grass-grown chalk. There he flung himself down, groaning with the weight of sheepskin on his head and shoulders, with the weight of the duty that he must fulfil if Marrag was to remain Old Man for another year.

And as he unwound the stinking thing from his head, to draw in the fresh air for a little space, he started back with shock. Rua Fish was sitting in the hollow behind the little hummock of earth, waiting for him, smiling at him, her old broad-lipped smile that showed her big teeth.

Only her eyes were different, empty now, or filled with

something that had not been there before, something which Garroch had seen in other eyes that looked up from the great stone before the Old Man's knife came down.

He saw that she too held a knife, listlessly, in her lap, as though it was the most natural thing in the world for her to have. He remembered that he had no knife, that his limbs and body were naked and unprotected, that he was weak with the sickness that had not yet left his blood. Rua Fish was strong. She had once killed a man, Garroch recalled, her own father, Kraka of the Fishers. Now she was waiting to kill him, he thought, there on the hilltop. And if she did, no one would harm her, for she was not like the others now, Earth Mother had visited her and made the change in her head. She must not be touched now, must never lie on the stone as another would have to do.

He half-rose to his knees and held out his hands towards her, wondering whether to try and pin her arms down, or whether he might beg her not to strike him in his weakness. A sudden surge of pride swept over him. He had killed the two wolves, then he could kill her as easily, he thought. He bared his teeth, showing them to her, hoping to frighten her, but she did not move. She only smiled back at him, drawing her mouth so broad that her face did not look like that of a woman, or of any creature he could think of. He knew that he could not frighten Rua Fish now and his own heart began to thud in his thin breast. Again the sweat ran down his neck and back, for Garroch was desperately afraid.

But Rua only laughed at him, silently, without moving the hand that held the knife. And at last, when he had struggled towards her, trying to touch the earth before her feet with his forehead as sign of reverence, he felt that his strength was going from him fast, like flowing blood, leaving him helpless. He knew that she would see that and he tried to speak words to her, saying that he meant her no harm, that he was the Corn Man and must not be hurt until the cutting was over. But the pain in his throat where the she-wolf had bitten came on him again and he could not form the words.

Then he fell down before her, staring wildly up into the clear blue sky of morning on the hilltop, powerless to help himself. And he saw Rua Fish bending over him, still smiling at him, her teeth coming down closer and closer to his face. He tried to close his eyes but was too powerless in her magic to make his lids obey him.

He saw her eyes near his own and felt the weight of her body upon his, savagely thrusting at him, again and again, as he lay spread out and helpless.

Then he knew that his face was wet with her salt tears and he heard her groaning sobs as she rolled him roughly this way and that until at last his senses left him and he lay still, stiff with the white clay, under the sky on the hill.

Below him, across the long fields, the folk sweated, chanting the rhythmic barley song now, the thumping drums driving them on and on across the flint-strewn earth. Beside the reapers walked their children, clasping the deep wicker baskets to them, staggering with the weight of barley ears before the day was over.

At last Garroch rose and stumbled down the hill to his father's house, his Corn Dance done. The singing reapers could not see beneath the sheepskin head-dress, or they would have wondered why the Corn Man's face was so fearful in the dusk.

Yet, even if they had questioned those staring eyes, Garroch would not have dared tell them his fear—that the Corn Man had been dishonoured and rolled in the dust, that he had lost his power, that he felt despised of Earth Mother and unclean. He would not have told them that his manly powers had left him, that he could not do with Rua what the Corn Man must always be able to do.

He would not have told them because they would have put him in the great brushwood fire after the last sheaf of corn had been cut, thinking him to be as dry and useless as the dead barley stalks that men were already rooting from the ground.

# 11: Barley Night

MARRAG SAT in the firelight of the great brushwood pile, the women of his house about him, Garroch's wives. They had decked him with leaves and barley straw, for now he was the Corn Man again, his son having passed back the magic power to him after the dance.

Garroch stood behind his father, the thong-marks still deep in his legs and arms, the white clay washed from his body.

And as they waited, the sounds of singing and drums came over the fields towards them, and the torchlight burst on to their eyes.

'They are bringing the one who cut the last sheaf, who cut the Corn Hag,' said Gwraig, knowingly. 'Let us hope he makes good sport before he goes to Earth Mother.'

Brach crept to her father and put her arm about him, afraid. Marrag stared before him, as he had done for all the many seasons he had been the Old Man. The Corn Man had nothing to do but be there for this rite; Marrag was relieved, for he was not strong enough now to do these things.

Then into the wide circle of women and old men, the reapers and their children came, pushing before them the cutter of the last sheaf, a white-haired man who usually tended the swine at the edge of the oak forest. He had no name. The children all called him 'Grunter' because of the way he spoke, for he had lived so long with swine that he could only say their words.

Grunter stumbled into the firelight, the great Corn Hag, a thick sheaf bound together and pulled in here and there to look something like a woman, hung heavily on his back.

Gwraig called to Brach, 'Look, child, he is carrying his wife on his back. He is a kind husband! Kinder than mine!'

Grunter heard her and smiled, a gap-toothed smile, and made a stupid gesture towards her with his hand, as though he would take Gwraig on his back too. She saw the gesture and called bitterly, 'Don't be too generous with your strength, Grunter! You will need it! See how long you can carry yourself, and we'll be satisfied!'

The other women began to laugh cruelly when they heard her words, for Gwraig was a fierce one and it was well to laugh at her jokes.

Grunter took the laugh to be one of friendship for him, and grinned round at the folk. But the young men ran forward and pushed him round and round the circle, 'Run faster, Grunter,' they said, 'the Corn Hag is angry with you for being so old and weak!'

The swineherd tried to do as he was told, stumbling on and on round the firelit circle, being pushed by all who could get near enough to him, until at last he fell face foremost and lay still, drawing in his breath painfully.

Then the young men raised him to his feet and hung stones round his neck on leather thongs.

'The Corn Hag is prospering,' they said. 'She likes you for her husband. She is getting fat under your care, Grunter. Can't you feel how fat she is getting, fat and heavy?'

Grunter nodded, smiling as best he could.

'Come,' they said, throwing him forward again, 'you must not keep her waiting, Grunter. Give the Corn Hag a ride, then! Be a good husband!'

The wretch shambled on again round the circle of mocking faces, the sweat running down his breast. Now Garroch reached down and covered Brach's face with a fold of his flax tunic. He felt her warm tears on his hand as he touched her.

Grunter had fallen again. He was gasping for breath now and could hardly stand when they put the bigger stones on his neck.

'What, man!' they cried, 'is this the sort of husband you are? How do you expect us to get a good harvest next year if you treat the Corn Hag like this? Run, man, and show what you can do!'

Now Grunter began to cry, high and wheezing, like a little baby who is little more than born into the world. He ran with long dragging strides, almost falling with each step. And at last one of the young warriors stuck out his foot so that the creature tripped over it and sprawled in the middle of the firelight, face downwards.

'Make love to her now, Grunter!' they all shouted. 'Now you have treated her so well, do the rest, and make sure we get a good harvest! Make love to her now!'

And so the young men rolled the swineherd on to the thick barley sheaf, and pressed his face down among the stalks, deep down until it could not be seen. And as his thin body twitched, trying to get air into the tormented lungs, they laughed and said, 'That's right! That's it, Grunter, make love to her man! Faster! Faster!'

And at last the limbs stopped twitching and the swineherd lay still across the tumbled corn-woman.

'Look, he is tired,' they shouted. 'He is a good husband, anyone can see that! Good Grunter! Good Grunter!'

Brach had heard it all and shuddered against Garroch's side. He patted her shoulder. 'Do not be afraid,' he whispered. 'That cannot happen to you. It must always be a man.'

Now they set Grunter's body near to the fire so that all could see him, and put the big round stones about him, daubed with red ochre, in honour of a good corn husband. In the old savage days these stones had been heads, those of other villages, but now it was stones.

'Aiee!' sighed the older men, 'times have changed. We are a

soft-hearted folk now!'

Then the Corn Dog came into the circle, a man dressed from head to foot in skins, barking, and running at the women and children with frightening gestures, making them scatter before him. He ran at Marrag once, great in his daring, because the Old Man was getting weak. But Marrag gave him so long and hard a look that the Corn dog turned tail and ran after the children again, wondering whether Marrag would hold it against him when it came the time for a meeting at the big stone.

And after the Corn Dog was tired and had taken off his skins, one of the young men stepped forward, elected to this duty, and said to the Old Man, 'Old Man, Old Man, come down from your chair and be killed!'

Then the crowd chanted, 'Old Man, Old Man, come down from your chair and be killed. The year has passed, the corn is got in, and now we must have a new Chief!'

Garroch looked over his father's shoulder at the young man. There was something strange about his eyes, as though he meant the words and was not saying them, as they should be said, as part of the festivities. Garroch looked down at the young man's hand and saw that it was clenched. He saw the pointed edge of the flint that the man's hand could not quite cover. This time they were going to kill the Old Man in all reality.

Garroch caught Gwraig's eye. She was smiling, her lips parted, as though she knew what was going to happen.

The young man still waited in the firelight. 'Come down, Old Man,' he said, 'come down and be killed!'

Old Marrag shuffled up from his chair, as he had done so many times before. He knew that nothing happened. Only a finger drawn across his throat. Then he must lie down until the folk had shouted three times, 'The Old Man is dead!' After that he must rise and then they would shout, 'The Old Man is risen!' And they would all eat and drink after that until the morning came.

But this time something strange happened. As Marrag was getting down from his chair, Garroch pushed forward and flung the young man away from him, into the circle.

'I am the killer of the Old Man,' he called.

The crowd was suddenly hushed. Marrag felt that something had gone wrong and tried to wave his son away. But Garroch caught him by the arms and forced him down on to the ground, drawing his finger across his father's throat gently.

'The Old Man is dead, People of the Hill!' he said. He looked round the circle so fiercely that no one dared accept the challenge. And so at last the folk shouted that the Old Man was dead, and then that the Old Man was living, and Marrag went back to his chair, a little puzzled, but generally pleased with the way things had turned out.

Only Gwraig dared to whisper to her husband, 'You fool! You fool! This was to be the night, you fool! Now you must go on being a slave to this old dog for another year!'

Now Garroch struck the woman hard on the mouth so that the blood ran on to her chin. But she did not turn her face away. She licked her mouth and stared back at him with dark and angry eyes.

'You will regret it, Garroch,' she said slowly. 'You will regret that blow, and before long, my husband.'

But no one heard her except Garroch. And then the folk began to eat and drink more than they had eaten or drunk for many months—and when they had filled their bellies they began the Pairing Dance, which would last until dawn came again and all were exhausted with their exertions.

Now in the firelight, the village compound was full of dancing shadows; the women putting up a token struggle before surrendering, the men sometimes fighting each other to possess the woman they had most desired during the corn-growing.

Even Garroch's wives were taken by one or more of the young men, and Garroch himself led a gentle young woman away into the dusk, whispering to her that his wound had left him weak for the moment.

But before he did this, he saw to it that Marrag and Brach were left safely in the Old Man's house, and himself set the sacred lamp before the door, the flame which must never go out and which no one must pass through.

From the hillside, Rua watched the couples in the dying glare of the fire, wondering when she might come down and search for the scraps of sheepmeat or cheese which they would have left. It was almost light again before she dared pass through the gates into the silent village and snatch up all she could find.

As she ran back, away from the village, munching hungrily, she skirted a hollow surrounded by birch trees and low gorse bushes. And there she had the fright of her life, for the hollow was full of men, wearing blue war-paint and with feathers bunched in their hair. Some of them were sleeping, but some lying in the attitude of those who listen for the least sound. She saw their javelins and wooden shields, their axes and sling-thongs, and she knew that these were the Hunters who had come up from the oak forest in the valley at last, choosing their moment when they knew that the People of the Hill would be least likely to fight fiercely.

Rua did not know what to do for a moment. It flashed across the darkness of her mind that she might run back and tell Garroch that his enemies were about him. But just as she halted, one of the men turned and looked at her, his eyes wild in his painted face. He did not speak to her, but made the strange cry of the owl and beckoned with his axe that she was to pass on her way and not turn back.

Rua was very frightened by the man's savage face, but in a way she felt that he had treated her kindly, more kindly than anyone else had treated her for many months.

She nodded and, not knowing what else to do, called by to him in the voice of a sea-gull and then ran on, towards the hill, where she would be away from anything that might happen.

The hunter watched her go as he lay between his painted companions. Then he smiled, showing his sharp white teeth between his ochred lips.

'She is the one these fools call the Fish,' he said. 'They should call her the sea-bird, it seems.'

His companion, a fat red-haired warrior, grunted and licked the edge of his knife.

'It is almost time,' he said, in a deep voice, like a bear. 'The light will strike down on to the hill soon. Be ready, brother Wolf? Our harvest should be easier getting than theirs was!'

# 12 : As a Wolf

GARROCH WALKED slowly across the compound, cold and yawning. The brushwood fire was now only a flattened heap of white ashes. It was hard to believe that the Corn Festival had come and gone. Then he saw the ragged bundle of straw that had been the Corn Hag and, a few yards away from it, the white body of Grunter, lolling among the stones.

Garroch turned his head away and walked on to Marrag's house, wondering whether his women had got back yet. He did not expect they would have done so; they would make the best of the opportunity, he thought. It would be another year before it happened again. He could think of them without any love or jealousy, for they did not mean much to him. He could get a woman somewhere else, anywhere, they were easy to get —but hard to look after once they were got. They always squabbled, each thinking she was better than the others, more beautiful, more skilled in this and that. And they all tried to pass the unpleasant work on to someone else; they did not mind grinding corn, or weaving, or mixing up the clay paint; but it was difficult to get any of them to go out and find fuel, or gut a sheep.

Garroch smiled sourly. 'All bitches,' he said. 'All bitches save Brach! And one day, no doubt, Brach will be a bitch too. I hope she will find a strong man for husband who will give her pretty amber beads and many babies and a big house to keep her busy. Brach, ah little Brach!'

Garroch loved Brach only among women. He did not love his sons, because he was not sure they were his. They could have come by reason of the Pairing Dances that had been before their birth. But Brach was his daughter. She had his nose, which was hooked like a little eagle's beak, and his slanting eyes, and his very long thin fingers. They were Garroch's things, no other man's.

Garroch stood in the doorway of Marrag's house. Then he gave a sudden gasp of shock. The sacred lamp had been kicked down the steps and now lay upside down, the fat run out of it on to the clay floor and the flame dead. Someone had passed through the doorway against the law and had been in such a hurry that he had kicked the lamp over.

Garroch did not know what to do. This would mean that whoever had destroyed the flame must be smelled out and punished or the Old Man would have to suffer the wrath of Earth Mother.

Then Garroch looked into the hut and was afraid. Marrag lay asleep, his thin arm about little Brach, who snuggled up to him like a bear cub to its father, but Garroch could not see his face. It was covered by a black cloth. *They* had put the black cloth on him while he slept. Whoever had come in had deliberately put out the flame and had covered the Old Man's face with the black cloth, as a sign that he was already considered dead by the People of the Hill.

Now they would do the thing that had to be done, as soon as

they found the chance to do it, perhaps when Garroch was away. Or they might even do it suddenly while he was in the village, just as they had meant to do it the night before, when the young man called him down out of his chair, with the sharp flint in his hand.

Garroch bared his teeth like an animal and turned his head about, as though he surveyed the whole village.

'People of the Hill!' he snarled, 'all carrion-dogs, eaters of old dead men, pigs grubbing for worms!'

Next to Brach, Garroch loved his father. Though it was clear now that the folk of Craig Dun no longer loved Marrag, because of his age and weakness.

Garroch drew the black cloth from his father's face gently, so as not to trouble him. And just then Brach's eyes opened and looked into his simple with understanding.

Garroch bent over her and whispered, 'They mean to kill the Old Man, Brach. They will put him on the hill for Hair, or make a hole in his head with a flint, if he stays here.'

Brach nodded. 'I know,' she said. 'Gwraig wants him dead, so that she will be the great one here. If Marrag dies, you will be the Old Man, she says, and then she will be great and not a slave as she is now.'

Frowning, Garroch said, 'I will tie her to the stone and let the Hunters find her if she does not change her ways.'

Brach's eyes brightened. She nodded, 'Yes, yes,' she said. 'Do that, and I will sit at her feet in the daytime and tell her stories to frighten her, stories about blood dripping and Hair smelling it from afar!'

Garroch could not help himself; he smiled at his daughter's hatred of Gwraig, who often hurt her when he was not about to prevent it.

Marrag began to stir, sensing that others were awake about him.

"Quick,' said Garroch, 'take his cloaks and some dried meat in a little bag and lead him over the hill, perhaps to the Dog Men. Take your necklaces and a bag of arrow-heads. The Dog Men make bad ones; they would let you live there for our arrows until I can come to you with men I trust and bring Marrag back again.'

He almost dragged her to her feet and pushed food into her hand. She brushed the hair from her eyes, tiredly, and began to gather the cloaks and arrow-heads from the clay jar where they were kept.

Garroch said, 'Do not go across the compound. Take him along the tunnel-way, and through the stockade behind the house. Then you will not be seen. You will get over the first little hills without any eye being on you. Go quickly when he wakes. Make him go!'

He touched his father's hair and bowed his own forehead until it brushed the back of Marrag's hand.

The Old Man woke easily, like a child and said, 'In my dream the worm was in my mouth again and the black cloth on my head. A man with horns came into the house and kicked over the lamp so that the flame died. Therefore, I am ready to die, Garroch. It is time that you became the Old Man, so that the village may prosper.'

Garroch did not reply, but placed his hands beneath his father's armpits and lifted him to his feet.

Brach took the Old Man's hand. 'Come, Marrag,' she said, 'we have a little journey to make. Only as far as the place of the Dog Men.'

Marrag looked down at her shrewdly and said, 'You have food and arrow-heads for barter, Brach. But they are a treacherous folk, the Dog Men. They will take your arrow-heads and then kill us while we are asleep.'

Brach began to say something but Marrag shook his head. 'Have no fear,' he said. 'I shall come with you. I might as well die there as here. It will be a change, to die out of my own village. I have died here in my dreams every night since Wraich was put under the floor.'

He kneeled and touched the floor with his white forehead and then rose and waited for the girl to lead him away. She raised the hide covering of the low tunnel-way and got down on hands and knees. He followed her, meekly, like a younger brother.

The hide curtain had hardly fallen back into place when the first of the Hunters leaped over the high stockade, his flint knife in his mouth. Garroch saw him come and putting his hand to his mouth gave the high shrieking warning-call of his folk.

Then, snatching up his long greenstone axe, he ran to meet the warrior. It was the red-haired one who had waited for dawn to come, in the hollow. He was bulkier in stature than Garroch, but was stiff in his movements. Garroch observed him as he ran towards him and thought that this man ate too much. Garroch saw that his belly was fat over the thong of his axe-belt. He wished he had his long knife for that would be useful on a fat belly; an axe was only of service against arm or shoulder or head.

The tiredness had left his limbs for the moment and his head was clear again. The smell of blood had come into his nose, at the back, just under his eyes, and that was a good sign. That is how it had to be if one was going to fight well. Garroch forgot all about his father and little Brach, and launched himself directly at the Hunter, who was still panting from his exertion of clambering over the stockade.

The man saw him in time and put himself into a position of guard, his long knife held up towards Garroch's throat. His lips were drawn back in his blue-painted face, but this did not frighten Garroch, who could look as fierce as any man.

So Garroch swept in like a hawk, with a flurry of pinions, swerving under the knife thrust as he came close and sweeping his axe out in a short arc. He felt it bite and drag as he went on, under the man's arm. He heard the Hunter grunt with pain. Then he was on the other side of him and ready to strike again.

The man moved round, painfully, and glared at Garroch with furious eyes. Garroch feinted with the axe, making to strike down on the man's head and then curving the stroke so that it struck outwards, across the man's right forearm. This time the blade did not bite, but caught the Hunter a glancing blow with its thick antler shaft. Garroch felt the shock run up the shaft, felt the horn shiver as though it might break. Then, as in a dream, he saw the Hunter almost fling the knife into his other hand and come forward, blind with pain and anger. His own guard was down, for the heavy axehead had carried on with its own impetus, bringing itself almost to the level of Garroch's knee. He could not raise his arm in time, but with the thoughtless speed of a snake, he kicked upwards as the man came in, hard into his groin.

He screamed and flung his knife with all his force into Garroch's face. It caught him across the cheekbone, laying it open instantly. The blood spurted down his chest and the sudden shock of the impact sent him tottering back a pace.

Then in his pain he saw the Hunter fall before him, clutching his middle, and Garroch forgot his own raw open wound to crouch over him and raise the waiting axe.

It was at that moment that he felt a stunning blow at the back of the neck, so that he let fall the axe and flung up his arms. They were taken roughly and dragged back until the bones almost cracked with the violence of the hold.

Through the swimming blood mist of battle, Garroch saw that he was surrounded by Hunters, their feathers nodding in the morning breeze that blew across the compound. And over their shoulders he saw the first of the hillfolk, roused by his warning shout, staggering half-drugged with sleep from the huts.

'Carrion!' he screamed at his own folk. 'Betrayers!'

The man who lay before him sat up now, his face grim with pain, and looked at him viciously. Then he reached for Garroch's axe and dragging himself to his feet, steadied himself, groaning still, to smash the hillman's head.

But Garroch suddenly found himself flung aside, even as the blow fell, and then he lay on his side, seeing another Hunter, whose body was streaked with woad in great concentric circles, take the red-haired warrior by the arm, trying to quieten him.

He could understand the words they spoke, for all his life he had lived on the fringe of the Hunter's world, and had even had a little slave of the Hunter folk for his own, when he was a boy. As he lay on the hard earth, he recalled that slave, a brown-haired boy with a flat face, like an otter's. They had taught each other many words and signs. But when the famine came one snow-time, the little slave had had to be left outside, for there was not enough for all in the Old Man's house. Garroch had been sorry, for they had planned so many glorious things to do one day, when they were men together.

And Garroch on the ground heard the woad-painted man say, 'You do wrong, Kaa Fox, to bring the darkness into this one's head. He is a fighting-man, fit to kill a wolf with this axe.'

Garroch could not help himself. 'I have killed two, and one of them with my teeth,' he shouted, throwing up his head proudly.

They stopped and looked down at him, smiling with thin lips.

The blue-painted one said quietly, 'Very well, kill him, Kaa Fox, he is a boaster. No man could hunt with his little teeth!'

Then Garroch was up and on to him, before the man could pull out his knife, clasping him round the neck and tearing at him with his teeth, spattering him with blood from the open wound across his face.

The man fell back and no one could save him, for the two rolled so swiftly over the ground that a blow dared not be struck.

Then Garroch felt a terrible pain run up his body, from between his legs to his throat, and he gasped for breath, trying to pull away from the man now, lest he should bring up his sharp knee again.

The blue-painted man bent over him, splashed with his red blood, but smiling.

'I swear to the trees that you *could* kill a wolf with your teeth, you misbegotten hound!' he said grimly. 'They shall not touch you while I have two hands to fight with.'

Garroch stared up at him, wondering whether to kick his legs from under him and then kneel on his throat bone till he died. He could do that before his fellow-Hunters could get to him, he thought.

But Garroch saw something which killed all his desire to hurt this man. He saw his own blood mingling with that which flowed from a gash in the blue-painted warrior's cheek; the two bloods running together as one.

'Aiee!' he gasped, pointing, speechless.

The Hunter put up his hand and touched the place, staring at the blood on his palm.

'The Gods of the trees have willed it,' he said quietly. 'What they command is no man's to deny.'

He bent and raised Garroch to his feet. The Hunters came forward, at first cautiously and then greatly daring, letting fall their weapons and smiling strangely.

Kaa Fox, the red one, he whom Garroch had first fought, said with a shrug of his broad shoulders, 'Asa Wolf, my brother, the Gods have decided that you shall increase your kindred, it seems.'

He held out his hands towards Garroch, a little self-consciously, but with truth.

'We came to carry away your harvest and a head or two,' he said, 'but we must forego that pleasure now that you and my brother Asa Wolf have been blooded together. Call off your folk, Chieftain of the Hill, for we wish no trouble between us now.'

Garroch turned and saw that his warriors had circled the Hunters now, their axes ready, their arrows fitted to the bowstring. He held up his hand and called, 'Let there be peace between us. It has been decreed by another greater than ourselves that I and this Asa Wolf are brothers, and now there shall be friendship between the folk of hill and wood.'

Asa Wolf leaned over to him and said drily, 'Now we are brothers we must set your people to rights. They are a lazy lot, my brother. The guards snored too loudly to hear a herd of oxen coming through the gates this morning.'

Garroch saw his smile, felt the hard muscles of his encircling arm. 'We shall see to it, Brother Wolf,' he said, breaking the taboo now and using the creature's proper name. 'We will cut their hearts out, you and I, before the sun rises any higher. It will be a seal on our brotherhood.'

Asa Wolf punched him lightly in the chest and said, 'No, brother, fierce little dark brother, a thrashing should suffice. Let us beat them, that will be enough!'

Garroch looked at him under lowered lids. 'You are too kind to be a great ruler,' he said.

Asa Wolf shrugged and answered, 'Perhaps you are too harsh my brother!'

The People of the Hill were not sorry to have an end to their constant fear of an attack from the wood folk. Nor after the pleasures of the Corn supper were they anxious for war that morning.

They welcomed another little feast, building up the fires again although the sun was shining, for the morning was chilly. So the two peoples sat together, eating and drinking milk warm from the cows, punching each other in the side to stress the jokes they made, testing each other's weapons, exchanging small gifts, the dark-haired women of the hill giving the only thing they had to offer, unstintingly, as though anxious to be thought generous.

And at last, when the Hunters rose to go, Asa Wolf still sat by Garroch's side. Kaa Fox shook him roughly and said, 'Come, Asa Wolf, we are waiting for you. There is work yet to do, we must find another village still sleeping after the Corn supper.'

But Asa Wolf shook his shaggy head and lolled back on the sheepskins by the fire.

'It is in my mind to stay here for a while, with my new brother Garroch,' he said. 'I would like to find out what it is that makes such men as these live under roofs and build walls about themselves. No, I shall stay.'

Kaa Fox shrugged his shoulders and said, 'It is lucky that you have no wives or children, or they would come up the hill and fetch you back to the forest by your hair!'

Then he kicked his brother playfully in the side and set off towards the open stockade gate, limping, but stalking as proudly as he could, his head held high so that his nostrils might catch any scent that travelled on the winds.

When the Hunters had gone a man of the village came to Garroch and said, 'Marrag and the little one, Brach, have gone from us in the night, Garroch. The old and the young have been taken. It is the work of Earth Mother.'

Garroch scratched the side of his hooked nose and looked the man in the eye. 'Why should Earth Mother do that, think you, friends?'

The man gestured with the back of his hand towards a group of warriors who already stood outside Marrag's hut, peering inside curiously.

'The men of this village say that Earth Mother is angry with us,' he said. 'She has taken Marrag because she is tired of his weakness and wants us to have a strong man for our Chief. She has taken Brach because you have given the child that love which Earth Mother asks for herself.'

Garroch stood up and squeezed the man's arm-muscle in his hand, making him groan to himself.

'Who are you to say what Earth Mother wants and does not want, you mannikin of sheep-droppings?' he said, looking closely into the man's eyes with his own dark eagle's eyes.

The man began to tremble with pain and fear.

'I only say what they are saying there, lord,' he gasped, though he made no attempt to break away from Garroch's hold.

Garroch pinched his arm even harder. The sweat began to run down the man's cheeks.

'And who is to be Old Man, do they say?'

Now the man could scarcely speak for pain. He groaned at last, 'You are the Old Man, now, lord. There can be no other.'

Garroch flung him on to the ground and stood over him, his lips pursed tight, his dark brows lowered.

'And what if Marrag has not gone away for ever?' he said. 'What if he has only walked over the hill and comes back when he has seen the world? Who will be Old Man then?'

The man bent his head and covered his face with his hands. 'They say that if he comes back, they will kill him,' he said, expecting Garroch's knife to strike him in the neck. 'They say that the village will not be great again unless Garroch is the Old Man,'

Garroch turned and walked away from him without touching him further. He stood by Asa Wolf for a while, thinking.

At last Asa Wolf stopped picking his teeth and said, 'There brother, they set you a task. Make the village great for them as they ask. You have your own harvest in; go out and take the harvest of other peoples. Bring back slaves, heads, sheep, cattle, and then you will be great. That is what they want.'

Garroch looked down at him and smiled suddenly, 'Is that what you would do, Brother Wolf?'

Asa began to pick his teeth with a thorn once more. He shrugged his shoulders. Then he said, 'I do not see what else you can do. In the forest, we are always busy tracking the creatures and skinning deer or wild pigs. But up here on the chalk, you have little to pass the time with. Yes, if I were you I would do as they say, brother. As for me, I have always longed to see what lay over the hill!'

Garroch said, 'Then that is what we shall do, Brother Wolf. For it is time that the People of the Hill knew what it was to shed and to lose blood. They have grown too soft. They will become dangerous to each other unless they are given fighting to do.'

# 13: Long House

BUT FIRST, there was something else which had to be done. Always when an Old Man had finished, what remained of him was gathered together and placed, daubed with bright ochre to signify blood and rebirth, in the stone walled chamber reserved for him, his place of rest, of the long sleep, in the great house of silence under the hill. That was the law, the never-changing way of things, for the long house was the body of Earth Mother herself, and the deep echoing chambers, the walls of her womb. And back into this womb must go all her children, so that they might one day be reborn and come again to rule the People of the Hill.

So men said, 'Marrag is dead! Marrag is dead! But where is Marrag? Where are the flesh and bones to put back into Earth Mother? Unless we can put them inside her again, she will feel cheated. She will punish us all. The rain will not come. The seed will not spring next year. The winds will blow down our roofs and Old Hair will come from over the hill and crunch the bones of our children. Marrag must be put into the long house of sleep if we are to prosper.'

They said this and looked through the smoke with their bright dark beads of eyes towards Garroch. And at last he agreed with what they meant to do to him. He said no word of this to Asa Wolf for he was of another folk whose ways were different. He might have laughed and then Garroch would have to lay him on the stone. So Garroch said nothing to Asa, but asked him to stay out of the Chief's house when the councillors met and spoke of this thing. Asa smiled and said that it was all the same to him. He was quite content to be free of such things.

So in the morning the villagers walked on to the hill, their bodies painted with the white clay, their heads covered with black cloth. They waited for the sun to strike across the land towards them and then in a loud voice they chanted, 'Marrag is dead, O Mother of all! The Old Man is dead at last! Only wait until night comes, Mother, and we will bring you his body to keep.'

As they stood, their heads bowed, it seemed that the hill below them heaved a little and shuddered, and a keen wind blew up suddenly from nowhere, whipping the black cloths about their faces.

They took that as the voice of Earth Mother, though they were not sure whether she had believed what they said.

That day Garroch lay still on the sheepskins in his house. His body was plastered with the bright red ochre and then bound round and round with broad strips of linen, so that he could not move. The pits of his eyes were covered thick with clay so that he could not open them. His mouth was bound shut with a strip of bark held in place by a wide thong of hide, so that he should make no sound to arouse the suspicions of Earth Mother. His head was pillowed on the carcase of a sheep; his feet rested on the body of a hunting hound. His greenstone axe lay at one side, his flint knife at the other. By his head stood a clay beaker, holding barley corns and dried sheep meat. He was ready for the long journey. No one must call him Garroch now, for Marrag must be his name until it was over.

Asa Wolf had been in the house when Garroch's wives had first begun to put the wrappings about him. He leaned over Garroch and said, 'Have no fear, brother, I shall bring you something to eat and drink at night, when the watchers are asleep!'

Garroch smiled grimly and shook his head. 'Earth Mother would see you, brother,' he said. 'She never sleeps. And she might ask me to lay you on the stone as a punishment, and I should not like to do that. No, Asa brother, go away and stay away until I come to you again, if I do come.'

After that they had bound his mouth and covered his eyes. He could say no more. Asa went out of the village with his sling to kill birds. His heart was heavy for his blood-brother, but light that he was not of this folk and so not subject to their strange laws. Those of the forest seemed much more sensible to him.

That day three slaves, with shoulder-blade shovels and antler picks, dug away the soil and then the tight-packed dry-stone walling which sealed the entrance to the long house. They worked hard in the sun, the sweat glistening on their bowed backs, but glad in their hearts that this was no real burial, for had it been their bodies would have formed the carpet over which the mourners must tread on their way to the chamber in which the Old Man must be laid.

When the night came, the many torches were kindled and Garroch was carried, stiffly, by his wives and the most fertile of the other women out of the village. Behind them walked the drummers and the hornmen, their music heavy on the rising night wind. And after them the People of the Hill followed, wailing, their heads covered by strips of black cloth, their bodies white with clay.

As they passed away from the stockade, the cattle in the corral on the next hill heard them and lowed mournfully.

So they took the body of the Old Man to the long house. As they entered, bending beneath the stone lintels of the doorway, the damp and musty scent of the place struck into their nostrils, making them catch their breath. This was the smell that they all feared, the smell which came in dreams before the times of sacrifice. In the dark damp air, the torches fluttered and almost went out. The women coughed with the stench and their coughs echoed along the stone corridor back to them, but with a mocking overtone, as though Earth Mother knew well enough what they were about.

They were glad to lay Garroch down on the stone in the little room that was his, at the side of the corridor. They wished they could run out of the place into the air again, but another thing had to be done first.

A youth whose birthday fell on that day was brought forward, the chosen one, the companion of the Old Man who must go with him where he had to go. This youth had not been told that this was not the real thing, the thing of blood, and he whimpered all the while they held him, thinking of the dog he was leaving behind and the new greenstone axe that his uncle had given him only that morning.

Then Gwraig, the eldest wife, passed her stone knife across his chest, not deeply but just hard enough to make the blood come. They forced him to his knees as though he had fallen, dead, and then each of the mourners dipped her fingers in the blood and placed it on her lips. When the real thing was done, the flesh of the chosen one was eaten in the long house, as a last and sacred meal in the presence of the sleeper.

But this was only a pretence to deceive Earth Mother. Though to the boy, it was the terrible thing, the thing one dreamed about before one woke sweating. He gave a little scream and struggled to get up. Gwraig clapped her hand over his mouth, afraid lest he should disturb Earth Mother, and the women forced him down again, on to the floor, pressing their bodies against him to smother his cries.

Then the torches were put out, one by one, each wife kissed the stiff face of the Old Man, and it was over. They all crept as silently as they could from the echoing chamber into the fresh evening air. The youth who had been chosen as the companion could hardly wait to get out again and see his hound and his axe. He jostled against the back of Gwraig's legs and almost had her down. Outside she gave him a cuff that loosened two of his teeth.

'Clumsy dog!' she said. 'I will see that you lie on the stone one day. Have no fear, Earth Mother will lay all the blame on you.'

The lad crept back to his father's hut and lay in the darkness, his hands over his eyes, his cut chest forgotten, afraid lest something should come to him out of the shadows and drag him back to that stinking place of dead echoes.

Garroch also lay in the dark, his back and buttocks chilled by the cold stone, his nose full of the stench of decay. Now it was so thick about him that it seemed a solid thing, something that blocked his nostrils and kept him from breathing. They had piled the earth back against the entrance when they left and no air from outside came into the long house of sleep.

He slept for a while, but came to his senses when he heard a low muffled wail sounding through the chambers. At first his heart began to thump with fear, then he remembered that there was a hole at the far end of the corridor, the hole through which the spirit might get out when Earth Mother had given it her permission to go free. The wind that came down the hill would blow over that hole, thought Garroch, and make such a noise.

As he listened, he heard another sound. It was something slowly dripping on to the stone floor outside his chamber. His fear told him that this was blood; his sense that it was water from the clay roof of the great mound.

He slept again, out of sheer exhaustion, his limbs cramped

and stiff already, his teeth chattering with cold through their binding.

He did not know how long this sleep lasted, an hour or a day. At times he did not know whether it was sleep or waking. They had bound him so that he could not move, could not make a sound, things which the waking man can do. But the pictures in the mind are the same in waking as in sleeping, when there is only darkness about a man. And Garroch did not know whether he woke or slept. He knew only the cold and the loss of self that great cold brings, as though one lived in the body of another.

And in this sleep it seemed to him that footsteps came along the corridor and stopped outside the little chamber where he lay. It seemed that he felt a touch on his breast at last, a cold touch, that stayed so long that he did not know when it went away, for it still seemed to be there.

And a voice seemed to whisper, so low, though, that it was hard to tell whether he was imagining it, whether it was the sound of the wind in the spirit-hole, or that of the blood-water on the stones.

And the voice seemed to say to him: 'I am Rua, daughter of Kraka of the Fishers. Rua, who killed Kraka so that she could go with Garroch of the Hill and be his wife. Rua killed her father for Garroch, but Garroch spurned her and treated her as he would a dog. And Garroch's folk spurned her, and treated her as a stinking fish, to be thrown into the midden; yet it was Rua who saved the folk of the hill, Rua's baskets of fish that saved them when they starved with hunger after a bad winter.'

Garroch shifted on the stone slab, wanting to cry out that it was not his fault. He had wives enough, he had not wanted another woman. He wanted to say that he had told her father so in her presence, that he was not to blame. She must go back to her own folk. That was where she belonged. We must all go back to our own folk, he wanted to say. That was the law, the old custom, the peoples must live in their own tribes, they must not try to join with other tribes for that angered the gods.

But he could not say this. Yet the voice answered him as though he had spoken: 'Rua whom you call the Fish could not go back to her folk for she has killed her father. The Fishers would wrap her in the skin of the shark, which is their god, and drag her through the shallow salt water till she choked. They would push their harpoons into her body and then hang her over a great fire, saying thay they had caught a wonderful fish that day. Rua cannot go back.

Then Garroch seemed to hear a great sobbing and the loneliness of that mournful sound woke him, weeping, to the other sounds of the spirit-hole and the dripping water. Yet the touch of the cold fingers was still on his breast as though he tried to move and shake them off, they remained, despite all his efforts.

It was after this that the cold became heat. Garroch's body, which had at first been numb, was now torn and shredded by shooting pains, through all his suffering organs. And his heart halted in her steady beat to flutter and bounce, until he thought she would come through the scar in his throat where the bitch wolf had bitten him.

Unable to stand it any longer, he tried to bite through the bark and the thongs about his mouth, but their pressure forced his lips between his teeth and he bit them to rags before the pain reached his knowing. Then he slept again and Rua came to him once more:

'Rua loved Garroch who despised her. Now perhaps Rua hates Garroch, for whom she killed her own father. What should Rua do? With this little flint knife, this scraping knife, Rua could cut Garroch up between the thighs, and on up into the belly, until he could love no one, no one ever again. How would that please Garroch as he lies bound on the stone? Would that seem a fair bargain to him, think you, Marrag?'

Garroch's throat filled with his own blood from his torn and ravaged lips. He choked in his sleep and the voice went away. But when exhaustion claimed him again, it came back:

'There is always blood in the land, the breaking of bone, the tearing of sinews, the slicing through of flesh. What does that matter, Garroch? The body is nothing; it breaks, it mends; or it breaks and one dies. That is nothing. It is the fear while it is breaking that matters, the agony of fear, the love for one's own flesh. That is all. It is silly, isn't it, Garroch, for a warrior to fear the breaking of the flesh?'

There was a silence then and Garroch began to jerk in agony as he thought the knife bit into him. Then he decided that the pain had been a dream and he lay still again. This time he slept without hearing Rua's voice. He heard only the water dripping and the wind at the spirit-hole.

And in this sleep he tried to count the number of wolves he had killed, Harvest Suppers he had eaten, Fire-sacrifices he had seen his father conduct. But always he lost count, for his hands were tied and he could not use his fingers.

Then the voice of Brach spoke in his ear: 'Father, Father, Father! I love you, father. Even if they break your body I shall love you, father. I shall lead you if you are blinded, carry you if they lame you, hunt for you if they cut off your bow-hand, eat for you if they cut your throat.'

This voice went quickly and Rua's came back in its place: 'It is time now; the moment has come. This cannot go on for ever. You will freeze, you will choke, you will starve to death. They have left you for ever, they have forgotten you, they will never come and fetch you out of this place. It was a trick, Garroch! You fool, you did not see through it! Now you are finished. But I could end it all for you, quickly, without waiting, with my little flint scraping knife. Look, I will show you, just there, on your throat, where the she-wolf bit and the flesh is still thin—there it would be easy. Come now, come now, Earth Mother would like that! Then she would not feel cheated! And I would not feel cheated! For I wanted Garroch, and so I might have him, for his other wives would not want him any longer, would they?'

Then Garroch heard another voice that he did not know; it was like Rua's and Brach's, but deeper, like the blowing of the wind over the spirit-hole and it was a damp voice, like the dripping of the water outside the chamber where he must lie. It said:

'Yes, yes, Garroch, I should not feel cheated! Just one little slash where the she-wolf bit your throat and I should not feel cheated, for you would be with me always and I love you, love you, love you, Garroch, my son, my father, my husband! Come, come, come to me, Garroch, for I killed a father for you, I am your father whom you will kill with your hatred, I am your wife, your daughter, yourself. Come, Garroch, it is easy—like this—don't scream!'

Then Garroch began to scream inside his thongs and wrappings, scream deeply in his throat, again and again and again, until the pain of the old wound spoke through his head like a voice, screaming with him . . .

Then the light burst in through the entrance door and the slaves stood away, with bowed heads, as the young warriors came into the tomb, holding their noses.

'There is the new Old Man,' said one. 'We have found him. He is reborn again.'

The other man bent over Garroch and said, 'Look at his throat, it is bleeding. Look at his eyes!'

The clay had dried and fallen from them in his rolling. He stared whitely up at them like a blind man, his eyes like clay themselves.

They lifted him roughly, trying to get out of the long house as quickly as they could. Once they almost dropped him, for his body was cold, cold as that of a corpse, cold to the bone, to the very heart.

'Look,' whispered one of the slaves as they passed between the stone lintels. 'Three days ago his hair was black as the crow's wing. Now it is all streaked with snow. It is pretty.'

Then they began to laugh, for the party had passed, and shovelled the stone and earth back into the entrance way. They were practical folk, and knew what it was like to suffer. They had each lost an eye after their capture, and the warrior who had used the thorn on them had not been gentle.

# 14: Awakening

IN THE days before Garroch at last threw off the nightmare of death, he lay in the house that had once been Marrag's house, and was now his. He was silent and full of thought, even when his throat had healed and the bitter chill had left his limbs, though it was not easy for him to think of things now. He saw the things about him, clearer than ever it seemed, when the blindness of hysterical exhaustion had left him—but he saw them only in their shapes and colours, and could spare no love for them, no insight into their life, no feeling. Even his precious polished greenstone axe lay at his side unloved. He knew well enough what it was and how best to use it, but he no longer cherished it, thought of it as a companion with an inner life of its own, as he had done once, in the days when he would speak to it, saying, 'Fight well with me in this battle today, Green Friend! Do not twist in my hand! Do not splinter at your edge! We shall gain glory today if you are true to me.'

When his dog, Mai Mai, came sniffing to his couch, Garroch knew who it was well enough: but Mai Mai was no more than the greenstone axe. Garroch felt the soft velvet of the dog's ear and then pinched it hard between finger and thumb, sensing the texture of the flesh, hearing the creature's high howling without emotion. When the little dog fled yelping from the hut at last, Garroch did not even look to see which way he went. Instead, he took up a length of hide-thong and wrapping it about both hands, strained at it until it broke. Then, incuriously, he observed that the leather had bitten deep into the flesh of his fingers.

Something had gone from his mind since those fearful nights in the long house. He was like a flint from which all the chalk, all the soft stone, had been chipped, leaving only the hard, vicious cutting edge.

And as he lay, he knew that power again which he had first felt when he was the Corn Man, but it was different this time, for it was with him all the time and filled his chest and head: nor did he need the sheepskin hat and the paint on his body to give him the power. He knew that it was inside him, the chill deathstone had given it to him to keep for ever. Now, he knew, he was the Old Man and was prepared to do everything that the Old Man must do. There was no more fear, no softness of heart, no love. He had left those behind him in the ghastly long house of sleep. Earth Mother could have them, he thought: they were not his any longer.

Yet, before he lost the past completely, there was something he had to do. He sent for the three slaves who had dug open the long house so that he could be put inside and taken out again. They came, bowing their heads before him, afraid down to the marrow of their bones.

He gazed at them for a long while, as though they were lumps of stone. Then at last he said, 'When I was lifted up and carried out of her house, what then?'

They waited until they had counted the fingers on one hand, as was appropriate for respect's sake, then the eldest of them replied, 'After then we closed her door, Old Man.'

Garroch said, 'Was it long or soon before you closed her door?' His voice was cold and they were desperately afraid.

'Old Man, it was soon, even before they had carried you through your gates.'

Behind his open eyes, Garroch seemed to sleep and sleep into eternity. The slaves grew more than ever afraid, their hope gone now.

Then Garroch spoke, as from the other side of the hill of death. 'Who came out of her house after they had carried me away? Think carefully and speak the truth. Who came out?'

The old slave's teeth chattered so violently that he could

hardly form his words.

'Old Man,' he said at length, 'no one came out. Only the smell of death. Then we closed the door quickly lest the old ones who were in there might come out and kill us.'

Garroch turned to them, his pale lips thin with a smile. 'They will not kill you,' he said. 'That is my task, my friends.'

He blew on the little bone whistle that hung from his neck and a guard came into the doorway, axe ready in his hand, his fellows behind him, waiting before the Old Man's house.

Garroch did not speak to the man, but merely nodded towards the shuddering slaves. To them, as they were dragged up the steps, he said, 'Go well. You have done your duty. Earth Mother will welcome such servants.'

Then he lay back and closed his eyes, as if he had forgotten all about them. Though he had not, for, as the hammers fell on to their heads half a mile away, a great shudder passed through all his limbs and a cold sweat burst out through the skin of his forehead.

And that night, when the wind blew down from the hill, Garroch wrapped his black cloak about his head and went alone to the long house. He did not stay there long, but crept round to the spirit-hole at the end of the stone corridor and put his mouth to it.

'My daughter Brach!' he called, 'Go well, go with love! My father Marrag! Go well, go with reverence! Rua Fish, go well, go with my hatred! Earth Mother, receive them all, for they are your children, the flesh of your womb!'

He waited a little while, listening for voices to answer him. But all he heard was the distant sound of water dripping slowly on to the stone floor. And a sour-sweet smell of decay came up through the hole into his nostrils, making him choke in the darkness.

Then he turned and went swiftly back to his house, where Asa Wolf was waiting to greet him. Garroch went up to him and pinched the man's neck and arms between his terrible fingers. Asa did not flinch, but only smiled up at him.

Then Garroch said, 'Such a brother, such a wolf, such an axe! Indeed, I am fortunate.'

Asa bowed his head, smiling gently, 'We shall do everything, brother, and no man shall stand against us.'

Garroch stared long into his eyes and then said, 'At last I am awake. Now no man shall gainsay me.' He paused a while and then added, with a smile, 'Only Asa Wolf.'

# 15: Preparation

ALL DAY long the drums had been beating, and the bare feet thudding in the compound. The dust hung heavy in the air. Garroch looked lazily through the doorway, Asa Wolf at his side.

'If I am to die for them, they shall obey me like dogs,' he said, waving his hand towards the sweating warriors. 'Like dogs, they shall be fed if they obey. They shall go with empty bellies and beaten hides if they disobey.'

Asa Wolf said, 'Learn not to be too harsh, Garroch. That can be as bad as being too soft.'

Garroch answered, 'The flint must be struck hard with the hammer, its edges chipped painfully, if it is to be sharp, to be useful to its master.'

Asa Wolf began to cluck humorously, casting his eyes over the warriors who trained for the war they had been promised. They danced in groups of ten—ten groups of ten—all over the hard earthen compound, the herons' feathers bobbing in their black hair, the thick horsehide bound in a broad strip round their bellies, proof against anything but the hardest axe-blow, their light wicker shields bouncing on their backs, and their cow-skin quivers packed full of new-knapped arrows. The People of the Hill had never before prepared for battle so carefully.

In every hut the women mixed the blue war-paint, ready for husband or brother or son, when the setting-out day came. In every hut the women ground the dried barley ears in their stone querns, to make the coarse flour that their menfolk would carry in skin bags by their side; flour which would mix with water into a paste, a porridge, to keep hunger away. And over the wood fires, they smoked sheep-meat and then cut it into strips, such as a warrior might suck and chew as he ran onwards, towards his quarry.

The flint-miners had grumbled these many days, sweating in the half-darkness for the best black stone, that they would knap on the spot, even in the galleries, to make arrows and knives for this war-band. Not a man of these workers but went now with raw palms from the speed of their chipping, for Garroch had commanded a hundred arrow-heads each day from every one of them—and no one dared risk falling below that number.

Garroch was no man to be played with now, they knew. And many longed already for the days when they had been able to slap him on the back and joke with him about his nose, or his hair, or his less mentionable parts.

All worked in Craig Dun; even the young boys, who were set to grope among the miners' spoil-heaps for sling-stones; even the young girls, who could be set to stitch water-bags with fine fish-gut.

But the warriors themselves were glad in their hearts to have a fighter-chief at last, after the long cow-years under Marrag's failing powers. They grumbled as they trained—but they would have grumbled more if Garroch had left them lolling against the sides of their huts, in the late summer sunshine.

Asa Wolf said, 'I shall send to my brother, Kaa Fox, and tell him that I go with my other brother, Garroch, to see the world. I shall tell him that he is bound to protect my brother Garroch's village while we are away.'

Garroch said, 'Remind him that his place is outside the stockade, until we return to welcome him inside again.'

Asa bowed his head. 'He will not break the law,' he said, a little hurt that Garroch should think so lightly of Kaa Fox.

Then abruptly Garroch punched one dark hand into another and said, 'Asa Wolf, forgive me. My tongue runs on, but that is because my head has many things in it and I speak in a hurry, like a man with a she-bear scratching his backside. You see, I have something to do now, which was not here for me to do before.' He paused a moment and wiped the sudden sweat from his forehead.

'Once I had a father and a daughter,' he said. 'I thought I needed nothing. But now I have no father, no daughter. Now this people is my father and my daughter and my son. I have a power inside me that was not there before. It is as though I am a woman in labour and must give birth to something that was not in the world before. I must bring forth a great people, a great village, many cattle and sheep, and great harvests, now. That is my wish, my new power.'

Asa Wolf said, 'It is right that you should have this wish, this power, for you are the Old Man, Garroch.'

Garroch was silent for a while, and then he leaned his forehead on the lintel of the hut and whispered, 'I have had a dream, Asa Wolf-brother, a great dream that has frightened me and has yet given me a sort of hope. It has come to me three times now, the sacred number, and I know it must be true.'

Asa shut his eyes and bowed his head, as one must do to show reverence. 'Tell me, if it is your will, Old Man,' he said, giving Garroch his title, which he did not usually do unless there were others to hear his words.

Garroch said slowly, 'I am sitting in a great house, whose walls reach out beyond the country of the Dog Men, whose roof lifts itself higher than the hill. I am sitting on a chair of blue-stone, brought by a thousand men from the west, and my feet rest upon a hundred otter pelts. There is music of drums and flutes about me, and many baskets of sweet berries and kid-meat are set before me. There is cheese from the cows and the sheep; there is smooth-ground flour; there are nuts and the sweetest of the fish, both of sea and of river. No Chief has ever provided such a feast for his people. And at last, when I have surveyed this feast, I blow on my bone whistle and from all the many doors of my great house come women, more than a hundred hands of women, all young and lithe-bellied like hunting-dogs, their hair full of sweet scents and their limbs supple as willow-wands. They are mine, but I am strong and do not wish to take them. They fall before me and beg me to give them what is in me, but I smile and shake my head. I tell them that I am my own man, not theirs to have, yet. They go from me, weeping, look-ing back to me sadly over their shoulders, their eyes wide as the roe-deer's with longing. They hesitate at the doors, but I wave my axe and then they are gone, with a sound like the night wind sighing over the hill.'

He paused for a moment and then passed his thin hand across his eyes, as though weary for the while.

'And then the flutes sound again, high like curlews, and I know that my guests have come, the great ones whom I await, whom I have always awaited, since Earth Mother first scattered the black soil over the face of the rocks to let men live. They come noiselessly, hardly parting the hide curtains as they enter my great hall.

And they stand before my great chair, in many ranks, their heads bowed, waiting for my welcome. And when I give it, they raise their heads, which are now but bones, but no flesh to tell their story. They fling aside their wrappings of bearskin and deerhide and otter-pelt; and their bodies are bones, all bones. They are the great ones from under the hill, those who have always been there, since the first light flickered over the earth. They have come without feet to walk to me, without hands to clasp mine, without tongues to greet me—yet they have come to stand before me as I sit on my great chair. They have come to do me homage, I, the greatest of them all.'

Asa raised his head and looked at Garroch. The young chieftain's eyes were closed and his head flung back, as though he spoke in a trance.

'Hail, Great One,' he said, with gentle irony. 'May you find pleasure in such a feast! But if I have the good fortune to be there, at least I hope you will let me go with the women, before your more famous guests arrive! I fancy the one more than the other!'

No one else would have dared say such a thing to Garroch in his new mood of power; but Asa Wolf could say anything to him, he knew, and he loved Asa for doing that, though he would have broken the teeth of any other man who had attempted such a thing.

Gwraig, his eldest wife, came scurrying in. She stopped when she saw Asa there and fell on her knees, to pay respect to the Old Man.

She waited for her husband to speak first, as was the custom. Garroch looked down at her and then poked her in the side with his foot, as though he were examining her for the first time. Gwraig giggled.

'What?' he asked.

Gwraing smiled unsurely. 'I come from the other women, Old Man,' she said. 'I come to speak their words for them, as is fitting for an eldest wife to do.'

She paused, then, hoping to rouse the curiosity of her man. He waited so long that she became quite cross with him. And then he said. 'What message do you being, you fat-bellied cow?'

She gasped with anger and could not speak for a moment. This was not how she had dreamed it would be when Garroch became the Old Man. She was glad the other women were not there to hear these words, or she would lose their respect, the respect of fear which she exerted over them.

And while she was waiting, Garroch bent over her and ripped her linen shift from her, leaving her back bare.

'Look, Asa brother,' he said, 'she is a cow. Look how she hangs down!'

Asa chuckled, for he hated Gwraig's insolent behaviour towards him.

But Gwraig smothered her rising fury and even smiled as she looked up at Garroch.

'What the Old Man wills must be allowed,' she said, wishing

every word were an arrow-head to pierce into his mocking eyes. Then she went on hurriedly, before he should do or say anything else to hurt her pride. 'I come to tell you, Old Man, that we, your wives, wish you well in the battles. We are your things to use before you go, should you need us. We are your things while you are away, to recall your visitations with respect and to await their new coming.'

Garroch scratched the side of his eagle's nose. Then his lips curled cruelly. 'The Old Man thanks his women for their good wishes in battle,' he said. 'He thanks them for the offer of their bodies before he goes, but that would not help him on his way. He thanks them for remembering him while he is away from them—and he sends them this message, that, because he values their love and would keep it safely for himself, he has made arrangements for them all to be sealed in his house until he returns.'

Gwraig gave a gasp and looked up at him in surprised anger. 'Garroch,' she said . . .

He waved her to silence and answered, 'The Old Man has already commanded his slaves to put food and water down through the chimney-hole until he returns, so that his women shall be happy in food at least. And should he not return, then those slaves and their sons shall continue their duties until the Old Man's women no longer need food. Is that enough?'

Gwraig glared up at her husband with fury. Now she forgot that Asa Wolf was still there. 'A stone can be rolled away, Garroch!' she said.

Garroch poked her again, lazily, with his toe and said, 'The Old Man is not such a fool, Gwraig Cow. He knows that only the long house will keep some women from giving themselves to the first swine-keeper they see, when their husband's back is turned. Indeed, Gwraig, I had even thought I might have you all placed in the long house, painted with ochre and bound round as you bound me, until I came back to fetch you out—but I was kinder than you were, Gwraig.'

He waited until his words had worked long enough in her head, and then he said, 'I shall have a great stone rolled against the door. If you wish to remain the women of Garroch, then you will not roll that stone away. But if you all push on it hard enough, for many days, perhaps then you will be able to shift it and come out into the light again.'

Gwraig looked at him, puzzled. 'What then, Old Man?' she said.

'What then?' he repeated, smiling darkly, 'then I have given other orders for that, Gwraig. The slaves have been given two choices—they may either take you as their own women, to use as they will; or they may split your heads with their hammers, to suit themselves.'

Gwraig was well-known for her secret cruelty to slaves. She shuddered to think what her chance of comfort might be.

Then Garroch turned to leave the hut. She reached out and grasped him by the ankle, to plead with him; but he kicked her aside roughly and went up into the sunlight where the warriors were still making the patterns of war.

As he passed away from her, she spat on his shadow.

'Die, dog,' she whispered hoarsely. 'Die, and good riddance!'

She gathered her torn robe about her, wondering how she would account for its tearing to the other women. Then at last she thought of an explanation that would not demean her, and smiling she went to the house of women to tell them her story.

# 16: Victory

THEY SAT together in a narrow gulley, overshadowed by couch-grass and gorse. They were talking, and waiting for night to come. The sunshine parched their mouths and the black flies crawled about their wounds, but they talked and gestured with spirit, for Earth Mother had smiled on them during the last days and had let them sack village after village along the chalk hills.

Now little more than half of the men who had set out from Craig Dun sat in the little valley. The others had either gone back to Earth Mother with an arrow in their throats, an axe-cut across the head, or they had started the long march back to their village under the hill, driving herds of sheep and cattle before them. The men who were left were those who had the greatest fame as warriors, or those whose wounds were the slightest.

Garroch and Asa leaned, back to back, chewing strips of dried meat, their faces and bodies filthy with dust and sweat now, their hair matted with dried blood, their hands scarred and raw with fighting. But they were as contented as warriors could be. The chipped edges of their axes told mutely of the good work they had already done. They lived in the present; it was unwise to do anything else.

Suddenly a man called out, 'There have never been such warriors, my friends! We shall run over the edge of the world together into the sunset. Men will never forget us, my comrades!'

The two friends only smiled. Men were saying such things all the time on a war journey, but of course, men did forget them, quite soon after they had fallen; for in wartime a warrior must not keep on remembering his dead friends, how they looked, what they said, or he would lose his own courage and soon be dead and grinning like them.

A spasm passed over Garroch's face. For a moment he did think of the past, of their first headlong rush into the weakly defended village of the Dog Men. It had all been over so quickly, and then he and Asa had run from hut to hut, looking for Brach and Marrag without really expecting to find them. But they were not in the village, and the headman insisted that he had never seen them, although they had almost broken his ankle bones to get the truth from him. Now Garroch did not know what to think. Perhaps one day the long house would be opened and the bones of three people be found there—an old man, a young woman, and a little girl. Then Garroch shrugged his shoulders and sneered at himself, for if the long house was opened again, it would be to admit his own body, he, the Old Man; and then he would not be able to see the bones of these people.

He turned to Asa and said, 'We will wait until nightfall. Then when their fires are lit, we will sweep down on them like the night-wind and spare no one. They are rich people here in this village under the rocks; they will provide us with cattle enough to keep our bellies full for three winters.'

Asa scratched his sides and yawned. 'I cannot think of three winters from now,' he said. 'Perhaps we shall all be dead long before then. Let us think about now, about tonight, when we go hunting again.'

He began to polish his flint knife on the skirt of his short hide tunic.

'But,' he said, 'it is poor hunting, this, after all. There is craft in stalking a bear or a badger, but men are so simple. They do the things a man expects them to do. There is no honour in killing them. Besides, a hunter can eat a stag or a wild pig, but what warrior would eat an old woman!'

Garroch turned away from him again, his face dark and flushed that his friend should jest about such a serious thing.

Asa saw this and elbowed him good-humouredly. 'Oh yes,' he said, 'I know you folk of the hills eat the "long pig" at certain times, but that is different; you do not make a feast of it, it is a thing to do with burial, and that sort of thing.'

Garroch said grimly, 'If my fight with your brother, Kaa Fox, had ended with my axe in his head, I should have eaten his heart at the least. That is the law. Why should the bravery of Kaa Fox be lost to men when he is once dead? Why should not the man who slew him enjoy some of that courage, to add to his own?'

Asa answered, 'Yes, I understand that. We, the Hunters, eat the heart of a swift stag or a brave deer. I have eaten the hearts of three wolves—but not a man's heart.'

Garroch spat in anger on to the grass. 'You should try it,' he said. 'It might help you.'

Asa stared him in the eye, his own face grave now, 'I shall recall that word, perhaps one day, Garroch,' he said.

Garroch's eyes fell away from the fierce stare of his blood-brother. He wished he could tell him to forget the words, that he had not meant them, but his pride would not let him say any more. He rose and went down the gully, kicking his men in their sides and telling them to be quiet or the folk of the village under the rocks would come up and catch them before night-fall.

Night came slowly, like a dying man dragging his weary feet along a tunnel that stretched to the edge of time. Yet it came at last, with a sudden cry of night birds and the silence of the grass-hoppers in the long dry grass. The men in the gulley began to breathe faster, their eyes wide and staring. They waited for Garroch to lead the way, crawling, over the edge of their hiding-place and then to the top of the round basin, in which lay the village of their next choice.

Below them the little fires started up outside the stone hovels in the compound. It seemed unbelievable that these folk could be so rich, yet the warriors had passed many broad fields of stubble which showed how great their barley crop had been, and away to the west, they had sighted the long hilltop corral where the cattle rested that night—more cattle than they had ever seen together before, behind the high, curving ramparts.

Asa Wolf lay beside Garroch in the rough grass. He had his axe in his hand and was just beginning to say a little prayer to it

when Garroch clapped his hand over his mouth, harshly, glaring at him with angry eyes, and pointing down towards the little fires.

The folk of the village were gathered in a circle in the compound, squatting cross-legged and eating from their clay bowls, singing snatches of songs, talking, laughing, ending their day together as they had always done.

Suddenly Garroch made the owl-cry which was their signal. 'Now!' he whispered hoarsely, and ran down the hill like a wicked fury. The warriors were after him, as swiftly as slavering dogs, their eyes wild, their silent mouths open with war-joy.

Then they were among the fires, scattering the hot ashes with their bare feet in the urgency of their striving, striking left and right wherever they saw a head to beat.

Yet there was something strange about this battle. The folk they struck were women, old women, and grey-haired old men, not a warrior among them. They fell about among the fires, without a scream, defenceless, silent, as though they had expected to be slaughtered, as though they were sacrifices to some hungry god.

Asa drew back, his axe-head black with blood. He looked round for Garroch, who was blind with war-lust now.

'Old Man, Old Man,' he called, 'I do not like this! Call off the warriors, Old Man!'

Only one of the slaughterers heard these words. It was the man who had crept into Rua's hut that night to betray her. He smiled, sneering, and said, 'So you have no stomach for fighting, Hunter? Stay with us a little while, and we will teach you how a man behaves!'

Then he ran past Asa, slashing at anything he saw.

But as Asa stared, wondering, at this scene of death among the dying fires and the purple shadows, there came a high scream from above them, answered at the other side of the basin, then answered again and again, and every time the screams coming nearer and nearer in the darkness, and the fierce feet thudding like those of devils down the steep hill.

Then a great whirlwind seemed to strike them all, and Asa saw little dark men about him, painted men, men with their black hair pinned up about their fierce heads, their chests daubed with woad, their eyes flashing white in the last embers of the fires.

Screaming they struck down the warriors of the Hill, without mercy, the dark death-bringers.

And Asa found himself surrounded by four of them, who lunged at him, their knives fastened by thin hide thongs to ash-plants. He roared like a bull and charged them, his heavy axe biting like a green thunder-stone into the dark heads. But always they came at him again, with others to help them. He felt their knives cut him savagely again and again in the darkness. He felt his blood running down his side, hot and wasteful.

At last, weak and bayed by these hounds, he shrieked, 'Garroch, to me, friend! To me, if you live!'

But Garroch could not hear him, He was standing with his back against the stone wall of a hut, swinging his axe about him, grunting with gladness when another man fell at his feet, the wounds thick on his painted breast.

And at length, when he stayed for breath, an old woman came out of the door beside him and struck him behind the head with a beef-bone, so hard that she howled with pain afterwards. The little dark men ran in upon him as he lay, his eyes rolled back, among the ashes, no longer caring that they burned into his hair and into the skin of his back.

As for the one who had slept with Rua, he woke from his dream of pleasure, striking down the old ones, to find true warriors about him. He dodged their blows for a while, then, taking his chance, swung round and ran wildly into the darkness, up the slope of rough grass that would lead him over the basin and into safety again. Even as he ran he praised his own craft in escaping so, and thought of the tale he would tell when he reached Craig Dun at last. There, he thought, they would heap praises on him, the last of their warriors; perhaps, he thought, they might even make him Old Man for his bravery.

Then something hit him, in the darkness, something hard, at the base of the stomach, even as his feet were rising on the tus-socky grass towards safety. A young boy had come out of a hut with his father's bow and for the first time in his life had let an arrow fly at an enemy. He saw the sharp stick plunge deep into the man's belly, and then ran back into the hut, afraid for what he had done.

The man was flung back with the shock of the thing and rolled a yard or two down the slope. Then he splayed out his legs, with much pain, and stopped himself. He thought that if he did not roll back into the fighting, he might still escape.

At last he understood what had hit him so hard in the belly. He tried to draw it out, but something else came with it and he began to scream without meaning to. It was a long time before he realised he would never go back to Craig Dun. Then he began to weep like a little child. It was long before he stopped screaming then. In fact, the fighting had ended before his strength was done.

Asa Wolf crawled past him, when the dawn was already streaking the sky. But Asa Wolf had not the strength to help him, to hit him on the neck with a stone, even if he would. He carried three arrows in his own side and was not concerned with this man's troubles.

As for Garroch, they had found the Chieftain's scars on his chest and had dragged him into a deep hut. There they had revived him for long enough to mock him, and to let him know what they were doing to him.

And even Garroch found himself screaming as they bent back his thumbs, and pushed sharp flints up into his body, though not too sharp and not too far, for they wanted their vengeance to last on this unjust raider, who broke the law of the hill peoples.

It would not do to end his punishment too soon. Now he must pay his end of the bargain fairly.

# PART TWO

## Light Folk

# 17: Waiting

ALONG THE reed-fringed margin of the shore, across the
Little Sea that separated the island of the flint-men from the
vast lands of the herdsmen, there had arisen a great commotion.

Cows lowed to their calves, in fear of being hustled together
and of losing them among the many tossing horned herds that
clustered nibbling at the coarse salt-grass; sheep bleated in terror
in the strange smell of the sea waters; horses whinnied, stretching
their nostrils wide, their red-rimmed nostrils, as though they
smelled battle from afar and were both anxious to be a part of
it and yet afraid of the whining arrow, the upthrust javelin that
brings ruin to the proudest stallion born.

And above them the sea-birds wheeled and screamed, white
in the morning sunlight, frightened of the many men and many
four-footed creatures that met together on the flat mud-banks
which were usually so bare, so desolate, so comfortingly
deserted to a gull.

They could not land there now, printing their pronged sig-
natures in the slime, sharp-eyed for eels, as they were used.
These birds smelled the biting smoke of wood-fires; with their
sharp salt-hardened eyes they saw the black fumes rise; with
their curiously hidden ears they heard the high yelling of herdsmen, the sudden thwacking of sticks on patient hides. This was
strange and different and frightening. They wheeled higher into
the salty airs for safety, then whirled about the place, screeching
that they did not like this, that they wished these men would go
back to the Baltic, to the great inland forests where they had
come from—anywhere, so long as they left the shore-reeds, and
let the white birds grub for elvers, crack open the shells of sea-
snails, as they had done since the sun first rose above the hills.

But the men below them hardly noticed their protests. It was
a bloody bitter East wind, they thought, clapping their red raw
hands about their thin and hungry chests, and cursing their
leader for bringing them so far on a dreamlike quest, when they
might still have been eating beef under the great green trees and
thanking the wind-dried horse-skull on the sacred oak for their
good fortune.

'May Barduca's bones rot inside his flesh and let him fall from
the saddle as he rides,' some of them swore, half meaning it, half

in jest. 'May this happen to him, and may his bastard son
Vedrix try to catch him, and be crushed in the tumble!'

Then they laughed and drank again of the raw fermented
corn-wine, their eyes running from the wind, their red noses
dripping with northern cold. Some of them, the more prosperous chieftains from the easy-lands, wrapped their thick woollen
gowns about them and ran their fingers along the sharp edges of
their copper swords, as though they resented being hurried along
by any tyrant, and would as soon use their expensive weapons on
him as on the simple folk they had been promised they would
meet.

Yet many of the common fellows, the cattle-men who loved
watching the steers mount and the cows bring forth and suckle
their young, rejoicing in these feats as though they shared them,
these men followed their tyrant leader without any wish to kill
him, believing that he knew best, and that they would come at
last to a land where they might graze their cattle and rear their
calves and lambs without any interference.

'Barduca is a fat bull,' they said. Then they would pause. 'But
he knows how many teats a cow has got. And that's more than
most of these lordly sun-worshipping swine do. All right they
are, for a basin of ale and a plate of meat, and riding round the
country on a horse's back. But when it comes to calving a cow,
Barduca makes fools of them.'

Under a great horsehide awning, with its back to the bitter
winds, Barduca held his court. He did not know that his lords
wished to cut his throat with their metal knives; he did not know
that his hundred herdsmen wished him well and thought him a
good judge of cattle. If he had known, he would not have cared.
He was above the judgment of common men of any sort. He
was almost a god, he considered; that is, after the Hornman and
the Bard. They were nearer gods than he was, he admitted. But
then came Barduca. And if Barduca said that milk came out of
the oak-apples and rain out of the sun's backside—then that
should be good enough for anybody.

Although, Barduca would not have said that thing about the
sun without smiling up into the sky and crossing his fingers as
he smiled. For, whatever a man might say in jest, he knew that
without the Sun-god's help, there was nothing possible on earth.

Barduca lounged in his great oaken chair covered with bear's
pelts and sheepskins, a beaker of mead in one hand, his long copper sword in the other. He sipped from the one and contem-
plated the other, his eyes red, not with the East wind but with

drink; his tongue slow with drink and with the tiredness that had come upon him from his age and from the long journey he had forced upon his many tribes.

They had come a long way; ten days of fast-travelling, over the upland roads, each tribe meeting the main body at the junctions of hill and valley, until they had formed a great gathering of wanderers, the men of the cows and the sheep, and the metal knives.

Barduca looked at the men before him in the wind-tent, but he could hardly focus them, for the mead was strong and he was getting too tired to bother about looking closely at folk. He did see the Bard, an old fellow, grey-bearded and dressed in his greasy black rags, mumbling to himself and counting his fingers to match the rhymes, for he was blind. Bards were blinded, when once they had given evidence of their talents—otherwise they went away to other tribes, discontented, as poets are, and gave others the benefit of their gifts, their communication with the source of life itself—*HIM*, the sun man, the smiling warmth-giver who brought life to everything—crops, cows, beetles, men.

'Poor blind bastard,' muttered Barduca, stroking his long red-golden beard. '*I* can see my sword, my finger-ring of gold, my jug of mead. I can see the women as I lie on them and make them squeal!'

He smiled inside his beard and long moustaches and took another suck at the beaker of honey-ale. He thought for a moment of his son's betrothed wife, Isca. The Bard would not be able to see Isca. He would not see her corn-coloured hair and her heavy white breasts with the little blue veins, oh so tiny, in them. He would not see . . . Oh, he would miss so much, thought Barduca, glad that he had not the gift of poetry.

He wiped his long red nose on the long sleeve of his red gown. He looked at the Hornman, the fearsome one of the tribes, the man—if one dared call him such—of the sacrifices, the one who cut the mistletoe, cut the man, too, on the flat stones at Mid-summer morning. The Hornman!

'Poor simple devil,' thought Barduca, drinking again. 'He thinks so much of his sacred black flint knife—but if I cared to step down from this platform, I could lop off his head with one sweep of my sword. Oh, the darling sword!'

The Hornman lolled on his sheepskins, already drunk, his stag-antlers wagging loosely, for his votaries had been careless in tying them on; his white clay paint already peeling off with the sweat that came from his unexercised body. Yet, even so, he was frightening; a man dedicated to sacrifice, one born to death and the sun, cut by his master-Hornman so that he would never be distracted towards creating a family, made to learn score upon score of spells and incantation, herbal remedies; organs, ligaments and bones, of man, beast and bird; punished in his apprenticeship, until he knew every phase of moon, every name and quality of rock, every plumage of bird, every feeding-stuff of beast. One who knew so much should have great possessions —yet this Hornman possessed nothing but his red-deer's antlers and the stinking cowhide that only half-covered his obese body.

A chieftain dared to say, 'The wind bites cold today, Barduca. Is this the day we sail?'

Outside, the sea-birds croaked for a century and the cows lowed for another century after that. Then Barduca spoke.

'When Bard and Hornman say we sail—then, we sail. *Unless* I decide that we do not sail.'

He rubbed his thick forefinger down his streaming nose and looked blankly round him in the smoke of the wood-fire. He held his cow-horn out and the slave-woman ran forward and filled it again. She gasped even with this effort, for Barduca was a constant drinker, and she was his hand-woman. She was heavy with his child too, and knew that he would not suffer it to live. That made her resent his mead as much as anything. He should have killed her six months before: that would have been kinder, and easier. But Barduca was not noted for his gentleness. A King must never be gentle or his lords would think him weak and would kill him as he slept, or as he rode carelessly back after the hunt.

The Bard sniffed the air, raising his head like a dog, his nostrils twitching, his eyes still closed. He began to intone in a high and sing-song voice.

> 'Lord of oak and ash,
> Of fire and of water,
> Of bird in the air
> And worm under ground,
> Give us a sign!
> Give us a sign,
> Lord of the stone and the snake!'

Barduca glared at him impatiently. The Hornman shifted his clumsy bulk, spilling the sticky honey-mead over his thighs and then chuckling, waving his grotesque head from side to side, his eyes, ringed round with red, fluttering stupidly.

He made passes in the air and it seemed for a moment that the wind dropped, for the tent sides stopped flapping, and in the silence they heard the mournful sound of a horn.

Then there came a great clattering of hooves and a small party of riders swept about the wind-break, led by a young woman. She dismounted with a laugh and a sudden flurry of garments and then ran forward to touch the back of Barduca's hand with her lips. He smiled down at her indulgently, tipsily.

'Uncle,' she said in a full deep voice. 'Look! the wind is changing! It is sweeping the white birds out to sea! It is a wind to carry us on our way! let us go!'

The Hornman nodded above his dripping cup. He looked towards the Bard and snuffled, 'There is your sign, blind one! Listen and be satisfied.'

Isca, the niece of Barduca, looked round at the men in the wind-break insolently. They bowed their heads. She was a fine woman, little more than a girl, yet heavy in her limbs, though well-formed. A thin fillet of gold held her rich corn-coloured hair in place; bars of black jet pierced her fine ears, dragging their lobes down. About her throat and arms, she wore spirals of heavy copper which jingled as she moved. Everything about her was rich and arrogant, the painted heavy-lidded eyes, the full lipped mouth, the thin and slightly curved nose, even the splash of red blood that streaked the front of her long white woollen gown.

Barduca saw it and said smiling, 'So you killed today, my child? I had expected Vedrix to do it, but you have beaten the fool to it. What was it, my Queen? A roe-buck?'

She showed her even teeth in a sneering smile. 'Nothing so useful, uncle,' she said. 'Nothing but a black bear, with teeth so small I'd have given him my own breast to suck; if there'd been any milk there!'

Barduca leaned forward and stroked her heavy breasts. She pushed against his hand, smiling, her eyes half-closed.

Then suddenly the old man roared, 'Where is the fool Vedrix? Why does he not come before me? Is he afraid, the dolt?'

Isca placed her arm about the King's neck and pushed one hand down into his shirt, caressing him. 'He is ashamed, I think, uncle,' she said, 'for his blow did nothing more than anger the animal. I had to strike it dead when it leapt on him and tore his horse's neck!'

Barduca stood up in his fury, almost flinging her from him. 'He let the bear maul his horse, did he?' he shouted. 'The misbegotten fool! How did such a thing ever come to spring from my loins? Did the Sun-god wish to drive me mad? Did he wish to punish me for all the faults of the world? Vedrix! Come in, Vedrix, you little suckling!'

A young man ran round the side of the hide windbreak, his thin face pale and smiling uncertainly. He twitched with fear as he stood before his father, the mask and paws of a young bear hanging from his belt, fouling his linen breeches with blood.

The King glared down at him for a while, relishing the young man's fear of him. Then, waving his hand so as to include all the lords he said, 'So, here we greet the great hunter, eh? The great warrior, the slayer of bears! Look at him, my lords, and fear his wrath—this lordly one, this killer of wild boars—this eater of dung!'

Vedrix fell before him on his knees, holding up his hands. 'Father,' he said in his high voice, 'may the gods take me, but I thought it was a full-grown bear. The wind had made my eyes water and I could not see.'

Barduca began to smile wickedly, and repeated the young man's words in mockery, imitating his voice with such cruelty that they all laughed openly, even the Bard. 'Well, and so you could not even kill a bear-cub cleanly, you fool? You had to put your woman in danger so as to save you, eh?'

Vedrix looked up for a moment towards Isca, who was smiling at him as wickedly as the others. His face was bitter towards her. 'Isca it was who told me to kill the thing,' he whined. 'She told me to clasp it to me as I rode, and hug it to death as its father would have hugged me. She said that so I could prove my valour and deserve her love!'

For a moment Barduca was silent, then he shouted, 'If Isca told you to cut off your thumb, would you do it, you fool? And what valour does that show? To let a bear cub savage a good horse for the sake of showing your crow's valour, what good is that?'

Vedrix lowered his eyes and began to snivel, waving his head from side to side in misery and humiliation.

Now the lords began to feel some pity for him, though they dared not show it before Barduca. Vedrix had always suffered thus, they thought; had always been made the scapegoat of any misfortune. Why did not Barduca kill the fool and put him out of his misery, they thought. He would never be a King and yet Barduca still spoke as though he would, one day, when he had shown his manhood, a manhood that did not exist and never would exist.

But Isca felt no pity. Her only feeling was of an immense

contempt that amounted almost to hatred, hatred that she was bound to this fool, this coward, promised to him as wife since she had been a little child.

Momentarily she recalled the betrothal ritual, the circumcisions. She shuddered to remember it again, how the folk had watched, smiling, as she and Vedrix suffered it; how the parts were pressed together so that their blood mingled and they were made one. She passed her hand over her forehead and found that a light sweat had sprung on to the white skin. Bound to this stupid coward! Had it been a warrior, a hawk-eyed man with great arms, the cutting would have been a pleasure, something to recall with passion—but this fool . . .

She suddenly spat at him as he knelt in the tent. 'Vedrix is a fool, uncle,' she said. 'He is such a man as will expect his wife to father her own child!'

Barduca laughed thickly. 'Must I kill myself to show the fool how to do everything?' he asked.

The lords nudged each other at their King's wit. It was no secret to them that Barduca had lain with Isca many times, for in accordance with the custom of their folk he was sworn to protect her from all other men until her marriage was celebrated with his son, and that meant keeping watch over her by night as well as by day. To make that easier, she slept in his bed while Vedrix lay outside the door, fulfilling his tribal function, too— that of protecting his father. It was a convenient arrangement for all but Vedrix.

As for Isca, a King was to be preferred to a thin-legged dolt, even though the King was an old man, and the dolt a young one. So she made no bones about her preferences, in public as well as in private.

Barduca leaned forward and pushed his son over with a sudden blow of the foot. The young man lay where he fell, looking up at the King with fearful eyes, wondering what he might do next.

And when they all went from the windbreak to see whether it was time for their great voyage, Vedrix was still left alone, lying among the straw and filth that littered the place where they had camped, afraid to rise and risk his father's taunts any further.

But when they were out of earshot, he punched himself bitterly in the groin and said, 'You bastard, Barduca! May your bones rot inside you. May you die! May you die in agony! You swine!'

And after a while, when he had vented his anger sufficiently on his own body, he grew more controlled to think of Isca.

'May she bear his children,' he said coldly, 'and may they come out of her as pigs and creeping snakes!'

Then he heard the King's great horn blowing, a sign that this day they would sail. He got up quickly, anxious to show that he wished to help in the preparations, desperate not to be found wanting again.

Those who watched him running after his father smiled to each other and pointed. 'Look,' they said, 'there goes Vedrix. He doesn't know a boat from a latrine-bucket! What good does he hope to do?'

All the same, they pitied him as much as they feared his tyrant father.

# 18: Sailing

THE SUN was high in the heavens before the first boats hoisted their leather sails and stood out from the shore. Then the great rafts were pushed through the reeds, men straining to free them from the sucking mud, for they were heavily laden with horses and cattle, hobbled and yoked together or lying on their sides, snorting and bellowing with terror, their red-rimmed eyes wide with the smell of death from salt-water.

Once, when the men were chest-deep in the slime, a great raft heeled over as the horses plunged with terror. Men screamed, trying to break free from the wooden monster that towered over them, taking them with it. Some hung for a moment in the air before they fell beneath its smothering bulk. Others stumbled and felt the mud fill their mouths before their fellows tramped them down in their mad rush, trampled them into forgetfulness.

Many cows were lost, for once they had slid overboard it was impossible because of their hobbled legs to drag them to the shore again. Once three calves slithered away into the water and went floating on the tide for a long distance, lowing plaintively, before they were at last swallowed up in the grey waters.

But at last the rafts were afloat, surrounded by the long dug-out boats and even by coracles. Men pushed their ash poles into the mud, urging the convoy out to deeper water, while others strained every sinew, plying their broad paddles, trying to

steer the unwieldy vessels towards the distant shore on which
lay their fortune, as Barduca had promised them.

The King sat at the prow of the leading boat, Isca beside him,
wrapped against the wind in a billowing cloak of deer-hide. She
held his hand and smiled back at Vedrix, who stood up to the
hips in the brackish water, watching them go, trying to hide the
tears of rage and disappointment that threatened to flow down
his cheeks and betray him to the laughing tribesmen in the boats.

Vedrix had put on all his princely finery, the blue and yellow
linen shirt, the rings and bracelets, the broad-bladed flint knife
and the long copper sword. He had bound his hair round with
gold wire and had even made tentative streaks of blue across his
forehead and the backs of his hands, such as the other warriors
had done.

And then, in the last tribal council on the shore before the
crews were sorted out and the beasts thrashed aboard, Barduca
had gone round from group to group, picking out the men he
wished to travel with him. He had chosen two-thirds of the total
mass of tribesmen, all young men, great fighters and cattle-own-
ers. The old men, the poor ones who had lost whatever they might
have possessed in the past and were bitter about it—these he left
behind for Vedrix to lead. And Barduca had taken all the women,
even the old ones, though they went on the rafts with the cattle.

'Stay here on the shore, my brave son,' he called mockingly,
'and when we have found a good kingdom, we will send for
you. See that you treat your warriors well, and do not let them
eat too much or lie with too many women. For that spoils a
warrior, the second more than the first!'

Vedrix had begged to be allowed to sail with them and find
himself a kingdom to rule, but Barduca had looked back into
the eyes of Isca and she had said, 'Stay here, little Vedrix. We
will find you a nice little kingdom where you will be happy. I
shall think of you, every night, my husband.'

The rowers laughed at this and punched each other in the
side, thinking what a she-devil Isca was, but wishing all the
same that they were where Barduca was.

So Vedrix was left standing in the water, watching them sail.
And as they gradually drew away, shouting and singing, their
harsh voices floating back over the waters, he shook his fist at
them and shouted, 'May the winds overturn your boats and
may the sea-monsters drag you down into the mud and fill
your eyes and your ears and your bellies.'

Then, afraid that they might have heard him, he turned back, wading to the higher mudbanks.

A group of his men waited for him, their faces grey and discontented. When he went towards them, they still stood, their arms folded, their eyes staring into his. He had expected them to show him some respect, as the son of their King. But they only stared at him and spat as he approached. He did not like to stare them out, and looked away, pretending to watch the boats. He stood for some time like that, until he felt a rough hand on his shoulder, swinging him round.

An old man stood before him, his face twisted with malice. 'Well, you little thing, you, and what are you going to do for us now?' he said, winking back at his fellows.

They came forward, putting on a great show of ferocity.

'Yes,' they growled, 'what are you going to give us? You are our Chief, aren't you? A Chief gives his warriors presents, doesn't he? That is the law, isn't it?'

Vedrix backed away from them a pace. But they kept coming on after him, making fierce noises that frightened him.

'He doesn't mean to give us anything,' said their leader, an old rogue whose back was deeply scarred with the lashings Barduca had given him in the past for theft and murder of his comrades. 'He doesn't mean to give us anything. He means to rule us and make us work for him and then give us nothing. His father was a better King, at least he gave us something—if only the whip!'

The old man went forward, pulling upon his shirt to show the scars, his face wicked with glee.

Vedrix stepped back again. 'I cannot help what my father has done, my friends,' he said, holding out his hands so that they would not hurt his face.

'He cannot help what his father has done, the coward!' said one of them, flinging a handful of mud into the young man's face.

They stood for a while, laughing at him as he spluttered. Then they crouched and moved towards him. He saw them coming and shrieked out, 'Father, Father, save me! They are going to hurt me!'

His last step backwards was into the slime again. His feet betrayed him, as did all else, and he fell into the water. They rushed forward and dragged him out again, stripping his finery from him, as they helped him up the bank and back to the wind-break tent.

He was weeping now and promising them anything he had. They let him sit in the King's chair and even made some pretence of drying him down.

'You treat us well, Vedrix,' they said, 'and we will look after you. We will do as you say, whenever there is a stranger about. But you try to betray us and we'll come on you at night and tear out your bowels with an oak-stake.'

They made such horrible gestures and rolled their eyes so fearsomely that Vedrix covered his face with his hands and wept like a child for the sheer hopelessness of his situation.

They laughed at each other and then, slapping him roughly on the back, left him, taking with them most of the food that Barduca had given him.

'Be a good boy,' they said, 'and do not try to run away. Or we shall follow you and hold you down while we pull your thumb out until it is as long as your arms.' They made horrible gestures to illustrate their words.

Vedrix began to love his father again and even wished that Isca was there to spit at him and lie about him. He was utterly miserable.

In the leading boat Barduca was holding Isca about the waist. The other men in the boat were too occupied in rowing, in keeping the clumsy craft heading to the west, to notice what he did or said. It made no difference, they could not have altered him, one way or the other.

It was Isca who spoke first. She pointed to the stern of the boat where they had hung a curtain and roof of cowhide on stout rafters.

'Come back there with me, King,' she said. 'It will be warm there and we can forget Vedrix for a while. Come, you are strong today, and so am I. Let us forget Vedrix.'

Barduca helped her to keep her balance as they shuffled between the sweating rowers.

Inside the shelter he said, 'Have no fear, my Queen, we shall never see Vedrix again. I chose his warriors carefully for him— they are all murderers, when they can find a weak enough victim; and Vedrix is that victim!'

Then, because they had other things to do, they did not speak of Vedrix again. And at last they slept in the stern of the boat, rocked by the freshening sea, lulled by the slow moaning of the cattle and the rhythmic grunts of the oarsmen.

There was a man who watched them from another boat: one Cradoc, a proud middle-aged lord, who had run foul of Barduca in the last stages of their long journey to the coast. Barduca had humbled him before all the others, who had not dared to speak up for him, and had then confiscated half of his horses and cattle as a punishment for offending a King.

This man, Cradoc, had accepted the tyrant's punishment meekly, while vowing in his heart that one day he would find and use the opportunity for revenge.

Now he watched Barduca smiling down at Isca before they fell asleep together, and he nodded gently, his lips curling as he thought that the time might not be so far away after all. Yet one must be careful, he thought. Barduca was not a man to forgive a blow, however slight. The man who struck Barduca must strike once and for all, he must not be allowed to rise again from the ground.

# 19: Escape

A FAINT grey light came into the prison-room below the ground. The ten who sprawled about the hard-beaten earthen floor lay in the attitude of men who listen to every sound that comes to them. They were all that were left of the prisoners of Craig Dun, and for them dawn was the signal to escape. They could stand no more of what was being done to them. They felt they had paid their debts now.

One of them, a tall young warrior, whose chest-wounds had scarcely healed and whose face had been laid wide open by a vicious axe-blow, stood up and went to the big stone that covered the door. He sniffed the air and listened like a hound. Then he turned back and limped towards a man who lay, listless against the stone wall; a man whose body was racked by his efforts to retch every few moments, though he brought up nothing.

'Old Man,' he said, 'the dawn is nearly here. Will you come with us, after all? Together we might find a means of getting up the hill and at least part of the way back home. Better to be caught and killed in the open out there, with our noses towards Craig Dun, than to rot here until they shall put us on to their winter fires.'

Garroch turned a grey face up towards him and shook his head painfully. 'Go you, Naga, with your five, and may Earth Mother bring you safely to Craig Dun. Tell them I shall come back to them one day, if She wishes me to. If not, they must find themselves another Old Man.'

The warrior kneeled down by Garroch and clasped his thin and twisted hands in his own, holding them to his chest to warm them.

'Come with us, Garroch,' he said. 'At least we should all die together under the sky.'

Garroch screwed up his eyes with pain and was breathless and silent for a while. Then he shook his head once more.

'Naga, I shall curse you if you do not go,' he said, trying to smile. 'Take your five and go. I shall stay here with my four friends, until we feel strong enough to run.' He seemed to consider for a moment, then he went on, 'Until we feel strong enough to take our killers with us, should they catch us again.'

The young man rose and went about the round hut, touching first this man, then another, on the shoulder. They rose silently as he touched them, and each kneeled before their leader and bent their foreheads towards his tortured hands. He kissed them and then turned away, his face to the wall.

All the men save Garroch went to the stone and, leaning their poor weight upon it, pushed with as much strength as their imprisonment and suffering had left them. It was long before the stone began to move.

Yet at last it did move, and slowly ground its way backwards from the door, letting the light flood into the deeply dug cell. Five of the warriors went up the steps and into the light. They each looked back and made the farewell sign before they disappeared.

The four who were left went back and lay beside Garroch, speaking in whispers. They spoke of the folk at Craig Dun, of the good harvest and the great number of cattle they had captured before they had been surprised, that night about the fires.

Garroch covered his face with his hands. He did not wish to remember how he had led his men into the trap. He wondered whether he could ever go back to Craig Dun, even if he grew strong enough to do so. They would not remember that he had given the folk great wealth; but they would remember that he had led half its warriors to death or imprisonment.

The men about him had stopped whispering now and had fallen into an uneasy sleep again, the cold dawn wind blowing down upon their naked bodies as they lay, unaware now of such simple thing as discomfort.

Garroch let his gaze wander over them, noting their wounds, their mutilations. He had been lucky, in a way; his captors had not marked him as his followers had been marked. At least his status as Chieftain had preserved the outside appearances, though they had done other things for which no thanks could be given. His stomach revolted again and his retching left him breathless and weak.

He recalled the hot wood-stakes they had used on him and the little flint-chips that they fixed into alder-stems. He groaned and wondered whether it would ever happen again. He would rather die now, he thought, than have that again.

Then he too fell asleep, wondering, and dreamed that he walked on the hill above Craig Dun with Marrag and Brach, with the sun shining down on them all out of a clear sky. Mai Mai the dog jumped about their legs, trying to trip them up and Marrag struck at the creature with his stick. Brach was very cross with the Old Man then and said, 'One day, Marrag, you might be a dog, like Mai Mai. Then how would you like some one to hit you with a stick, just because you were happy in the sun'

Garroch woke, crying, for he loved Brach, and it made him sad to see her again, even if only in a dream. He was remem bering the things she had said when she was first learning to talk, funny things, when she used the words all wrong and then laughed, screwing up her little beak of a nose and shaking her head so that her thick black hair sprayed about her shoulers and covered her face . . .

He was still thinking about Brach when a shadow fell across the floor and he looked up to see three warriors standing on the step, looking down at the prisoners, holding their great green- stone axes menacingly before them. They had been standing there a long time, waiting for the sleepers to awake. Now that the leader had come up from sleep, they came down into the hut and shook the others into wakefulness, dragging them roughly to their feet.

'Come,' they said to Garroch. 'Come, Great One, you must come. It is commanded.'

They treated him with respect, though they did not hesitate to force his body to do what they wished. Even their Chief had made that clear to Garroch—that as a Chief, the Old Man of Craig Dun, he was respected; but as a wicked body that stole cattle and killed the folk, he must be punished. It was the law among the chieftains that they were brothers and must not harm each other—as chieftains. They could only torment one another as wicked men. So now, as they rammed the hafts of their axes into his back to make him rise, they still bowed their heads with reverence to his spirit as the Old Man.

Garroch wondered why he must go up into the light. He thought that perhaps they were to be punished because their comrades had escaped. He even thought that they might be going out to freedom. But he soon smothered that thought, for it was almost impossible that this revengeful people would set their enemies free.

Then the five were up the steps and above ground again, blinking in the daylight which they had not seen for a moon's time. At first they rubbed their eyes, almost blind, and then the black turned to grey and the grey to white, and they saw again, clearly and in a great start.

The Chief and his councillors stood in a group in the middle of the compound. The folk ranged about the outer rim of the great circle. Everyone was smiling, waiting and smiling.

Before the Chief and his older men lay a small heap of bodies. Garroch gave a little cry as he recognised the five who had gone through the doorway at dawn. They had got no further than the middle of the compound, then; not up the hill, not on to the rolling plain, not on the way to their home, to Craig Dun. Just a few yards, nothing more. and now they lay still and white, their limbs stuck out stiffly, their eyes rolled back and the whites showing in the sunlight.

Garroch fell to the ground with exhaustion and disappointment. They did not need to tie stones to his hands and feet, as they did to the others, before they flogged him with heavy plants. He was too weak to move, they knew.

It was fortunate for him, in its way, because his senses left after the first blows and he suffered no more until he came much later. It was the worse for the strong ones among his band, whose fury kept them conscious until the last beater had sworn to the ground with his efforts. They suffered much, the strong ones.

# 20: Landing

THE FISHERFOLK, about their tasks along the estuary, were the first to see the rafts and dug-out boats, rolling towards them on the morning tide.

'See, see!' cried one, pointing, 'they float as thick as seeds upon a pool! Let us tell Tula. He will know what to do.'

They ran to the hutment and told the grey-bearded elder who had looked after them, praying for their welfare to the Sea-Mother since they had lost Kraka, their Chief of the true blood.

But Tule did not know what to do, for such a thing as this had never happened before.

One of the young men said, 'If they are strong, let us make friends with them, whoever they are: if they are weak, let us meet them in the water and kill them before they set foot on land.'

The older men looked hard at him, as though they did not wish to hear his unfledged opinion; nevertheless, they had to accept this youth's advice, since no one had better words to offer.

So Tula sent the women, with their children, out of the village and beyond the hill for safety. Then he and the menfolk made ready their arrows and harpoons and waited, watching keenly, behind the rocks at the water's edge.

They need not have feared: Barduca's folk and his animals had suffered too dreadfully during their stormy voyage to harm anyone for the time being.

'Look,' called out the youth, 'they are both strong and weak —strong in their great numbers and weak in their salt-sickness.'

Of the great fleet of dug-outs that had pushed off from the salt-marshes two days before, half had been swept away or swamped in the rising seas, they had capsized among the treacherous rollers or had sprung leaks which their sailors had no moss or rags to plug. The dug-outs which came in slowly with the tide wallowed, half-full of water, their crews sick and exhausted with effort and hunger.

Yet the horses and cattle had suffered more. Some in mid-channel, terrified by the unfamiliar seas and the rising winds, had burst their leather bounds and had plunged, lowing or whinnying, into the deep waters, dragging their fellows with them. One raft, laden with cows and calves, lashed down on their sides, had turned turtle in the heavy seas, and later turned back again to keep on its course, bearing with it a pathetic load of death. The other creatures, scenting this mute cargo, had turned as wild as their thongs would let them, goring each other's sides or kicking their neighbours to death.

The Fisherfolk came from behind their sheltering rocks to gaze in wonder at this strange sad landing.

'Aiee!' said Tula, shaking his grizzled head, 'but a people who dares such a voyage must be brave.'

One of the elders said, 'Let us find their Chief, if he is alive. It would be wise to have such men as our friends.'

They soon found Barduca. He was staggering about the shore, cursing and striking out at all who seemed too slow for his liking, bellowing like a man possessed, almost as though he blamed his followers for the misfortune which had overtaken them. He vented his anger especially upon Cradoc, the lord who hated him more than did the others. Cradoc only smiled in his thin-lipped way, and pledged himself silently to pay Barduca back in the same manner one day, one day, when the luck turned.

Even Isca came under the lash of the angry King's tongue. He began to call her a bitch for enticing him away from his work as a leader. She tried to brazen him out, but her face was pale and her lips were quivering. Her heavy woollen robe was drenched with salt water and clung to her, so that she could only restrain her shivering by the most extreme effort. Yet she did so, anxious not to let this tyrant appear to rule her as he did silly Vedrix.

Barduca pointed insultingly at a part of her body and roared out, 'Do you think *that* is worth the loss of so many good cattle and men? Do you think it pays for the fine horses that have gone under the sea?'

Isca's eyes blazed for a moment and then she said, in almost as loud a voice, 'What have you that could equal a billy-goat, much less a horse, old King?'

Now Barduca's rage flared up, for he could hear the many little rustles of laughter among his men, especially from such as Cradoc, whom he had treated shamefully. He stepped towards her and raised his hand to strike her, even before the folk. But she stared back into his eyes, despite her shivering body and the great fear that suddenly jumped up inside her.

'If you strike me, Barduca,' she said coldly, 'I will have your head. Never fear, King, I will have your head.'

He stopped, glaring back at her as though she had flung a stone in his face. No one had ever said that to him before, no one had ever as much as looked into his eyes when he was angry, not even his mother, who had shrunk from him though he was a young boy.

If Isca's words had been heard by anyone else, Barduca would have had to strike her, perhaps with his long copper sword, to keep his place among the warriors. But she had spoken in a low voice and they were standing away from the others. He mastered his fury and said to her, 'I will not punish you now, woman, but do not tempt me again with such a threat, or I will show you what pain can be.'

She bowed her golden head before him, in mock humility, thinking that at last she had begun to understand this tyrant King, thinking that at last she knew how big, and how little he was.

Gently she said, 'I hear your words, Barduca. That is enough, between two such as we are.'

Then Tula and the elders of the Fisherfolk came between them, speaking words of peace. Barduca turned to them, straining to understand their words, for their dialect was very different from that of the herdsmen, yet with some trouble it could be understood.

Tula said, 'Welcome, stranger King. Our houses are yours, our fires are yours, our food is yours, until you shall go onwards to find these things for yourselves in another place.'

Barduca nodded and said, 'Lend me all your men, my friend. We must drag the rafts ashore before the tide turns. There is much for us to do.'

Then he went to another part of the shore to give his orders and to beat his slower followers with the flat of his great sword.

Tula stared at the shining weapon. 'It is a golden thing,' he said, 'a sword out of the sun. Truly this must be a great one, my folk. His friendship is such that a man might cherish.'

The young man who had spoken earlier said, 'At last the Sea Mother has sent us a friend. One who will get revenge on the People of the Hill for us. This King will bring suffering on Garroch for killing Kraka, my friends! A King with a golden sword!'

Tula said, 'Garroch did not kill Kraka. Rua, his daughter, killed Kraka, her father.'

The young man said with a sneer, 'Garroch killed Kraka with Rua for his weapon. She loved Garroch and so she killed her father.'

Tula did the only thing he could do, and struck the young man to the ground for speaking so insolently to his elders.

Yet, as the old men walked away, they said to each other, 'The young fool is right. We must tend these strangers carefully, and then persuade them to fight with Garroch's folk. We will not go with them to fight, but we will send someone to show them where they will find Garroch's steading.'

So Barduca came to the Fisherfolk, and so the Fisherfolk gave the strangers what food and warmth they had. Yet before the golden-haired ones left, driving their thin cattle and their dispirited horses before them, Tula was glad to see the back of them, for they were a proud and demanding people, who treated the Fishers as though they were slaves.

Yet principally he was glad to see Isca go, for her beauty and great hunger of the body had already turned the heads of the young men, who wanted her so badly that many of them pledged themselves to Barduca, so that they should at least be near her.

As for Isca, she had had her moment of revolt on the sea-shore, and now her temper had been quenched again before they left. Before these simple stinking Fisherfolk, Barduca had treated her like a Queen, with respect and courtesy. And in his bed he had treated her with that sort of savage abandon which best suited her desires; though his motives had been those of revenge, rather than a wish to give pleasure to the woman who had dared to stand up against him before his followers.

As for the common folk of that sea-shore village, they had eaten cow-meat and horseflesh for the first time, and many who had spent the greater part of their lives naked, now strutted along the mud-flats dressed in the hides of calves and stallions— the cattle that had not survived the voyage to this dark island of flint-men. And so these Fisherfolk kneeled before their rotting shark-goddess on the leaning pole and thanked her for bringing such good fortune over the seas to them.

Tula thanked her especially, for at last, by this King with the golden sword, there was a chance to bring proud Garroch to his knees.

# 21: Farewell!

IF TULA could have been in the damp dungeon, he would have seen that Garroch was already on his knees, with exhaustion and hunger, which left him little opportunity of showing any pride he might still have.

Of his followers, only two had survived the beating after their attempted escape, and now the three seldom spoke to each other, so weak and downhearted were they. Yet each morning the two tribesmen slithered across the floor from their sleeping place and touched their Chief's hand, to show that they were still his men.

But Garroch hardly looked at them as they did this. He kneeled, or sat cross-legged, all day, his head bowed, his tangled hair filthy and lice-ridden now, the bones of his shoulders sticking up, pointed, as he folded his arms to relieve himself of their weight.

Now even his dreams had deserted him. He did not see the blue sky over the hill any more, or walk with his father and daughter and Mai Mai the dog. Earth Mother withheld such pleasant pictures from his mind, almost as though she too was punishing him.

He tried to think why this misfortune should have happened to him, and the answers were many—he had sheltered a woman who had killed her own father, he had shown weakness in the Corn Dance on the hill, he had deceived Earth Mother by taking Marrag's place in the Long House, he had robbed the other flint-folk of their barley and their cattle so that his own folk might prosper. All these things might have offended the Gods.

He went over this every day, again and again, but now it did not seem useful any longer to pray to Earth Mother. She seemed to have made up her mind that he must die forgotten. Besides, he had nothing to offer, no sacrifice—unless it was part of himself. But even as he thought of this, his body shuddered with fear. It had suffered too much in the last weeks. It could no longer bear pain. Garroch lay down and turned his face to the wall, hoping that he might die in his sleep.

Yet he did wake again, to hear the big stone being rolled away from the door, and then in a sudden burst of sunlight to see Asa Wolf standing on the steps, his arms held out to embrace his blood-brother. And behind Asa there was the great sound of many cattle stamping the earth and lowing, so loudly that it sounded to Garroch like the beating of surf on the sea-shore.

For a while they looked at each other silently. Then Asa's face lost its smile and he knelt before Garroch, weeping at his sad condition.

Garroch spoke first. He said. 'Are you a ghost, my brother?'

Asa shook his head and said, 'I am not ghost, Old Man. Though I was nearly a ghost before I crawled back to Craig Dun with the arrows in me. Yet I have survived.'

Garroch had to wait long before his thudding heart would let him speak again. Then he whispered, 'Why are you here, my brother?'

And Asa said, 'I come to take you back to your people. I come to pay your ransom to this Chief, so that he will set you free.'

Garroch said, 'I hear the sound of many cattle. Is that my ransom?'

Asa answered, 'Aye, that is your ransom—all the cattle we have, each bull, each cow, each calf.'

Garroch said, 'That is a big price to pay for one so weak as I am. My people must love me to offer so much, to offer all their profit in our raids, for me.'

Asa lowered his eyes and said with a wicked smile, 'My brother, Kaa Fox, and I told them that if they did not bring you back, we would leave them to their fate. They have relied on my brother's warriors for some time now, for your own are scarcely ready to fight for their village. We told them that they must pay the ransom or we would take the cattle, for ourselves, so that they must lose it in any case.'

Garroch shook his head in sorrow. Then he clasped Asa's hand and said, 'I have two good brothers, I seé.'

Then he gestured towards the wretches who sat with him in the dungeon, sharing his misfortunes. They smiled back, bright eyed at the prospect of freedom.

'Will these friends come with us away from here?' he asked. But Asa shook his head. 'The Chief is a hard man,' he answered. 'He will set you free, Garroch, but he says that these must stay and take your place in whatever is to come.'

Garroch turned towards them and held out his hands. 'There, you see, my brothers,' he said, 'our friend Asa has done what he could. What will you have me do now? Shall I stay with you so that we die together, as we expected; or shall I go back with Asa?'

They touched their foreheads on the back of his hand. 'Go back, Old Man,' they said. 'We are but dogs. We are worth nothing. Go back and leave us.'

Garroch beat his head on the floor and wept. Then he said, not looking at them this time, 'My brothers, I will come again for you, to fetch you from this place of death. Be alive when I come, for if you are not, I shall have yet another load to carry on my shoulders through my dreams.'

He got up then and went out with Asa. The two bowed down before him as he passed and did not raise their heads again until the stone had been rolled back across the doorway, shutting out the sunlight. They sat in silence, as they always did now, staring at each other.

Garroch stumbled forward, leaning heavily on the broad shoulder of his blood-brother. As he appeared from the depths of the prison-house, a gasp went up from the folk in the com-

bound, for their enemy who was to be ransomed seemed so changed a man. His haggard face and dark-ringed eyes were those of an old man, they thought, remembering the hawklike glory of his body when they first took him.

In the centre of the compound, sitting amongst his wives and many children, was the Chief of the Village Under the Rocks. He had put on all his ceremonial splendour, the green-dyed lynx skin that acted as a hood, its foreclaws dangling down on either side of his face, his cloak of white bullhide, rubbed so thin and so shiny that it had the appearance of the finest cloth, his triple necklace of wolf-teeth, his great bone rings, his loin-cloth of blue linen, trimmed with the fur of the pine marten. His fleshy face was streaked with the juice of the woad plant and his beard and eyebrows had been redyed a deeper shade of black, which contrasted strangely with the long grizzled hair that hung down on to his bent shoulders.

As Garroch approached, he wrinkled up his eyes and began to chew more strongly on the barley grain with which he had filled his mouth while waiting for his prisoner to appear. He stroked his black beard, wondering whether he had done the wise thing in letting this man go for the ransom he had agreed on, or whether he might not have screwed more out of the folk at Craig Dun if he had waited. He wondered whether to send Garroch back into the prison and tell Asa Wolf that he needed even more cattle, and also many bags of barley, before the man could go home.

One of his wives, a woman many years older than he, sensed what was in his mind. She had that talent, which was why he feared her and kept her on as his wife—she always knew what he was thinking. She leaned towards him and said, 'If you send him back he will die before his friend can fetch the new ransom. I see it in his eyes. He would not stand imprisonment any longer after being promised freedom.'

The Chief spat at her feet, meaning that she should hold her tongue on such an important occasion.

'I shall do as I think best,' he said, not knowing what he would do.

The woman inclined her head, as was befitting for a wife before a husband; but there was nothing slavish in the tone of her voice as she whispered, 'I promise you, if you break your word now, that man who is with him, whom they call Asa Wolf, will leap on you and tear out your throat with his teeth. It is written in the pebbles at your feet.'

The Chief gave a start. Then, hurriedly, he reached forward with his right foot and scattered the little flints so that they lost the pattern they had had.

'What now, O Knower of All Things?' he said with a smile.

The woman sniffed with an endless cold in the head. Then she shrugged her shoulders and said, 'The pebbles now say that if you send him back into the death-house, a stone will form inside your belly and swell there until it bursts you open, one night, when no one is with you to put stitches into the hole and save your blood from leaving you.'

The Chief said, 'Have no fear, woman, I shall let him go.'

When Garroch stood before him, swaying, he said, 'Hail, great Chief! Your folk have sent your cattle-price. You may go from us freely, and may Earth Mother be good to her son.'

But Garroch only stared into his eyes, unwaveringly, his hands clenched by his sides, his white lips twisted with hatred.

The Chief said hurriedly, 'What has been done to you, was done to the body, not to the Chief in you. The spirit of the Chief in you has not been touched, you know that. We love and respect that spirit, my brother. It is only the wicked body that we punished for what it did to our folk and children about the peaceful fires.'

For a while, Asa Wolf was afraid that Garroch would use his last strength to drag the fat Chief from his chair and gouge out his eyes, for Garroch's fingers now began to twitch uncontrolledly. The Chief saw this too, and tried to back away as far as he could from the wild beast who stood before him. But then a shudder passed through Garroch's body and his hands were still. The mood of killing had left him.

'I understand,' said Garroch. 'What of my friends still in your prison house? Can they not come with me?'

The Chieftain shook his head sadly. 'It is too late, my dear brother,' he said. 'For I gave orders that when you were taken from them, they were to be sent on the last journey, so that they should not suffer the loneliness of being without their Chief. They are already dead.'

Garroch muttered, 'That is another load I must carry then.'

He turned away from the Chief, without a word or a sign of respect and began to stumble towards the hillside that would lead him out of this place of pain. Asa turned and followed him closely, lest he should fall down.

The Chief and his people watched the two go without a word. When they stood at last on the top of the basin, the old wife of the Chief said, 'Those two are great ones, husband. You would have done well to grant Garroch's request. Because you kill his friends, he will come back one day and put an axe-head into your neck.'

In fury the Chief turned and knocked the woman away from him, so that she fell on the ground. Losing all control, he shouted now to the group of warriors who stood nearest the prison house, 'Roll back the stone! Go in and kill those dogs! I will not be brow-beaten by this woman any longer. She is no longer my woman. She is a witch and must die at the next burnings.'

But the woman did not seem to mind his words. She lay where he had knocked her, smiling up at him strangely and spreading a little group of pebbles with her hand.

At last she whispered to him as he watched her, wide-eyed, 'So it has come to this at last! Very well, my husband, you shall see that you cannot escape the death. These pebbles bring something worse than Garroch's axe to you!'

Suddenly he gave a choked cry and shambled at her. No man dared step forward to drag him from her. But at last he stood up, his broad-bladed hunting knife red, his flushed face moving in a silly smile.

The old woman coughed again and again, but still smiled in her mocking way.

'You will never enjoy Garroch's cattle,' she said. 'What a shame! Oh, what a shame!'

Then she began to laugh aloud, but in the middle of her laughter, she sank back and did not move again.

The folk lowered their eyes and went back into their huts. The Chief was left alone in the middle of the compound, weeping over the body of the only woman who had ever been of use to him.

That night his oldest son, the child of the woman he had killed, pushed a bone bird-arrow into the Chief's ear, deep, with a savage thrust that broke the thing inside his head. There was no one else in the hut to help the Chief, though all in the village heard his high screaming, but were afraid to go to his aid for fear that someone else might be with him in the darkness, someone they all feared by day and by night.

They tried to make out what their Chief was yelling, but his hoarse words were not for men to understand.

As for Garroch and Asa, they passed away from that village in the daylight, pausing many times because Garroch was so weak. Once they sat on a little hillock and saw below them the vast herd of cattle, that had been Garroch's ransom, being walked by many herdsmen and dogs towards a high hill corral. The lowing and the shouts and barking came clearly to Garroch's ears, like taunting words.

'My brother,' he said, 'this poor body is not worth a half of those.' He pointed towards the great moving stream.

Asa Wolf took his hand and stroked it gently. 'You are worth many hundreds of such herds, my brother,' he said. 'Yes, worth all the cattle that the hills have ever bred.'

Garroch looked at him strangely and said, 'I would die, my brother, rather than let you speak a lie like that. Help me to be that man you boast of, Asa Wolf. Help me, I beg you, brother.'

And Asa Wolf put his arm about the Chieftain's thin shoulders. 'I shall help you, Garroch,' he said, 'or may this hand rot from my body, and the worm come inside my mouth.'

They slept in a little hollow and when the dawn came, they began their march once more towards Craig Dun. The buzzards hovered over them, but Asa Wolf only smiled, baring his teeth up at them.

'Fly another way, little brothers,' he called, 'for down here you cannot hope to feed. Down here there are two who would pluck you from the air and crunch you up, wings and claws and all, if you came too close! Fly, fly, little brothers.'

The birds wheeled and flew away, far towards the east.

Asa Wolf shook his fist at them and smiled.

'Coward hawks,' he called. 'If you but knew, there are two here who haven't the strength to eat a dish of barley porridge!'

He smiled towards Garroch, who smiled back, happy now.

But it was not Asa's threat that had called the birds away. The message had just reached them that a great army had landed at the place of the Fisherfolk, strange men in dug-out boats, with many dead cows and horses laden on their rafts. Better it was to fly far to such a feast than follow two men-things over the dry hills, waiting for one of them to fall. The pickings would be greater, if less sweet.

# 22: Meeting

VEDRIX WALKED alone in a dripping oakwood, his thin cloak drenched with a sudden shower of rain. As often as he was able, he would creep away from the crowded and stinking encampment on the salt-marshes, where the men mocked him and when they were drunk, which was often, pushed him from one to the other, as though he were a blindfold boy or a half-wit.

There was one whom he hated especially, a squat cross-eyed fellow with a tumour on the side of his neck, who felt that the world had betrayed him and so was always anxious to make suffer those who had been born more fortunate. This man made Vedrix weep with weak vexation, and when he was in that state he became almost inarticulate and quite unable to answer the sneers and taunts of his tormentor.

As Vedrix walked in the wood, looking for something to kill, something on which he might vent his anger, he thought of the man with the growth on his neck and kicked at the trunk of an oak tree in his sudden access of rage. But the tree did not suffer; it was Vedrix who sat down in the damp moss, to rub his foot and to swear that everything below the sky conspired against him.

He was sitting like that, his bright sword across his knees, when the bushes behind him rustled. Vedrix began to rise to his feet, his fallen sword forgotten, his heart suddenly jumping up into his throat. He was about to shout out in his terror that he would harm no man, that he would give what little he had if the man would treat him gently. Then he saw who had stirred behind him and his manner changed. He stopped and picked up the bright sword and, flinging his cloak away from his shoulders, put on the stance of a warrior, a kingly leader, his mouth curling proudly to drive away his own tremors.

A woman was standing there, suckling a babe at her heavy breast and looking at Vedrix with wide-open eyes. He could see from the colours of her rough woollen shift and the thick coils of her dark brown hair that she was not of his people—he guessed that she was of the distant mountain folk, who seldom came out of their cold high land to travel through the woods and over the great plains.

She stared at him for a while, then, slow-footed and weary,

she pushed on through the bushes and came towards him.

'I have come far,' she said, 'and I am tired. Have you got food, man? Have you got a camp nearby, where I can rest with the bairn?'

Vedrix said proudly, 'I am a Prince, woman. Do you speak so rudely to a Prince?'

The woman looked him up and down and then shrugged her shoulders. 'Needs must when the Horned One drives,' she said. 'Well, Prince, I beg your help, I who was once a Queen in my own land. I ask for food for myself, and shelter for my bairn, who does not need your food but only mine. Will that do? I want no more than a barley crust and a jar of the warming mead; my tastes are simple. They needs must be!'

Vedrix said, 'So, you are a Queen, are you? And where, may I humbly ask, is your great kingdom?'

The woman looked strongly into his eyes, though he did not give way to her immediately, but tried to stare her out. He was unsuccessful, of course, but at least he had made the effort. That encouraged him a little.

She said, 'I come from the high Snow Cantons, and my father was Maelguna, he of the three bronze swords. My brothers were Fynn and Goduin and Brann. They slew the giant of the Middle Sea and set up his horned head in the caverns of a little island there. Men still pray to it, the fools!'

As she spoke she went on suckling the baby and ceased gazing at Vedrix. He came closer to her and examined the thin gold bracelets on her strong arms, the little half-moon of bronze above her breasts.

Then he bowed his head before her and said, 'I know that you speak the truth. Your father and his family are told about in our own stories. You are a great one, one of the first of the golden families. I salute you!'

She looked up at him as though he spoke no sense. Then she said, 'My father and brothers are dead. The mountain fell on them while they were hunting and the folk have sent me away, for they say I am a witch. I loved my father and my brothers, but I swore at them when they galloped off that day, and the folk think my curse brought down the mountain.'

Vedrix said, 'Are you a witch, lady?' His voice shook a little.

The woman took her sore breast away from the baby, who began to cry immediately. She disregarded it and said, 'I do not know. I only know that I did not mean what I said that morning. I only said it because my father was angry with me for burning the oat-cakes.'

Vedrix said fearfully, 'What was the curse you said to them then, lady?'

Yet from the look of this heavy-limbed woman, her strength and confidence, he knew what reply he would receive.

She answered simply, 'I only said, "May the mountain fall on you as you ride!" But I did not mean it, you understand, lord?'

Vedrix stood back from her and nodded. 'Yes, I understand, lady,' he said. Then an idea worked in his mind. He dared to step closer again and say, 'Will you come with me? My camp is yours. I welcome such a great one.'

The woman looked into his face keenly. 'You need my help,' she said.

Vedrix lowered his sword and nodded miserably.

The woman said, 'All over the world there are little men like you, born into the beds of Kings. They do not ask to come, nor do they ask for Kings to be their fathers. Yet they suffer the shame of being Princes when they have not the courage of mice. They would be far happier with a crook and a dog, watching sheep on a hillside.'

Vedrix began to protest but she looked him in the eye and he was quiet again, already fearing her because she looked into his heart and saw the fear there.

'I am a Queen,' she said. 'I did not ask to be such. Yet the Sun was gracious to give me courage as well as high blood and so I do not mind being a Queen. Yes, little one, I will help you.'

She rose and walked beside him. After a few paces she said, 'Here, little Prince, carry the baby, for I am weary of the thing.'

He gave her his sword and took her burden. He had never carried a baby before and had no idea how difficult it was. But he carried out his end of the bargain, even though the little thing wet him through.

At the edge of the wood he said, 'Whose child is this, Queen of the Snow Cantons?'

He was amazed at his daring as he spoke such words. The woman only smiled and chopped off the heads of the cow-parsley as they went along, with the bright copper sword. She used it as though it was not the first sword she had held.

At last she stopped and turned towards him, her eyes afire with roguishness. She drew Vedrix towards her and then reaching down touched him in a tender spot so that at first he drew away, then, thinking better of it, came closer to her.

'You see,' she said, with a little smile, 'it is your baby now. Whose else could it be?'

Vedrix was not so convinced, but walked on with her and at last reached the camp. The squat man with the tumour on his neck came running to meet them, his face aflame with anger.

'Damn you, you mannikin,' he shouted. 'Where have you been, you cowardly dolt, all morning?'

The woman looked sharply at Vedrix and said, 'If we are to go together, this must not happen.'

She took the baby from the young man and almost with the same movement put the sword back into his hand.

'I am a Queen,' she said, 'whose father was a warrior, whose brothers were warriors. They would have looked at this kitchen slave and he would have fled. You can do no less than chop off his brutish head, my little Prince.'

Vedrix took the sword and his heart was cold inside him. He did not shiver, he was too dead even for that sign of life.

As the man ran towards him, his tongue lolling from his mouth, his fat red hands open to clutch this coward by the neck and humiliate him once more. Vedrix stepped to one side and with as much force as he had, drove in the sword, just under the man's breastbone.

The man gasped and stared at Vedrix with the wide eyes of surprise. He even grunted out, 'Why, you little swine! You little . . .'

But he had fallen speechless before he could finish the words. Then Vedrix mastered his repugnance and stooping hacked off the man's head, and so went with it and the woman, negligently into the camp. He was glad to be walking for when he stood still his legs shivered violently.

The elderly warriors who saw them coming thus fell on their knees as the two entered the encampment. They too knew who this woman must be and they too knew that now Vedrix would want to use his copper sword again, just to prove it was not all a dream.

'We are your servants, King,' they chanted.

Vedrix looked at them like an emperor and said, 'One day, my friends, we go to claim our kingdom.'

Then pushed the woman inside the hide tent, a new power come upon him. She turned towards him when once they were inside.

'Little Prince,' she said, 'always remember this—they say I am a witch. You know what you were before I came here. You know what you think you are now. But I know everything. And I ask you to treat me carefully, and I ask you to treat this boy carefully. He is the son of a great one.'

Then she began to nurse the little thing, changing the wrappings about it and talking to it in a tongue that Vedrix did not understand. He waited a while, until he felt sure that she had forgotten him, and then began to walk towards the door, crestfallen and small again.

The woman looked up at him, almost in anger. 'You little thing,' she said, 'how dare you go out of this tent so soon! You will lose all the respect I have won for you. Come here, you mouse, you, and have your nibbling!'

Vedrix laid his sword on the chair that his great father had once sat in and went to her. She had put the baby on the heap of sheepskins. It slept gently, like a little King.

Vedrix wept with the joy this strange Queen gave him, but she stared up at the roof of the tent all the time, her eyes never moving.

Afterwards she said, 'Little king, we need boats. Tomorrow you must send those slaves into the woods. They have axes. Let them cut down trees and make us boats.'

Barduca's arms reached round Isca's body in the darkness of their tent. It was at such moments, before the birds began their dawn chorus, that his age came upon him so strongly and he could not get back to sleep. An old man needs comfort, he thought, his dry fingers hooking about the warm softness of the woman.

Isca stirred in her deep sleep, turning over to him, her breath sweet as honey. She murmured, still dreaming of a love she had never known, her throat vibrating against the old man's breast.

'Isca! Isca!' he said in the darkness. 'It is not love I want. Tell me, Isca! Tell me! Give me your counsel!'

But Isca slept on; whatever soul she had might have been her own: her body was outside her governance. She lay warm in sleep against the frightened King. He sighed deeply, almost wishing his son Vedrix back again in that firelit tent, to take the burden of the young woman away from him at last.

As the dawn light came through the open flat of the tent, Barduca the Sun King watched the tired guard blowing on his chilled fingers, his copper sword wedged under his arm.

Barduca wished he might leave the warm bed of this woman and go to the man and speak to him as a hard soldier should.

He wanted to ask him what he would do: whether he would

kill more and more of these little black-haired men, taking their cattle and their women, laying them down on any stone that was handy and slashing them to the glory of the sun—or whether he should turn back on his tracks and sail again, over the Little Sea, in whatever dug-out boats he could find, to the woods and plains of the bigger land, where a King could at least make sense of the men he met.

But this guard was a young man of good family. He did not pause long before the King's tent, but having blown on his raw fingers, went back to his patrol.

Barduca sighed and groaned. Isca stirred out of her sleep and flung her arms about him.

'My King,' she breathed, 'we go towards our great kingdom.'

'Yes, yes, my dove,' whispered the old man, hardly daring to stroke her hair, 'it is as you say.'

His pale eyes glared at the shrieking light of dawn with all the hatred of age.

'Lord of the Sun!' he groaned, 'Oh, take this, your daughter, from me. She burns, my lord, she burns!'

In Craig Dun, Garroch lay beneath the sweating body of the Hunters' medicine man, who was drawing out the fever from his weakened body. Asa stood near, nodding as the sweat poured out of the back of the painted tribesman who worked on the Old Man.

'Garroch burns,' grunted the man, 'he burns at last!'

So three men burned in their separate houses. But only one of them was pledged to build a boat.

And in the morning all three rose and walked among their fellows as though the night had held no terrors: Vedrix, towards the weeping oak-woods; Barduca, towards the stone where a dark-haired one lay cursing him with his eyes; Garroch, towards the hilltop—healed at last of his worst torments, though weak in the healing. Asa walked behind him, anxious lest he should fall down the slope again, in the sight of his anxious folk.

But Garroch did not fall. He stood at last on the hilltop and, raising his arms, he called, 'I am free, Mother! Free at last! My arms are my own, my legs are my own, my heart is my own—and Asa is my brother. Mother, I will meet all corners—even the Sun King!'

Below him, the folk of Craig Dun shouted their praise, all except his wives. They stared sullenly at the ground, the women of slaves now, for they had rolled away the stone when he had lain in the dungeon, suffering in that distant village, forgotten of all save Asa Wolf.

And when Garroch came down the hill at last, a messenger rushed forward to greet him, kneeling before such a Chief.

'Old Man,' he sobbed, in his fear, 'the Sun King comes to meet you. His men more like devils in their wrath, beyond the far forest.'

Garroch looked at Asa. 'Will your folk let us pass that way to meet them?' he said.

Asa said, 'If they do not, then let Kaa Fox, my brother, out of one mother, hide himself in the rocks with the stoats and weasels—for I shall be seeking him with this axe!'

So the talking-drums began to beat from hilltop to hilltop, linking tribe to tribe and so Garroch of Craig Dun called the folk together in the compound, to talk of the struggle to come.

# 23: Dancing

THE BONE bull-roarers whirred viciously and moaned like hornets about the compound, their undulating ground-bass broken at curiously recurring intervals by the stammering drums, the thin hides stretched tightly across the mouths of resonant clay pots. Above this foundation of savage music, rose the high squealing of the thigh-bone flutes, last relics of twelve tribesmen of ancient times, taken from them while the breath was still in their bodies, for potency's sake, each flute still called by the name of the man of whom it once formed a part.

The dust bellied in a dark cloud above the place as the hard feet of the warriors rose and fell, rose and fell, keeping hysterical time with the brute passion of the music. Women squatting round the beaten earth of the compound clapped their hands harshly, their heads wagging as they clapped, like grotesque mannikins jerking on wires.

> 'Aiee! Aiee! Ai-eeee!
> Breast makes milk,
> Tree makes wood;

Flint makes axe,
And axe makes blood!

Aiee! Aiee!
Suck my breast,
Pluck my tree;
Chip my flint,
But don't kill me!

Aiee! Aiee!
When my man
Came to me,
He shed my blood
Upon his tree!

Aiee! Aiee!
When my man
Went from me,
He left his blood
All on me!

O, cloth will wipe
And water clean,
But we shall know
Where you've been;
We shall see
Along your tree
Blackening wood,
Another's blood.'

As they chanted the women grinned and gestured with an ageless guile, inciting the menfolk to blood, scarcely knowing what they did, yet compelled to sing these words by a ritual as old as the blood that pulsed in their veins.

The men danced on, their faces set and empty of expression, stiff like masks now, daubed with clay. They had worked themselves into a battle-fury in which they would fight like men in deep sleep, neither feeling compassion for the wounds they inflicted nor sensing hurt in the gashes they received.

Garroch came from his house with Asa Wolf when the frenzy was at its height. They looked across the broad compound and Asa said, 'Your dark folk are demons, my brother. Now I know why they took our lands. We are not a folk like that. We will fight when the occasions come, but our blood cools quickly and then we are sorry for losing our temper.'

Garroch smiled, his lips dry, his throat working. He placed his

hand on Asa's arm, and said, 'My brother, let us not trust them
too far. Yes, they are brave now, with the music in their ears
and the women chanting, driving them on. But let them run for
a dozen miles to meet their enemy, and you will see, their
courage too will die away. It is not that they are cowards, Asa
Wolf; they are not that; but they must be led into battle when
they are hot; then they will fight like demons. Leave them even
a little too long and they begin to be hungry, or to want their
women, or to wonder about their barley fields or their sheep.
Then they melt away like the ice when the first sun throws his
hot breath down on it. If we can meet these Sun folk soon, we
shall overcome them. But if they make us wait, then this day is
our last one as great ones in Craig Dun.'

Asa said, 'You are still weak, Garroch my brother. Your
heart shows you black dreams of a world that should be white.
You will see that these men of yours are little wolves. They
will tear the throats out of the Sun folk, I promise you.'

Garroch shrugged his shoulders and did not speak. He smiled
slowly, his head turned away from Asa.

A little boy pranced up to the two great ones, his head turned
by the maddening monotony of the war-chant. He had painted
his thin body with red clay and carried a stick in his hand like
a man-harpoon.

When he reached Garroch he nodded his head before him
like a proud horse and then began to stamp so that the dust rose
about him, waving his spear above his head and shouting.:

> 'Greetings, warrior!
> Greetings, warrior!
> About to die,
> We bring you greetings,
> Old man of Craig Dun!'

A tear ran down Garroch's cheeks as he looked at the boy.
Then he bowed his dark head, set with its great bone pins and
bound about his forehead with coloured thongs of hide.

He touched his own forehead with the back of his hand in
salute and said, 'I receive your greetings, Warrior. May the
kill be quick and the blood flow free!'

The little lad, delighted that this great one had accepted his
words with the ancient reply, nodded and pranced back among
the warriors, who danced on about him, their eyes staring above
them, never noticing such things. He danced on with them until
he fell down into the swirling dust, too tired to move another

step, yet happy that the Old Man had spoken to him.

Asa Wolf watched it all. 'There,' he said, 'even the children wish to die for you, my brother.'

Garroch put his hand to his painful throat but could not answer.

Asa said then, 'And even if the warriors forget too soon what they have vowed to do, there is one who will not forget, my brother.'

Garroch did not turn his head, but felt out blindly for the hand of Asa Wolf. When he found it, he gripped it so tightly that even Asa grinned with pain for a moment.

Then the two went forward to speak to the warriors and to tell them of the journey before them.

And when they had done, the dancing broke out afresh, only to cease for the Proud Walkers. Three young warriors, painted until they resembled totem-poles rather than men, walked with high prancing steps across the dusty compound. They called, high and piercing, across the village, like hungry hawks. Their axes flew into the air with each call, and were caught again with each taking of breath. They were the signs that war should be bloody and carried to its end. Each axe-shaft was notched with at least five notches. Each triangular white scar on the shiny antler shaft meant a man.

# 24: Little Dog

A DAY had passed since the hot dancing in the compound. Garroch and the men of Craig Dun crouched among the gorse at the edge of the wood, looking down the slope. Asa Wolf lay at Garroch's side, testing the edge of his flint axe proudly with his thumb, then kissing the keen blade again and again, along its length. Garroch saw him and smiled. He was glad to have Asa Wolf with him now in his weakness; glad that they were blood-brothers, though of different folk. Asa Wolf was more to be trusted than any five men of Craig Dun, the small dark ones, even the Proud Walkers, who so often craved to get back to their fields and their sheep when the arrows began to fall and the men to scream.

Suddenly Asa sniffed the air and held up his hand. He was like a dog on the scent.

'They are coming,' he said, in his strange guttural voice. 'What shall we do, Old Man?'

The dark eyes of the waiting tribesmen were upon Garroch. He must choose right for them, that was his task as the Chief of the folk of Craig Dun, that was why he was their leader, to choose right, always. That was the frightening thing—he must be right.

Garroch licked his dry lips secretly, but smiled for his people to see, and said, 'I have a plan, my warriors. I may not tell you yet. But wait, and you will see that it will be well with us.'

He was not at all sure of himself, not as he would have been if his enemy had been the careless Hunters, or the cowardly Fisherfolk, or one of the other villages in that high chalk country. But these were the Strangers, these new ones, and it was always frightening to meet strange men from over the sea.

Garroch pressed the haft of his flint knife into his groin hard, once, twice, thrice, until he almost groaned with the pain. Then he said, in his head, 'Help me to choose, Earth Mother! Help me now. I offer three sheep, Earth Mother. Make me strong enough to choose, I who am weak!'

As he pressed the knife in again, waiting, a skin drum began to throb in the gulley below them, and then a horn started its high howling. The dark watchers at the edge of the wood shuddered and stared at each other, their eyes even more terrible because of the blue streaks of war-paint across their faces.

Asa Wolf began to rock back and forth, chanting low, the ancient spell of his people, 'Send me a fat stag! Send me a black bull! Send me a rutting badger! But do not send me death!' He said the words over and over again, until Garroch could have screamed with the tension, or even have struck Asa across his flat red face.

Then, out of the deep and dried-up watercourse, the strangers emerged. The grim-faced men of Craig Dun watched them with a curious horror, almost exposing themselves among the gorse bushes to get a better sight of the men who came to the chalk country. And as each one appeared, a little whisper went up from the watchers at the wood's edge.

Barduca was the first to appear, as he was leading the column. The men of Craig Dun gasped and pointed excitedly, for he was sitting astride a horse, and so were two others who followed him, two or three paces behind.

'Such a man! Such a horse!' gasped Asa Wolf, looking down and shaking his red head.

'A man on a horse! Look! Look!' whispered the warriors, pointing.

Barduca held up his right hand, as a signal to those behind him to halt when they had reached level ground. The copper bracelets glimmered in the dying sun and caused wonder in the eyes of those on the hill. He sat still for a while, a hunched and massive figure, his cross-gartered legs dangling on each side of his shaggy pony, his sky-coloured woollen cloak hanging down heavily behind him, hiding the pony's rump. The men on the hill gazed at his long golden plaits and the strips of dull bronze that were riveted to his leathern jerkin. Their keen eyes picked out the great round coral studs of his belt, the blue beads at his throat, the round copper-plated buckler that was slung at his pony's side. They saw the heavy greenstone axe at his saddle-bow, the criss-cross tartan of his linen skirt, all blues and reds. But what struck them most into wonder was the sword—the sword that lay, almost negligently, across his broad thighs as he sat looking up the hill towards them.

"Aiee! Aiee!" wailed the little dark men. 'A sword out of the sun.'

And almost as though the sun had heard their words, the naked blade glimmered suddenly in a sullen reddish glow below them.

Asa Wolf reached back and took Garroch's hand in his own. He did not speak, but that grasp told Garroch that whatever the men of Craig Dun did, Asa Wolf would stay to see fair play. Garroch swallowed hard. He had already heard the little rustling sounds behind him in the bracken that told him the men of his village had remembered their fields and sheep. He held Asa's hand firmly, trying to say that he valued such a friend.

Down below them others had joined Barduca. There was a cloaked figure on his right—that was Isca, in her white woollen robe; and a black cloaked man at his left—blind Cormac, the Bard. Close behind them, in a skin-hung litter, lolled the Hornman, though no one had seen him yet in his savagery of antlers and white clay. Then came the tribesmen, each with his axe or copper knife, his oxhide buckler or his javelin. And on each head, each flaxen head, a conical leather helmet gleamed with bronze and copper; round each waist a broad hide belt glittered with polished stones and metal. Though there were no more than two hundred in Barduca's tribe, even including the herdsmen who were still struggling along the watercourse with the cattle, the men on the hill felt their hearts sinking at such an enemy. These were the men of the sun, whom no one might overcome.

'Look at the golden woman on the horse,' said Garroch.

'A bitch!' said Asa Wolf.

Once more the long horn howled from the valley. The war-party below them had halted and were waiting. A man came running and leaping up the hill, as though in joy. He wore a stag's hide about his shoulders and carried a white heron's feather in his right hand. His face was bare of war-paint. He stopped thirty yards from the place where Garroch crouched.

'A herald!' said Asa Wolf. 'I could place a shaft where his neck joins his body.'

He set an arrow to the string, but Garroch gripped his arm firmly.

'It is wise to hear what he offers, first,' he said.

Asa shrugged his shoulders. 'He will offer only death,' he said.

Garroch said, 'We must all come to that in the end. The long house under the hill waits for us all.'

The man below them began to speak, in a high sing-song voice. They were amazed that they could understand what he said, for he used many words of their own, though spoken differently, as though he had a stone in his mouth. This was different from the Hunters, who spoke like the trees or the creatures that lived under them.

'Hear now,' the man called. 'You in the gorse, hear now, for we speak but once, we men of the Sun!'

Garroch passed his war-painted hand over his dark forehead. He had heard his followers melting away into the woods behind him, and knew that the battle would be a desperate one.

Then, in a voice that he did not know he possessed, he said aloud, 'Speak on, herald, speak your last words freely. We are just men, we men of the hill.'

He saw the herald's eyebrows twitch and a little spasm of surprise pass over his face, as though he had not expected such a reply. The man was brave, for he came a pace nearer, and setting himself with one foot well before the other and his head thrown back, he called, 'It is well that strong men should meet just men. May the just men also be strong, or we gain a battle too easily!'

Asa Wolf spat into the grass. 'Let me set a shaft in his liver, Garroch,' he said. But Garroch held him close.

'Wait,' he said. 'There will be time.'

Then the herald said, for all to hear, 'My master, Barduca, bids me invite your Headman to come down the hill and to speak with him. Nothing more.'

When he had spoken the man stood still, a contemptuous smile playing about his thin lips. He set his right hand on his hip as he waited and the watchers saw that his fingers were laden with copper rings. His right hand was worth a flock of sheep, thought Garroch, enviously.

'Do not go, Old Man,' whispered Asa Wolf. 'When you are down there, they will stick their knives into you and then the crops will fail and the ewes bear no lambs. Do not go!'

Garroch answered, 'If I do not go, they will ride to the village and burn it to the ground. I have heard of such folk before.'

He tried to think what his old father, Marrag, would have done. Probably he would have drawn a circle on the ground and put criss-cross lines in it, as he always seemed to do when in doubt. Though Garroch could not recall that this had ever helped him in settling any problem—certainly not when the Old Woman was alive, for she would shuffle her foot over the drawing and give Marrag a knock over the head. She always got her own way, drawing or not. Garroch smiled as he recalled the Old Woman. He even wished she were there to tell him what to do. He leaned back among the gorse and felt for the head of his small hound, Mai-Mai. There was a sort of comfort to be got from the touch of that cold damp muzzle, those long silken ears. The dog crept closer to him, as though sensing that his master was in trouble.

'What shall I do, Mai-Mai?' asked Garroch.

'Do not go down,' said Asa Wolf. 'Do not trust what a dog tells you. They are born liars, Old Man. I know dogs.'

The herald glanced back at the knot of smiling men below him, as though to ask what he should say next. Barduca leaned sideways on his shaggy pony, his thick lips drawn back from his great teeth. Isca, wrapped in her white woollen robe, caught his glance and said, 'It should not take long. Once their Headman is dead, they will fight no more. These dark ones are all the same. Get him down, Barduca, and push your sword into his belly and you will see that I speak the truth!'

Barduca scratched his beard and glared at her. He saw how her heavy breasts pushed the woollen robe outwards and he wished that it was night-time. He began to bite at his horny finger-nails, for he was an old warrior and knew enough to distrust the advice of civilians. Who could tell how many men were in that wood? And they need not all be the cowardly dark ones that Isca had mentioned. He had himself sighted a red one, a pace before the bush where their chief's voice had come from. Perhaps there were more, and if so they would be Hunters. Barduca had met Hunters before, in his own country. They were not like the other men, these cave-dwellers with magic in their skill with bow and broad hunting-knife. They knew with a ghastly assurance which tendons to slash, so that a bull fell forward helpless and bellowing, or a great stag screamed and rolled over writhing. Barduca had a healthy respect for the Hunters, even though most of them were like speechless children, and no good at bargaining.

He said, 'You talk like a green girl, Isca. But then, perhaps you are one and should be forgiven.' He thought of her body again and bit his thumb-nail until the blood came from the side of the quick.

'We shall see,' he said, 'we shall see.'

Then he nodded to the herald. The man caught his eye and understood what he was to say.

'Come down, come down, Headman of dung-eaters! Leave your swine and come down to the King. Come with your weapons, or come with your shirt off. Come when we call, or the birds shall feed full!'

Garroch felt the blood pound in his head. He was a prince as old as the hills and he knew it. He knew it by story and by the strange tensing of his muscles, that brought his head upright against his will. Garroch felt himself to be as old and as pure as the great stones at the edge of the village, as the grass that came anew each year on the hill above the chalk, as the very flints themselves, deep deep below the soil, below the earth, the first of things.

Garroch stood upright, like a man entranced, like a man walking in his sleep, a troubled sleep, the sleep that started with the beginning of the world.

'Sit down, you fool!' said Asa Wolf, who was even older than Garroch, for he knew the language of the otter and the wren.

Mai-Mai the hound stood up with his master. Together they began to walk down the hill.

Barduca and his men stared upwards and smiled. Such a small man! Such a small dog!

Asa Wolf said once more, 'If you do not sit down, Garroch, I will place a shaft between your shoulder blades!' He drew his bow.

But Garroch and Mai-Mai kept walking down the hill as though they had not heard him. Then he knew that he was powerless and waited to set an arrow into the breast of Barduca or Isca, or whoever seemed the most dangerous to his brother.

As Garroch came nearer, stepping daintily, a lord of the ancient world, his slight dark head flung back, so that the blue war-marks on his cheeks could be seen by all, his hands by his sides, their palms open and empty towards his enemies in the old way, the rough men of Barduca, the bronze-men laughed. They saw the flimsy wicker shield slung at his back, the short flint knife, the delicate stone axe. They saw that he wore his thick black hair now streaked with grey in a bun on top of his head, held up with bone pins, but no helmet. They saw that his light leather tunic was plated with horn from elk and horse—and they laughed.

Isca, leaning forwards, her lips parted, saw something else. She rose to meet the great horn of her pommel and then fell back again with a little gasp. Garroch was a comely man, she thought, though small; such a one as she had never seen before, a prince of the first days.

Ten paces from the war-band, Garroch halted, his right hand held upwards to signify that he came in peace. The little hound stood at his right side, his head against the Old Man's calf.

Garroch said quietly, 'I come, as you ask. I come to tell you that we are a peaceful folk. I come to tell you to go away to whatever land you please. I come to tell you that we do not wish to kill you, if you go back in the way you have come. We do not wish your company in the chalk hills. Go, and peace go with you!'

As he spoke, his heart thumped with tiredness and fear, for he knew that not more than twenty men of Craig Dun lay back there in the gorse, to fight with him should the need arise. Yet he did not show this in his proud blue-lined face.

Barduca stared at him, amazed. Then he turned to Isca and said, 'What shall we do with this one?' But his quick eyes noted her expression, saw what she would have done, and he turned back.

'Come closer, chieftain,' said Barduca, as gently as he was able. 'Come closer and let us talk of peace. It would be a shame for two such men as you and I to spill the blood of our people. Let us settle our differences otherwise.'

Garroch stood still and said, 'There are no differences. I only tell you to go away. That is what I said. I am the Old Man of the land.'

Barduca turned back to Isca, and this time she smiled.

'But all the same, we must not waste the blood of men,' said Barduca, amazed at his own tolerance. 'We cannot afford to let men die in an argument, can we, little Chief!'

The word had slipped out before he knew it. He saw the sudden startled look come into Garroch's dark eyes; he heard the low rustle of amusement form the men behind him.

'Look,' he said, trying to make the peace once more. 'we must not fight. Let our dogs fight instead.'

Garroch stared, for he could see no dog beside Barduca. Then as though he understood what the enemy had said, Mai Mai pushed his head hard against Garroch's thigh. Garroch nodded. He could think of nothing else to do. He did not like the way this golden woman was smiling at him, sneering with her lips. Besides, he was afraid, very much afraid, to be amongst these strange men who smelled differently, and who were always closing round him, putting *him* in the middle of the circle. He was the Old Man, he knew, and must never be enclosed like that. All the men of Craig Dun knew that. No one ever closed a circle about him, for that was against the ancient law. Yet these men did such things. Garroch was afraid because they did not understand what was sacred. So he nodded.

Immediately a man behind Barduca whistled, three times, and then the others stood aside to let an animal pass into the circle. It was a sheep-dog, huge and grey and matted, its hair hanging down almost to the ground, unkempt and stinking. It seemed almost blind, for the long hair covered its face. At first Garroch started to laugh. But Barduca said, 'Hey! Hey!' and the creature stopped dead and turned towards the man on the horse.

'Who-iee! Who-iee!' whistled Barduca, and the great dog swung round to face Mai-Mai, his legs spragged back, so that he might be ready to stand any assault.

Barduca called to Garroch, 'That is the warning of wolves, my friend. This dog has torn the belly out of twelve wolves, He is a good dog. We can rely on him to settle any argument.'

Garroch felt down and touched poor Mai-Mai's head. His hair was bristling. Garroch spoke to him gently in the sheep language, but he knew that his hound was badly matched. Then Mai-Mai licked his hand, but instantly turned back to face his enemy, on guard. Garroch knew that there was nothing he could do. He stepped away from his dog, saying, 'Fight well, brother, and may we meet under the hill!'

Then little Mai-Mai seemed to shrug his shoulders and run forward to meet the great sheep-dog of the bronze-men.

The scuffle did not last long. Soon Mai-Mai rolled on the ground writhing, his entrails bare, his eyes wildly searching for Garroch who hid his face in his hands. A man leaned forward and smashed the tormented dog's skull as he shuddered past him. Barduca smiled, but Isca leaned forward, her eyes wide, her nostrils dilated, the pommel pressing against her, hard.

The great sheep-dog lurched back on to his haunches, waving his shaggy head from side to side. Then he began to howl shrilly.

A man said to Barduca, 'The little hound has blinded him, King. He has torn the eyes from their sockets.'

Barduca smiled again and said, 'Well, we have other dogs.'

Garroch looked up to see the man thrust his copper sword easily through the creature. The dog dropped, still crying. Garroch knew then that he might expect no mercy.

In the gorse, Asa levelled his arrow at a point just below Barduca's jaw. He was about to release it when he saw that jaw move. He held back expecting words of peace. But what Barduca said was, 'So, you have lost your land. My dog was the victor.'

Garroch's anger was cold now. He shook his head slowly. A bone pin fell out, letting a great dark wave of hair fall over his shoulder, the hair that must never be cut. Isca gasped, shutting her eyes.

Garroch pointed to the still twitching bodies. 'Who is the victor,' he said, 'when both lie dead?'

Barduca rocked in his saddle, angry at the force of the dark chief's argument. A slave-woman ran forward towards him, bearing a long horn of mead which Barduca drank off at a draught, signing for more. The woman hastened away, she knew already how urgent that gesture was, and with what severity it could be enforced, should the need arise, or even seem to arise.

Isca was leaning forward, her eyes still closed, as though she did not wish to see Barduca's anger vented on this strange lithe dark man, who stared up so arrogantly at them, whose muscles twitched lightly, like a hunting-hound's, whose deep brown eyes were proud and afraid at once.

Barduca tore at his thumb-nail until it gave him a sudden agony. He swore quietly and then putting on a smile said, 'Where did you become so wise, little one?'

Garroch stared back at him, his long fingers now on the

bone handle of his slim flint knife.

The slave woman hurried forward and thrust the second horn of mead into her master's outstretched hand. He drank it noisily, and belched, flinging the bronze-mounted horn behind him for the woman to snatch up before she ran back among the others.

Barduca wiped his thick lips with the back of a scarred hand. His eyes were bloodshot and fiery, but still he kept his great furnace of a temper in check. When he spoke, his voice was like oil flowing slowly between two rubbing stones.

'My friend, my dear friend,' he murmured, 'you and I are masters, not slaves. We can talk freely, can we not, without such words as victor and death coming into the talk, like ill bred dogs that shove their muzzles between their master's hand and his plate?'

Garroch's face began to twitch now. He had not understood all that Barduca had said, but he had sensed the smiles on the mouths of the great men about him, and Garroch was sensitive. He resented smiles on the faces of other men unless his own words had put them there. Slowly his own face hardened and with an almost imperceptible movement, he assumed the posture from which he might best put his throwing-knife into the fat throat of Barduca.

As he did so, Barduca winked to the men on his left and they drew their own knives slowly, ready for the cast should this savage make another move. The air was tense with death. Even Asa Wolf, up there in the gorse, felt it rubbing along his shoulders, like fur, making them twitch as they did in the frost-time.

Then Garroch suddenly bared his long white teeth at the man on the shaggy horse. Barduca started with surprise that such a mild little man could make himself so frightening, and so quickly.

Isca, who had opened her eyes, shut them again quickly and decided that she was a fool to think of this little cannibal as a man.

At that moment the man in the black robes pushed his pony forward, signing to Barduca as he passed by him, with a pale hand.

His gaunt face was half-shrouded by a fold of his thick frieze garment, yet Garroch saw that he was blind. His great eyes stared before him like moonstones in the afternoon sun, opaque and pearly, shot through with dangerous amber glows that seemed to come from nowhere and to disappear as instantly. An ivory mask, set with two bloody-hued stones. Garroch did not like this man. He wished that he might have put his little knife into the neck of that fat headman without any interruption.

Barduca was lolling in the rawhide saddle now, heavy with mead. He waved his hand and the copper bracelets jangled. 'Listen to this man, little chief,' he whispered. 'He will decide everything for us. Have no fear!'

The men behind him laughed quietly. Garroch heard that laugh and felt the blood rising in his temples again.

'Why should I fear him?' he said.

The blind man said gently, 'Aye, indeed, why should you fear me? I am nothing. A leaf in the wind. A shell on the seashore. A dry stick beating against a granite wall. Indeed, why should any fear me?'

And so gentle was his tone that many were deceived and gazed at him as children do at a kindly old man who gives them honey-cakes when they expected blows from his white stick. But others, who knew more, nudged each other and set themselves to wait for what would happen.

'I do not fear you,' said Garroch, his pulses pounding and his inner heart thrusting at him to be away, to run, and run, and run, into the sunset, anywhere, as long as it was not this awful place with these strangers about him, closing him in, making him a little man, not the Old Man any more . . .

'Come here,' said the blind man, reaching out his thin hands from his horse. 'Come here, my son. Let there be no fear between us.'

Garroch found himself walking towards the black horse, as though a great wind were pushing at his back. Once he tried to break the power of this wind, but it became even stronger and thrust him on, in spite of himself. He saw that the blind man was holding out his two hands now. Amazed at his own foolishness, he let fall his dagger and his shield and held out his hands to meet them.

The blind man's hands were very strong, surprisingly strong, and cold, like a stone, or like the hands of a dead man who goes into the long House of Sleep. Garroch shuddered as he grasped them, but he could not take his own away. He even heard the chuckles of the men who clustered about Barduca, but he could no longer make himself interested in them. His whole mind was concentrated on what the blind man was saying to him.

'Come, come,' the grey voice was saying. 'Come into the long house and rest, my son, my son, my son . . .'

Garroch gave a gasp and broke away. He did not know how he did it, or why—but there was something in the old man's voice which told him that he was doomed if he did not break away, like a frightened wood-creature out of a trap.

Garroch found himself sprawling on his haunches, three paces from the horse of the blind man. And then he realised with what force he had flung himself backwards.

He heard himself screaming then, trying to impress his own importance on the creature who stared at him and could not see him, who smiled though no man had made a joke.

'I am the Old Man in this country,' his shrill voice said. 'I have the magic in my fingers and my stick. If you have power, then test it now. Step over this line which I draw on the earth before you.'

Swiftly Garroch traced a line before that black horse, making it deep, thrusting down with his flint knife, as though cutting the throat of an old man lying on the midsummer stones.

It was a good line; as good a line as any he had ever drawn. But the blind man on the black pony smiled and kneed his mount forward. They passed over Garroch's magic line, without any hindrance. The blind man was smiling.

Garroch said, 'You may smile, rider, but you know nothing yet.'

He tried to convince himself of his courage as he bent and took up a pebble from the ground beneath his feet. His eyes saw that it was a perfect instrument for the task it was to perform—a round thing, grey, streaked with white.

'Look you,' he called, in a high voice, 'here is a mouse in my palm!' He held it up for all to see. Barduca saw and turned to Isca. Her eyes were round with amazement. The tribesmen behind her muttered and whispered, 'This is a wizard. He is a Great One!'

'What do you see?', called Garroch to Barduca.

The chieftain shrugged his round shoulders and shook his head to clear his vision. Then he said, 'I see a mouse!'

The blind man half-turned in his saddle, shaking his head. His face was angry.

'You fools,' he said, 'it is a pebble. An ordinary stone that this cheat snatched up from his feet. It is grey and streaked with white. It is no mouse. That is what he made you to say. It is a pebble.'

Barduca alone among the gathering knew the truth of the blind man's words, for he had blinded him, to keep the magic in the tribe. He had seen the red sticks pierce through the damp orbs and let another liquid out. He shut his own eyes and said, 'He speaks the truth. It is a stone.'

Then Garroch fell back, for he knew that his magic was not

strong enough to win this fight.

The blind man came forward, urging his pony step by step towards him with the gentle pressure of his old knees.

'Look you,' he whispered in a soft voice, 'the thing in your hand is a flower, is it not?'

Garroch looked at the stone, his dark eyes wide with fear. It *was* a flower; a little blue flower, with petals shaped like a star. It had a gold centre. The petals were streaked with green, in three fine lines. 'Yes,' he said, nodding his head, 'it is a flower.'

A great laugh went up from the men about Barduca, for they saw now that it was a stone. Garroch did not hear them. He stared at the flower, thinking he had never seen one so beautiful.

The blind man said, 'Is it a flower you know, friend? The cornflower, perhaps?'

Garroch answered, 'Aye master, it is the cornflower.'

The blind man smiled. 'Or is it the flower of the flax?'

Garroch seemed to smile at his own stupidity. 'Aye master, it is the flower of the flax.'

Then the blind man nodded, as to himself, and turning towards Barduca whispered, 'It is well.' He slowly dismounted from his pony then and groping with his hands before him, went towards Garroch. Now he smiled like a pale wolf. He said, 'For such a pretty flower any king would give up his kingdom, my friend. Is that not so?'

Garroch frowned a little, but answered nevertheless, 'Aye, master, his kingdom for this pretty flower. May I keep the flower, master?'

The blind man reached out for Garroch's hands and said, 'Put your hands in mine and tell me that you will sell your bare chalk hills for this splendid flower, than the bargain will be settled.'

The warriors held their breath as Garroch slowly came to meet their bard, his dark hands before him, like those of a man who must walk through sleep to find his dreams.

And even as their fingers touched, the blind man gave a violent start, stiffening his back and throwing up his vacant head. A strange harsh gasp came from him and he flung his hands up towards his throat. Garroch felt that someone had flung a pannikin of icy water over him. He shook his head. His sight came back, clear as a hawk's. He saw the feathered barb of an arrow showing between the blind man's scratching fingers, too firmly fixed to be moved by any man now.

'Asa Wolf!' he yelled. 'Asa Wolf!'

In battle-fury he reached down for shield and knife, the blood coming before his eyes like a red cloth and into his nose, smelling thick and strong with death.

Isca clenched her hands suddenly and cried, 'Kill! Kill, Barduca!'

Then Barduca had kicked his horse drunkenly forward and was slashing at Garroch with the long shining sword.

Now that he had reached the climax of this meeting, what he had expected deep in his heart, Garroch lost all fear. Even as Barduca reared over him, Garroch set his legs wide and began to chant, his dark eyes staring and ecstatic, the old words coming unsought into his head from behind a thousand camp fires since his folk had moved perilously to the north from the hot lands that first bore them.

> 'Sweat on spear-haft, blood on blade!
> Come, warrior, lean on my flint;
> Set your white breast to this white stone.
> Blood will come from your wound
> And your mouth and your nostrils.
> You will speak, but none will hear you.
> Then my flint will know that you are hers.
> She will be proud, for the heat of your blood
> Will harden her—and sharpen her,
> Against deadlier foes!'

Barduca bellowed and struck downwards. Like a quick thing of the woods, Garroch moved aside, sliding his wicker shield above his head as he would have done against a stone axe. But Barduca's sword was of metal. The angry glinting blade sheared through the light shield, cutting Garroch's left arm deeply.

He fell sideways, flinging the tattered shield away from him in the pain of the wound. On his knees, he clutched at his welling arm, staring at the gash in amazement and terror. He was the Old Man and this stranger had spilled his blood on the ground. That was a crime which nothing could wipe out. It was as though his father's blood had been desecrated, the blood of all his fathers, back to the dawn times. And now, when all men sucked in their breath, expectantly, Barduca came at him again, his thick lips spattered with froth, his red eyes rolling horribly. Garroch heard the man's breath almost wheezing above him and then, forgetting his wound and remembering only that he was the Old Man whose power had been sinfully challenged, he slid under the pony's belly, coming up by Barduca's left side where it would be harder for him to strike with that cruel sword.

The pony suddenly screamed with fear, smelling blood near his nostrils and reared. Barduca clutched at his saddle-girth. And as he did so Garroch clasped his left foot, twisting it outwards with all the strength of his fury. There was a hidden cracking sound as the ankle bones gave way under this vicious attack.

Barduca flung up his hands to cover his face, crying hoarsely, wordlessly. The bronze sword clattered down at Garroch's feet. In the next instant, Barduca was sprawling on the stones, trying to rise and falling again helplessly, like a lamed bird.

The watchers stood unable to move, amazed at this sudden turn in the combat. They saw Garroch, his thin lips drawn back in pain and triumph to show his white teeth. They saw him steady himself and then slash downwards with the metal sword. Barduca's head rolled at his feet then and the spell was broken.

Now men rushed forward, closing in on the swaying Garroch, yelling abuse and hatred. Isca was among them, screaming as they screamed, when suddenly there was a whining in the air and her horse sank beneath her, grunting, a long arrow deep down to its heart. The woman pitched forward on to hands and knees, her eyes staring with terror now, afraid that the next shaft from the forest would be hers.

Garroch stared towards the trees, trying to smile, waiting for the blows that would knock aside his terrible new sword and send him to join Barduca.

But instead there was a shocked silence about him. All men were looking at the writhing horse. And then Isca scrambled up and came forward towards Garroch, holding out her shaking white hands, on which the bronze and gold glistened with heavy wickedness. Her face was very pale, but her red lips were smiling strangely.

She came closely up to Garroch so that he smelled the perfume of her body. Then she touched his wound gently, as though sadly, and so knelt before him. There was nothing else to do, now that the King was dead. Better to kneel than to die, she thought. One may always rise again, one day.

She said, 'His sword is yours. His horse is yours. His folk are yours, and I am yours.' She bowed her golden head before him then.

Garroch stared down at her in wonder. She looked up into his eyes and said, 'We have an old song which says, "When I am

King, you shall be Queen." Come warrior, lead me to the kingdom I am to share with you.'

Garroch felt himself powerless before this woman. He had not known her like before. She was different from Gwraig and Garreg-wen and the others.

'Come,' she said, rising and taking his hands. She saw the admiration in his eyes. 'Your new folk must promise themselves to you, as is the custom of this people.'

And so Garroch stood faint with weary sickness still, astraddle, above the entrance to the little gulley, while all men walked beneath his legs, accepting them as their yoke of loyalty. And when the last man had passed, the boys drove the dogs and the sheep and cattle forward to pay their homage, while Garroch swayed with exhaustion, his feet slipping on the great stones which had been set for him.

At last, like a man in a dream, his legs dangling on each side of the pony, Barduca's pale head slung on a hide thong round the creature's neck, Garroch rode before his new people, taking the lowland road towards Craig Dun. He had gained a woman and a tribe with one blow. It was too much to believe. Isca walked heavily at his side, her hand on his thigh, warm and possessive. Cradoc strode, some paces behind, smiling secretly.

'Where are your many warriors?' asked Isca. But Garroch did not answer.

Asa Wolf waited until they had gone beyond his vision. He had no wish to walk with these strangers. Then he loped swiftly from the empty wood until he came to the place where the blood had been shed. As he passed the dead sheepdog and its headless master, he spurned them savagely, spitting on them. But before Mai-Mai he stopped and kneeled, then, drawing his sharp hunting-knife, cut gently and with love down into the stiffening body. The little dog's warm heart lay in his hand.

'Oh, great Mai-Mai,' he prayed, 'give me your courage, hound of the Hill. Give me your courage, for now we shall need it. The woman is a witch!'

So Asa Wolf did what Garroch should have done, and ate the heart of Mai-Mai as the sun sank over the hills of the West. And when his shadow had melted into the twilight, he rose and ran back into the darkening forest, towards Craig Dun, singing quietly as he went, a sad little song of the Hunters, as dark as the bramble-fruit, as bitter as the crab-apple, and almost as old as the chalk hills.

# PART THREE

## Day and Night

# 25: Fire

THE OAK trees stood almost bare, their yellow leaves fallen. The cattle had been brought from their summer pasturage and lodged wherever they might find shelter from the harsh winds that blew across the high chalk hill. The flint miners worked only a short time during the day, since they could not light fires in the low galleries for fear of suffocation, and dusk came early now.

In Garroch's house the air was warm, the sheepskins thickly strewn about. All was comfort there.

Isca lay smiling, gazing towards the chimney hole, watching the blue woodsmoke curling up and then out into the deep blue-black of the sky. Garroch kneeled beside her, his hand hidden in the long rich waves of her hair. His lean dark features held the expression of a man who is at last contented, a creature come to peace after many grievous trials.

Garroch was a changed man. A thin gold circlet ennobled his high forehead. His once black hair had been cut at last, so that only two short plaits hung down from his temples, in the fashion of the Sun Men. He, even he, had dared to let them cut his hair. Though each strand had been burned immediately so that it might not come into the possession of an enemy who would make a medicine from it. About his scarred throat gleamed a heavy bronze gorget. The bracelets of copper jingled and glistened as he moved his arms. Over his white woollen tunic dropped the thick cloak of tartan cloth, such as the King of the Sun men himself had once worn. Barduca's great sword stood propped against a stool, beside the bed.

Isca reached up and clasped his hand as it stroked her hair. She put it to her mouth, caressing it. Garroch looked down on her like a wondering child that cannot believe its good fortune in possessing a toy which it had always envied and thought never to achieve.

Then she said quietly, almost as though she spoke love-words, 'The old year is dying, husband, and the ghosts are wailing about the doors, begging to be let in to smell the warmth.'

Garroch smiled, for he did not understand her. She had said this to him twice before, in the days since the first leaves had fallen from the trees. Nor was she the only one to say it. When he had walked round his town, as a King must do each day to give praises or punishments, the stranger men, the golden-haired ones, had come out of their skin-tents, for they would not build themselves houses, being cattle-followers, and had knelt before him humbly. 'The old year is dying, King,' they had said, 'The ghosts come to our doors each night, wailing to be let in.'

This was something which Garroch did not know about, and so he smiled, waiting for someone to tell him, for a King may not ask a question like a common man or that would show his ignorance, and a King must know everything. That is the law.

But when he did not answer this third time, Isca sat up and said, 'It is the time for lighting the big fire, my husband. We must burn the old year and give a welcoming light to the new one. That is the custom with my people, and we must not break it.'

Garroch felt a sudden chill run down his spine. The hairs at the base of his skull stiffened. He almost groaned, 'Is there no escaping this?' But Isca looked away and did not answer him.

At length he said, 'Tell me, Golden One, what must a King do then?'

Isca held him close in her arms and said, 'He must set the torch to the wood and make the fire burn. He must leap through the highest flames of the fire.'

Garroch drew away from her, already feeling the heat and the burning of flesh.

She went on quickly, 'Then when the fire is going out, he must run from it to the safety of his hut before the last spark dies.'

Garroch said quietly, 'And if he does not reach his house?'

Isca smiled gravely and said, 'Then the Black Sow takes him for her own, and we mourn his passing before we crown the new King.'

Garroch rose and paced the room, beating the fist of one hand into the palm of the other. 'Why must it always be death, death, death!' he said savagely. 'Why must the King always suffer so!'

Isca lay back slowly upon the bed and said, 'The King must suffer so that his people may flourish. That is why there is a King. That is why he has his pleasures, to repay him for what he must risk every year.'

Garroch stopped by the door and then sat down suddenly on the step, his head in his hands.

'I have suffered enough to save all the people of this land, Golden One,' he said. 'My body is not strong enough to suffer any more. My heart is ready, but my body will not obey my heart any longer.'

Isca said, 'The fire eats up the ghosts that howl about the houses now, frightening the children; the fire will make our bulls hot and our cows fertile; the fire will bring the sun to shine on our pastures in the coming year. A King who loves his folk must light the fire.'

Garroch ran towards her and flung himself beside her, like a little boy, afraid and wishing to be consoled. She stared at him for a while and then said softly, 'It will be easy, my brave one. The Hornman will arrange it all for us. He will not dare to hurt you, husband, for he knows how much I want you. He fears me, Garroch, and that should drive your fear away.'

Garroch rolled over, his body shuddering in revolt after its many privations. For a while he had not the command of his tongue and so could not speak to this woman who had made herself his Queen.

Isca smiled at him and ran her hand up and down his lithe body, as she liked to do. 'You are only a little lad, in spite of your big sword and all your finery,' she said.

He let her say it and did not protest, for suffering had purged him of his pride.

'If it were battle, with the blood-smell coming quick into the nose, I could do that. I could run to meet three champions and never cry with fear. But this thing, this sacrifice, is more than I can bear now. Perhaps in a little while my courage will return. Perhaps I can grow to be a worthy King of your folk, Isca. But now I am afraid.'

Isca said, 'Can you not trust the Hornman to treat you well? To send you though the chillest part of the fire? To fan the spark until you have reached your door in safety? Not to hold you down over the ashes too long?'

Garroch shook his head and suddenly rose from the bed and took up the sword. It glimmered wickedly in the light of the clay-lamp. He ran his thumb along its edge, then felt its keen point. He rested the hilt against the heavy wooden stool, setting the blade into his groin.

'Rather than the fire, I would fall upon this sword now,' he said, breathlessly, his dark eyes wide.

Isca had watched him curiously while he had the set the weapon in position; but now she almost leaped from the bed and ran towards him, snatching the sword away, her own eyes wide with anger.

'You fool,' she said. 'Would you end our life together in such a way? Would you tell the folk that you are a coward?'

Then she repented of her hard words and pulled him to her, rocking him back and forth like a little child, and weeping.

'A little thing,' she said. 'Even the greatest of men—only little things, despite their loud words.'

And when she had quietened him with her body and with the heavy honey-mead that her folk brewed, she left him sleeping and went to the house of Asa Wolf, who sat sharpening a new sword which Garroch had given him. Asa rose, out of respect for the Queen, but she smiled and waved her hand to him, telling him to be seated again.

'What I have to say to you does not need respect, Asa, my new brother,' she said. 'I am the begger, not you.'

'You are a Queen, lady,' said Asa, turning his eyes from hers, in fear of her body.

She came towards him and put her hands on his broad shoulders, looking up at him and touching him with her breasts very lightly.

'Brother Wolf,' she said, 'Garroch is still sick in his mind. He sends me to beg your help, to do something for him until he is strong enough to do it for himself again.'

Asa did not know how to read her eyes. He guessed at something other than her meaning. 'I cannot do some things for Garroch. There are some things which only he can do for himself, lady.'

Isca slapped him lightly on the chest and moved away from him, smiling, knowing well that her nearness troubled him.

'Have no fear, Asa Wolf,' she said. 'Garroch has not sent me to make you do that thing for him, yet. Perhaps it may come, my brother—but not yet.'

And when she told Asa that he must be the Sun King in Garroch's place, he bowed his head and said, 'What Garroch wills, I will, too. There is no more to be said.'

But Isca said, 'You are a real man, Asa. It is a pity that your folk are savages who worship the forest things and not the true God. You are the Sun King's colour, being red. Your offering will please the Sun King and will bring fertility to his folk and his cattle.'

Asa smiled grimly but did not answer her. Yet she understood his smile and said, 'I drink the juice of a little plant that an old witch once showed me. Believe me, Wolf, I shall be fertile enough when I find the man whose sons will come to rule a great kingdom.'

She went out then, and Asa bowed his head before her as befitted the occasion.

And when the fire was lit at last, it was Asa who wore the thin gold circlet and the tartan cloak, acting the part of the Sun King. It was Asa who leapt through the hot fire and raced away from the Black Sow to the very door of Garroch's house. And it was Asa who let himself be held down over the hot embers until the Hornman had performed his grotesque dance to the drums and the bone flutes. He did this without a groan. He did not groan until he was alone in his own house.

Garroch had lain in his dark hut, hearing the shouts and drum beats outside in the great compound, shivering in his weakness. The Hornman had told the folk that he was communing with the Sun God, that the God had sucked forth Garroch's spirit for the time being and that he had appointed Asa to perform the necessary ritual.

Garroch had heard them shout in approval at these words. He had lain shuddering until the festival was done and then, when the last man had staggered to his hut, Garroch the King had gone to Asa's house, to weep over his scarred back, to fall before him and beg his forgiveness.

Asa Wolf had grinned with some effort and had said, 'We who are of one blood should not begrudge each other a little of that blood, my brother. Do not fret, I was getting over-fat!'

Garroch held Asa's hands and kissed them again and again. 'For you, my brother,' he said, 'I would kill the world—yea, even her! Though I love her, even her!'

Asa grimaced and said, 'Do not lie to me, brother. You could never bring yourself to hurt that woman. You know it. She has bewitched you.'

Garroch punched himself between the eyes and said, 'I swear it, Asa! I swear before Earth Mother, I would kill her, for you.'

But Asa only smiled patiently and patted Garroch's hand, as though soothing an hysterical child.

# 26: Golden Moments

THERE ARE the golden moments in life, as well as the moments of ice, of flint; and they may last for some a year and a day, a millennium; and for some they may last—but a moment. Yet while they are there, they are of gold, as though the sun shone through clear water with no thing, no dross, no obstacle, to hinder its pure brightness. And though such moments may be as fleeting as the life of the May fly, yet for ever afterwards they live on in the mind, as though they had lasted a hundred years.

After the terror, the darkness of suffering, Garroch knew his golden moments. Now, in the chill brilliance of Autumn, he knew security for the first time since he had been born into a doom-driven world. His people had come to regard the golden ones, the warriors of the bright swords, as their brothers, their protectors almost. They laughed and danced together to the sound of flute and harp and echoing drum. Their flocks mingled and their young men and women married. Gold head and black head lay close together on the sheepskin pillows. And now Garroch, whose work as a Sun King was so different from his hard-held and precarious state as the Old Man, had willingly handed over his magic, his sacrificial knife to the Hornman. That was a great relief to Garroch's mind. His hands seemed clean at last. He could allow his heart to soften a little now.

Kaa Fox met him once walking at the edge of the forest and said to him, 'Brother of my brother, things go well with your village at last. You do not need the help of my Hunters any longer. Now that you have such a body of warriors, we can go back to our caverns and our glades. We can forget you, Garroch.'

But Garroch clasped the Hunter's painted hands and said, 'Brother Fox, do not go yet. Stay at the edge of the forest a little while longer, for if you go, my brother Asa Wolf will want to go with you too, and he is a dear friend to me whom I cannot lose yet awhile.'

Kaa Fox said, 'Have no fear, brother. I do not think that Asa Wolf will ever leave you while you need him and love him. He would rather lose me than lose you, I have read it in his eyes.'

Yet Garroch still held the big man's hands and said, 'Kaa Fox, listen to me; I am like a man who comes out of the long night of blackness into a valley of gold light. Now all things are glorious and sweet; yet my bones still feel the last chill of that night I have travelled through, and I am afraid that the sun will go in and the night will come again. I am a man who dreams a golden dream, but who shudders even in his joy, for fear that the dream will shatter like an outworn beaker of clay and crumble to pieces in my hands as I drink from it. Do not leave me yet, Kaa Fox, lest the dream breaks in my hands.'

And Kaa Fox said, 'You have spoken the word, Garroch. I shall not leave you until you tell me that I may go, for I am bound to you because you have taken my own brother as your blood-brother and to leave you would be to leave him.'

Garroch said, 'If I ever hurt you, may the hawk eat my entrails.'

Kaa Fox saluted Garroch and went back into the shallow glades of the wood, where his folk had built their fires for many weeks now. But before he went through the bushes he turned back to see where Garroch was.

Garroch was still standing where he had left him, smiling gently now like a young child, comforted in the night by a strong friend who can drive the whispering ghosts away.

And once Asa Wolf said to Garroch, 'My brother, in these weeks since the strangers came to Craig Dun, we have begun to do things differently. We no longer pray before the Old Woman stone outside the village; we no longer call on Earth Mother so often. The folk of the Hill no longer speak of the Long House as though it was a sacred storehouse of Chieftains. And you, who were once the Old Man, now turn up your eyes towards the Sun and not down towards the earth, when you make an oath.'

Garroch said, 'All that is true, my brother. Yet what would you have us do? These strong strangers have made me their King, and so I must follow their Gods, not the old ones I knew before. And these strangers are prosperous ones, men of cattle and horses and fine swords of copper. Are they not a fine golden folk, Asa? And have we not prospered under the Sun God since they came? Is it not fine to fly under the sun with the eagles rather than burrow down under the earth with the worms?'

Asa Wolf said, 'I do not know, Garroch. It *seems* that we have prospered since the Sun folk came — yet who knows but what She, sly Earth Mother, is waiting her time to punish us? One day we may be sorry for changing our ways.'

Garroch smiled gaily and said, 'When that day comes, let us

weep; but until that day comes, let us be merry together!'

And Asa, who in any case was of a much older religion and had only paid the merest lip-service to Earth Mother, shrugged his shoulders and told Garroch that the King's word was law and must be obeyed.

Now in the steadings, the dark folk put on the gay garments of the strangers, and the flint-miners learned to make their arrow-heads with two sharp barbs and a little tang to fit into a hollow stem. The women learned to turn their clay lumps to the shape of the strangers' beakers, and to mark them with cord-patterns and herringbone whorls.

And the strangers learned to eat barley cakes as often as they ate the flesh of cows or sheep. But both folk drank mead and barley ale more often than milk or water now, and the drums and flutes were seldom silent, nor the bright songs stilled.

And now the folk of other villages further along the sharp chalk ridge stared in wonder. pointing, as Garroch rode with Isca and Asa Wolf, proudly glistening in his metal finery and gay colours, over the sunset rise.

'Look! Look!' they cried, half-in-fear. 'The King and the Queen of the Sun! Look, my friends, *they ride on horses!*'

And in the dreams of many children under other hills, Garroch became the King of Fairyland, the Sun King, the man on the horse, the Noble One, the God himself. But to their fathers he was secretly *the upstart who ride on a horse, and carried a sword that did not belong to him.* Though none now dared show Garroch anything but the deepest reverence, even the greatest of the flint Chiefs.

One day Garroch rose with Isca and Asa above the basin that contained the Village Under the Rocks. They reined in their fierce stallions, jingling, and looked down at the steadings, their gay cloaks floating behind them on the late breezes.

Isca said, 'It is chill, my husband. Why have you brought me here?'

Garroch pointed down the hill. 'It was there that Asa took the arrows in his side,' he said. 'And there, in that great prison-house of grey stone, men tormented my body until I became less than a man. I wished to remind myself of this, for it works in my head to come here one day and wipe out this village.'

Asa urged his horse forward a pace or two and said, 'Let the past go to its own grave, Garroch. We shall gain nothing by recalling those hours. Sufficient that they have gone and left us alive.'

Isca seemed undecided. She pouted at Asa and then smiled at him. 'It would be good to see my man, Garroch, using his new sword on these savages, riding them down and making them scream. Besides, I would like a black-haired slave and I cannot choose one from the folk of Craig Dun who hold equal rights with my own folk in Garroch's kingdom.'

Asa Wolf said, 'If that is all you want, I will surely ride down there and bring back a slave for you, as long as you treat her well.'

Isca pretended to be cross and said, 'Slaves must be bought with blood, otherwise they do not realise how serious a business it all is. Besides, I want a he-slave, not a she. I know all about she-things, being one, but a he-thing would be amusing to learn about, when Garroch is away from the house.'

Garroch slapped her hard across the backside with the flat of his sword and said, 'You are a witch! You wish to anger me, but those days are over! No man and no woman either shall ever anger me again. I have learned that much. And as for having a he-slave, what do you think I am? Learn about men from me, or my brother Asa, not from some shivering wretch who will bring you no pleasure because he is afraid to hurt you.'

Isca turned in her sheepskin saddle towards Asa. 'Hear what the King says, slave,' she said. 'He commands you to give me pleasure and to hurt me!'

But Asa only smiled, a dry smile, and began to whistle. This annoyed Isca who never before had been refused so lightly by a man. She vowed secretly to get her revenge on the Hunter, the little revenge, that leaves no mark on the body, but a deep one on the spirit of a man.

Garroch had seen all this happen and was glad that his blood-brother had not accepted Isca, for in his heart he wanted her for himself alone. He had never felt like this about a woman before, and it made him very warm in his feelings to Asa that the man should act in such a considerate way to him.

'There is no woman in the whole of Craig Dun that you cannot have, married or not, my brother,' he said to Asa then. But Asa only twitched his shoulders and said, 'It would please me more to have a mare to put to my stallion, Garroch. Then I would breed a race of horses and think of nothing else.'

Garroch slapped his friend on the back and said, 'Such a stallion as that needs more than one mare, my brother. I shall give you three, and then do not hope to get him snorting into battle, for they will cool his blood and pump the courage out of him!

He was about to swing his horse round and gallop away gaily, when Isca gave a sudden cry and pointed to the side. They turned their heads to follow her pointing, and Garroch's heart began to thump wildly.

Coming over a little humped rise in the chalk hills was a war-party, just such a band as once swept down the hillside and captured the men of Craig Dun in their battle-pride.

They ran easily, in their scores, their bodies painted, the war-hide wrapped about their bellies, their hair bound up with thongs so as to be out of the way when the blows fell. As they sighted the horsemen thay gave a great shout and loped forward like wolves, their wicker shields held high, their axes poised for the strike. Garroch, white-faced now, noticed that their Chief ran well before them. This was a man he had a score to settle with. Garroch kneed his stallion forward to meet him.

Asa saw that movement and swung his horse before that of Isca, drawing his long copper sword from his hide belt and flinging his red hair from before his eyes. His knee touched that of the woman by accident and she smiled at him, secretly, but Asa was not thinking her thoughts and he allowed a sign of anger to cross his face. Isca noticed this and her own features hardened for the moment.

But Garroch knew nothing of this. And as the company of warriors came within twenty paces of him, he leaned low over his stallion's neck and, gripping his sword, prepared to charge into them.

Then something strange happened. Their Chief held up his hand as though to a pre-arranged signal and every man fell forward to his knees, his head bowed. Only the Chief still ran on until he was within a man's length from Garroch, who had reined in the horse. Then, flinging himself upright, standing as tall as he could, the dark Chief swept wide his arms, the shield in one, the flint axe in the other, and holding up his head he chanted, 'Hail, King of the Sun!'

The warriors, on their knees, chanted in unison, 'Hail, King of the Sun!'

Again the Chief called out, 'Hail, King of the Sun!' And once more the men echoed his cry with, 'Hail, King of the Sun!'

Never before had Garroch been greeted with such prepara-ation, for each syllable fell into place, each voice struck the same note. On the hilltop the effect caused his throat muscles to tighten. He sat bolt upright in his thick saddle.

Then the Chief flung himself almost under the hooves of the

black stallion, his osier shield and flint axe flying away from him. He stayed silent for a while and then at last he said humbly, 'We who were once great now offer ourselves to a greater one. We who once demanded humility from our foes now give humility to our master. Hail Garroch, King of the Sun, we salute you! We serve you! We will die for you! Lead us!'

As he came to the last phrases of his offering, the warriors joined in with their Chief, lending their deep voices to make even more solemn a declaration which, coming from him, held sufficient gravity in itself.

Garroch sat silent for a while. Suddenly he recalled how they had mauled him down there in the great hut; he felt again their hard murderous hands, their little flints set into alder stems, the hot stones they had pressed upon the tender parts of his body.

As they all gazed at him, their dark eyes wide, their haunches quivering, Garroch kicked his stallion forward until he came alongside the kneeling Chief. Then with all the savagery he was capable of he leaned over and kicked the man at the side of the head, sprawling him into the mud. Then he sat motionless, waiting to see what might be the outcome of this humiliation. The Chief lay still, as one who must obey a greater than himself. The warrior's eyes did not flicker. They stared on at Garroch as a child will stare at a rainbow, sensing that it is something beyond fear or love or envy.

And at last Garroch gestured with his right hand towards the man and said gently, 'Rise, my friend. The past is past. Now I accept you. You shall march with me, members of my family.'

Beyond the hillock, they found a great herd of cattle already waiting, tended by many herdsmen. The Chief, who now walked at Garroch's side said, 'I pay my debts, King of the Sun. These are the cows we took from you, together with many others. Is it well?'

Garroch nodded curtly. 'It is well, Chief,' he said.

And so the great party made its way towards Craig Dun.

On the way Isca, who rode behind Garroch with Asa, saw a young warrior whose stomach was heavily scarred with great raised circles, one within another, until the final small one was only broad enough to enclose his navel. She smiled at this young man, for his markings interested her, as another woman might have been interested in the markings of a calf or a linnet. She beckoned to him to walk beside her horse.

'What will your family do,' she asked, 'now that the warriors and the cattle are all gone?'

The man grinned and said, 'They must fend for themselves, Queen. They must get other sons and their cattle must get other calves.'

The spell was shattered; the young man's teeth were broken and irregular. Isca looked away from him in disgust.

At last he shrugged his broad shoulders and went back to walk with his comrade. 'Women,' he whispered, 'are as fickle as the morning breeze, my brother. I could have sworn that Queen wanted me.'

His friend said, 'If such as she wanted me, I would run a knife across my throat when she sent for me. She needs a spring stallion, not a man, my brother.'

And so Garroch brought great glory to Craig Dun once more, without meaning to; and this, too, was a golden moment.

# 27: Cradac

WHEN THE host of men and cattle were still far away from Craig Dun and dusk had fallen over the village as though a giant had clasped it in his dark hand, a lank-haired fellow with a cast in his right eye shambled inside the stockade and stared towards the fires in the compound, about which the warriors of both folk stood gossiping or boasting of their prowess with horse or arrow, sword or sling-stone.

At last his questing eyes picked out the man he looked for and pulling his drab-coloured cloak up about his neck he moved like a shadow towards his quarry.

'Cradoc,' he whispered at last. The man he sought turned with a little shock at the voice he knew so well.

'Come away from the fire glow,' said Cradoc cautiously. 'We may talk more freely near the stockade gates.'

And when they stood in the shadows there the man with the cast in his right eye said suddenly, 'Vedrix has landed and rests for a while with the Fisherfolk. They have sworn vengeance on Garroch the King.'

Cradoc said, 'That is good. What did he say when you told him the news of Barduca's end? It is serious, the death of a father.'

The man answered, 'He was mad with joy. Then his woman spoke sharply to him and he tried to look like a man worthy of a crown. He said that he would come to claim his rightful inheritance as soon as his men had rested.'

Cradoc said, 'I think it is his woman who looks for a crown rather than the little mouse, is it not?'

The man nodded with a smile of contempt.

Cradoc said, 'Very well, my friend. Serve me well and you shall profit in the end more than most folk.'

The man bowed his head and whispered, 'I obey you, King that shall be.'

Cradoc's mouth twisted into an ugly little smile in the shadows. 'Good, my friend,' he said. 'Go back to Vedrix then and tell him to wait awhile until I send for him. Tell him that Garroch is too strong for the moment and would conquer the men of Vedrix if he came yet awhile. Tell him that soon I will find a way of getting rid of the Hunters who watch over this place; then, when they have gone, and the men of Barduca have quarrelled with those of Craig Dun, Vedrix must come swiftly and lend his help.'

The rogue nodded and smiled. 'But master,' he said, 'you are perhaps too generous to this little man, Vedrix. How do you know that he will help you in return?'

Cradoc said wearily, 'That is arranged, my friend. When Vedrix has lent his men to overcome Garroch, why, then we can push him into the midden pit and choke him one dark night! It is not hard to whip the crown from a fool's head, my friend!'

The man chuckled, 'So, you will gain both his crown and his woman, eh, Cradoc?'

Cradoc wanted to hit the creature's head against the gateposts, but restrained himself for the fellow must be used a little more yet. 'No,' he said, controlling himself. 'I shall give his woman to you, my friend.'

The man slapped his thighs and grunted, 'Oh, now! She'd be too much for me to handle, Cradoc! Too stern and strong in the arm!'

He paused then and scratched his thin chin and said as an afterthought, 'Though I must say I've often wondered what it would be like to have a Queen! One with royal blood, not ordinary blood like mine.'

Cradoc sighed in boredom now, 'No different,' he said. 'No different, my friend. They are all alike, women. All bitches!'

From afar they heard the sound of horns blowing and of many

cattle lowing and bellowing. Cradoc sniffed the air like a dog.

'Go swiftly now, man,' he said, 'for I think Garroch the King returns. He brings new victories it seems. That will be all to the good when we come to share them out, eh?'

The fellow began to chuckle and almost slapped Cradoc on the shoulder in familiar merriment. But a look in the lord's eye quelled him.

'I shall obey your commands, King to be,' he said. 'I shall deliver your message, every word of it. And may we soon know greatness, you and I.'

Cradoc said, 'May we soon know greatness, my friend.' But when the man had gone into the darkness on his way back to Vedrix among the Fisherfolk, Cradoc spat against the stone wall and said grimly, 'But may it last for you only the time it takes for an axe to spill out your dog's brains, you stinking thing!'

Then Cradoc went back to the fires and ordered the warriors to be ready to welcome their King and his woman, for they were bringing more wealth and prosperity to the settlement under the great hill. All men rushed towards the gates, for now both dark men and gold had learned to like this little King with the courage of a spring lynx and the swift skill of the adder. Then the drums began to throb and the flutes to squeal.

And at length Isca lay again on her sheepskin bed, staring up at the chimney-hole as she often did. Garroch and Asa sat by the fire, shaking the knuckle bones and wagering this and that on their throws.

And Isca said, 'The head of Barduca is well-dried now, King, up there in the smoke.'

They looked up and saw the shrivelled yellow thing with the straggling grey beard that had once been a King of the Sun.

Asa said, 'We of the forests do not keep such things.'

But Garroch answered him, 'Why, in the days of my boyhood, I remember that my father, the Old Man, had them strung all round the walls of this house. And afar, when he took me visiting the other Chiefs, I have been to some steadings where they set them on the roof of every house, and on pikes round the stockades, too. We have grown too peaceful in these last years, and we have neglected the old customs.'

He said this with a wry smile, which Asa had grown to understand now. But Isca did not see his face, only heard the words, and she said, 'Such things create respect, Asa Wolf. Among your people, no one seems to respect anyone else. Not even their own Chief, your brother. And when I have passed among your folk, why, they have even lifted up my robe to see what was underneath!'

Asa said in mock reverence, 'Alas! Alas, lady! But my brother, Kaa Fox, likes them to forget that he has power of life and death over them. And as for yourself—well, I have often considered making that particular act of exploration myself.'

Isca looked at him narrowly and said, 'Why have you not, my husband's brother? Is it because you are afraid that I might not like it? I will tell you that you need not be afraid.'

Garroch's lips were pursed together tightly. He stared back at the fire with a look that was every bit as hot. Asa saw that look and he said, 'No, lady, I have since come to the conclusion that my only reason for lifting your clouts would be to smack what is kept warm under them!'

He saw the quick glimmer of joy in Garroch's eyes and so he did not bother to observe the effect of his words on the Queen. If he had looked at her face, he would have seen only an interested amusement there, for Isca was no fool.

And then Asa rose and stretched his long limbs and said. 'I go to my bed, Garroch, with your permission. I wish to hunt with my brother Kaa Fox tomorrow and he is an early riser.'

Garroch nodded and smiled at him warmly. Isca said to him, 'I hope you come upon a woman in the forests who would welcome such a hunter. I shall want to hear your story of how you ran away from her.'

Asa Wolf turned at the door and flung a ball of clay at the girl, striking her on the side. As she rubbed the place, pretending to be annoyed, he smiled and said, 'I have never run away from any beast in my life—but you, O Queen!'

Then he went slowly and with a Hunter's lithe dignity through the door into the darkness.

And when he had gone, Garroch said, 'Asa Wolf is my best friend, my love.'

And Isca said, 'I do not deny it, my husband. He is a great one, I tell you. There has never been a man whom I could not bring under the magic of my body but Asa Wolf. If he ever accepted what I offered, I think I should despise him.'

Garroch said easily, 'You will never despise him, my Queen, I think. If you had cause to, I think I should kill you first and then myself.'

Isca turned over towards him, smiling, and said, 'Why not kill Asa, my King? That would seem the thing to do in such a case.'

Garroch looked into the glowing ashes and said gently. 'Why should I kill him for you? He is worth more than we are, both together, is he not?'

And Isca nodded, still smiling. 'I think he is,' she said. 'Yes, truly I think he is. He is a great one, though he does not know it.'

# 28 : Building

IN THE hours when the bat and the owl come into their own kingdom, Isca turned to Garroch the King as they lay in their bed. In the last glow of the wood fire she saw that his dark eyes were still open and that he was awake.

'Garroch,' she said, 'I have had a dream. In my first sleeping a vision came to me and a great voice that bellowed like a rutting bull spoke the words to it.'

Garroch smiled wryly at this, for he too had had a dream. That was why she had suddenly caught him awake. His dream had frightened him into waking, for in it the worm had crept into his mouth and had made there a home for itself. He had sprung awake, his throat dry and ready to scream, his heart thumping wildly. But before he had yelled in his terror of the death sign, Isca had turned to him and had looked sharply into his eyes. That look chased his dream away and he cherished this woman more than ever for her powerful magic over the darkness.

'Yes, my Queen,' he said, 'and what was your dream?'

Isca said, 'At first all the darkness, all the world, was swirling before my eyes in a great wheel. Then in the centre of the wheel I saw the head of Barduca; not the yellow wasted bundle of rag that it is now, but as it used to be in his time of power and glory when he would look down on me in the firelight as we lay on such a bed as this.'

Garroch felt his muscles shiver at her words. 'Tell me your dream, my love.' he said.

And Isca said, 'The voice of Barduca bellowed down at me like the roaring of the wind in the winter trees.'

'Have done with Barduca!' shouted Garroch, rising up in his angry bed. 'Tell me your dream!'

But Isca spoke back at him calmly. 'The voice was the dream,' she said, 'for as the voice spoke the words, I saw their pictures as I slept.'

Garroch grunted with impatient anger. 'Then speak the words of the dream,' he said, 'Barduca's words.'

And Isca said, 'These are the words that pale mouth roared at me:

"I was once the King of the Sun.
Now my head is drying on a stake
Over the smoking fire of another King.
Let him beware—I still can speak.
I tell him that his house is no fit place
For a Sun King's head to dry in;
No place for the Sun to be remembered.
Let him beware—I shall speak again
Until he has housed me afresh
In a place that is worthy of the Sun".'

Garroch looked at the woman as she chanted. Her eyes were wide and fixed above his head. Her body lay stiff, away from him. He bowed his head in respect and listened to her words.

' "Let Garroch the Sun King build afresh!
Let Garroch build to the Sun or lose his crown.
So, in a place high on the hill
Shall he prepare a house fit for a King.
Let him dig the foundations deep,
For it must endure to the ending of the world.
Fetch greenstone from the West for all the walls,
Sun asks no common flint.
The King post of this house is finest oak
Plated with coloured ornaments.
The roof is first of osiers, whitely peeled,
And over them the hide of blackest bulls.
And there shall be, within, a pit for fire
Ringed round with glistening quartz;
And after that a dancing-floor of pine,
Where men shall see a vision after wine.
Then shall there be a gentle feasting place
Where men may set their meat on stools of stone.
Last, and in memory of me, the sleeping-stalls,

> Built close against the wall, of slate cut smooth,
> Furnished with beds of bracken, covered deep
> With skins, with fleece of whitest sheep,
> Where men shall rob the honeyed hive of sleep".'

And when Isca had said these words, her eyes closed again and she lay on her back, breathing gently. Garroch spoke to her at last in his bewilderment but she did not answer.

And in the morning when he asked her about her dream, she only smiled and shook her head. Then she repeated those words again, just as she had spoken them before, but where she had heard them she did not know, she said.

Then Garroch was sure that these words were a message that must not be disobeyed, and so, although the cold time of the year had almost come upon the village, he set about building the great house that would be a fitting home for such a one as he, the King of the Sun.

And all the time Cradoc watched, stroking his thin beard, waiting for his moment to come, sending back word to Vedrix by the shore from time to time, and already wondering how it felt to wear that thin gold circlet which he had seen so often and had always envied.

The house grew swiftly, for there were many folk to work upon it. While the dark men of Craig Dun levelled a great shelf half-way up the hill with their shoulder-blade shovels and their antler-horn picks, the golden men rode to the west dragging light sledges behind them for the famous green stone. And they were scarcely out of sight before the red men of Kaa Fox lit a fierce fire beside the trunk of the straightest oak they could find, and brought it crashing down with their hide ropes and their heavy stone axes, chopping deep into the charcoal that the fires had left, spattering each other's faces and then laughing to see their comrades so black with soot.

And the women gathered osiers by the river, many bundles of the lithe green withies, even the women who were lightly pregnant: and at night by the fires in the compound they would peel the whipping rods and weave them together, until at last they had made hurdle after white hurdle that would be lashed to each other to form a tall roof about the smooth oak kingpost soon.

And hardly had the great kingpost been sunk, deep into its foundations in the chalk, its red-haired hauliers cheering at their success as it rose on the tough thongs, when the King himself,

arroch the Dark One as he was now called, went over the hill
) the corrals and himself chose the black bulls whose hides
.ould gain honour as his roof, selecting this one, rejecting that
.e, choosing the shiniest black bulls, refusing those that had
.e slightest patch of sable, the smallest tuft of white hairs . . .

And as he chose, indicating his wish by a movement of his
.ng antler wand, the small dark killers would run forth, leap-
.g on to the back of the doomed beast, clasping its muzzle to
raw back the puzzled head, and then with the other grim hand
ragging the keen flint knife across its throat. The corrals were
.ll of bewildered cattle that day, both living and dead, for such
slaughter had never been known on the hills before.

And when Isca saw the flayed carcases she said, 'Such meat
.ould not waste, my husband. To celebrate the building of the
:eat house, let there be a feast. We shall all eat well on this bull-
.eat!'

Garroch said, 'Then we must tell them all, and they will
urry with the building, for they will know that the fly will
.ste the meat first if they do not hasten!'

And as he had said, the workers hastened, their bodies gleam-
.g with sweat to raise the great hall in time for the feast. The
.ders came back from the west, short of many horses that had
ragged out their guts with the heavy rock, the magic green
)ck; but they were content when they heard of the feast. So
.ere those who quarried the bright quartz and set it about the
.re pit. So were the patient men who felled the pines and then,
.ith their heavy axes swinging between their legs, chipped and
.hipped the awkward wood until they had made smooth
.lanks for a dancing floor, as the King had commanded.

So the house grew, and the children both black and gold in
.e village below looked up at it each day pointing and said,
'Aiee! Look, it is higher now than it was when the sun awoke!'
.nd later in the day they would point again and say, 'Aiee!
.ut look, my brothers, it is as tall as the sky!'

And the sheep were killed as the bulls had been killed--their
.eeces to make comfort, their flesh to fill the cooking-pots at
.east-time.

And the tribes from afar who had received peremptory mes-
.ages from this terrible Dark King came into the steading at last,
.ragging great slabs of flint on sledges for the walled cubicles
.f the palace, cursing Garroch with every breath but the one
.hat brought them inside his stockade—then praising him as the
.reatest of Kings, as indeed he was, for no man of authority in

the land had ever before raised such a monument to his power and to the power of the God he served.

This Garroch, son of Marrag, was the first great King of a land that would one day have many great Kings. But he was the first. Though he made no laws, he was a Great One and a Great Captain. Yet he is forgotten, and his palace has long since been only a dream—a dream that breathes past the end of the corridor of forgetfulness, to be caught as a fleeting vision only by the poet, the seer, the magician, and sometimes the warrior. Yet he built this house, on the hill, because Barduca had spoken in Isca's dream. He built it because he was now the plaything of a greater King, the Sun Himself.

And many times Garroch toyed with the notion of tearing down the Old Woman stone—which signified Earth Mother—just outside the village; but each time he wavered and then told his dark ones to leave the stone for yet another day. He did not tell them of his dreams, of Marrag shaking a warning finger at him, of Brach weeping at his feet for the stone's sake. Marrag and Brach were precious to him still, though now they were ghosts who only came to him at night in his sleep. He had loved his father and adored his daughter, and they were gone from him and were dead, he thought. Dead and locked for ever in the House of Sleep—had he not heard them as he lay there, bound with the thongs, painted with the blood-clay?

And sometimes he thought of Rua—poor Rua! He pitied her for she had loved him though he had not wanted her love. Once, with a cold shock, he had realised that she had killed her father, Kraka, for his sake. That disturbed the sleep of Garroch for many nights, for it was taboo to kill a father, or any of one's blood. Just as it was taboo to go into one's sister. That began to trouble Garroch too and he said to Isca:

'My Queen, are you certain that you are not my sister?'

Isca struck him across his backside, not too gently, and said, 'Yes, of course I am your sister. I am your grandmother as well. You can see that by my hair—it is golden, and yours is black. That is the law; the brother is always black-haired and the sister golden! No cattle are ever the same colour, out of one mother!'

Then she took his mind away from this matter, and by the morning he had forgotten what had troubled him.

And so, almost as by a miracle, it was the time for the feast, the feast in Garroch's great hall, set above the village, on the side of the hill.

Asa Wolf had watched all, and when the place was ready, he

said to Garroch, 'My brother, you may make many mistakes as the years walk on, but the greatest mistake now could be not to ask my brother Kaa Fox and his folk to your feast. They love you and have helped you; do not forget them in favour of the black and the gold ones.'

Garroch said, 'My brother, may this hand rot from me if I ever forget their goodness to me. Without them I would not be a King now. They *shall* come, the greatest of them, and sit in the house with the greatest of the others. I will ask Kaa Fox, our brother, to bring fifty of his men. Is that well?'

And Asa Wolf bent and kissed the hem of Garroch's tunic.

'Yes, brother mine,' he said, 'it is well. That is the fulfilment of my dream.'

And when he had gone, Isca said to Garroch, 'My husband, my little black husband, I think I love you as much as I have ever known how to love anything, including myself! I love you so much that I hardly notice the other men in this steading— hardly, my husband, for I am not yet an old woman! Yes, I love you, Garroch, the King, and I would let them cut from me any part they wished if it would save you in your distress. But make no error, my love, no error at all, this Asa loves you more deeply than I ever could, though I let them rip out my breathing heart. You must never betray this man, Garroch, or the hill above us would crumble to dust and the world fall from under our feet.'

And Garroch placed his arm about her strong waist and drew her to him. He said, 'My Queen, I hear all that you have said, and for my part I would do as much for you. The women I once knew are no longer living, as far as these eyes may tell me. And I also know what you say of the hill and the world. And I say to you now, here on the great hill with our palace below us for witness, that should I ever betray Asa Wolf, my brother in blood, may the Sun Himself strike me down, and may Earth Mother come up for vengeance and tear from me my claim to manhood with her teeth!'

A curlew swung low over the twilit hill, almost screaming in their ears. Isca shuddered and pulled her robe about her.

'Let us go down to the fires, husband,' she said. 'We are two fools to speak such words up here, at such a time.'

Then the two frightened ones went down towards the glowing fires, trying not to run lest each should accuse the other of cowardice, and laughing secretly at the same time, when they glimpsed each other's eyes in the light of the rising moon.

For that is the way the creatures are—they know the game,
they know the delusion, both in themselves and also in the
others. Yet they also know the fear, and that comes from the
deep truth that they both share, the truth that they would hide.
And though they jest, the fear is still there; and it is the fear that
is with them when they die, not the jesting, in that last lonely
moment.

# 29: Feasting

IT HAD been the greatest feast the dark folk had ever
known. Never before in Craig Dun had such quantities of food
been eaten at one time—beef and mutton and pig, venison
brought up the hill by the Hunters, barley bread and millet
porridge, great flat cheeses of sheep's milk and goat milk, and
all washed down with barley beer and sweet honey mead drunk
from bulls' horns and clay beakers, decorated with cord-
patterns wound round and round about the swelling sides.

Family after family of the folk had gone up to the slate
tables to eat their fill and had then joined the others about the
round fire hearth, or had retired to lie in the sheltered cubicles
round the greenstone walls with the women of their choosing,
gold or black.

Now the air was thick with wood-smoke and the fumes of
mead, the talk was wilder, the laughter less constrained. And
the golden haired ones laughed the loudest, for they were a
great-voiced people; the dark ones of Craig Dun talked much,
and swiftly, gesturing at every sentence to make clearer their
points, the bone bracelets clicking on their narrow painted
wrists. The grave Hunters of Kaa Fox sat together, in one group,
drinking horn for horn with their chieftain, neither more nor
less, and talking only when something needed to be said, the
high heron's feathers nodding in their hair as they shook their
heads.

Barduca's shrivelled face gazed emptily down on them all,
his dry white lips curled in a sneer.

There was much to talk about that evening. There had been
both food and singing—a slave woman had played on the small

harp with its five strings, made like a beautiful little bow, while her man, a blind one captured at the same time, sang a plaintive song about their country. The song told how the sun always shone there and the trees stayed green; there was no frost, no snow, and the fields were always heavy with barley whatever the season. In the forests, the song said, the deer wandered, fat with the green grass, waiting for the hunter's arrow; the cows upon the hill gave milk so rich that no man could drink more than a cup of it at a meal. The song ended by asking where this country was, and then replied, saying that it had sworn never to tell, or all men would want to live there.

The slave women, playing the harp, smiled bitterly as she strummed her fingers across the strings to stress her man's words. She remembered that country only too well; the old Chief there took every woman as soon as she had ceased to be a child, and sometimes before that; the grass was thin there and the cattle stumbled from tussock to tussock like moving skeletons, wrapped in lousy hides; few men had ever tasted milk there, and the crops were never enough to keep the families through the snow time, so that many died every year and the babies born in winter were put out upon the hill so as to save the milk of the women for the older ones.

But the folk in the great house of Garroch did not know this, and many of them called out, half in jest, half-seriously, asking again where this wonderful country was. The blind singer shook his head, smiling; but the slave woman whispered grimly to the nearest of them that if they made it worth her while, she could tell them with pleasure, provided they took an oath to go there and not come back.

Then a fat-bellied warrior, with a great hide belt and golden plaits that reached down to his broad chest, had swayed to his feet and had sung on the spur of the moment, beating out the rhythm of his words with a stick on the bottom of a cooking pot. There was no sadness about this ditty, which told how a man staggered home drunk from a feast one night, to find that his wife had already gone to bed. He lay beside her, complimenting her on her beauty of form, on the sweetness of her smell, and so on. At last, becoming suspicious that another man had been with her in his absence, he asked her where she had got her thick new cloak. But she remained silent. This angered the drunken warrior so much that he struck the figure beside him a great blow with an ash staff, whereupon it turned the bed over with a great kick, running from the room, bellowing, 'Moo!'

As the singer came to the last line of his song, he struck the pot such a resounding clout that it shattered in his hands, drenching all around him with dirty water.

Then, when the laughter had died down again, Garroch the King, feeling his new power, had called across the great hall to the Hornman, asking him to show his skill for the pleasure of the guests. The Hornman had lolled, perched high on skins, the whole of the feast, his face greasy with meat, his eyes bloodshot in the thick smoke. He had drunk more than any other man, which was saying a great deal, for many of them, the golden haired ones, were immense drinkers of mead and seemed almost immune to its effects, having known nothing else since childhood.

The Hornman heard Garroch and at first shook his head, the mead-jar already at his lips again. But Garroch was in no mood for refusal that night, and once more he asked the Hornman to rise and perform for the pleasure of his guests. Those who knew the Hornman well saw the anger in his red eyes, but this was no affair of theirs, it lay between the King and the Priest, they would not interfere.

Garroch was about to make his command for the third and fateful time when the Hornman staggered unsteadily to his feet, belching and wagging his grotesque head from side to side clumsily. Those who did not know him, such men as the Hunters, began to smile at his clumsy antics. Was this the famous and fearful creature they had heard of? They asked each other. Why, he was nothing more than a buffoon, an idiot fit only to sweep out the stalls of cattle and horses.

'I hear, O King of the Sun,' said the Hornman in his high cracked voice. 'I hear and obey!'

Then, with a sudden violence, he flung his mead jar straight up above his head, so that it disappeared in the smoke that billowed about the pointed roof. He stood still, looking up after it. there was silence in the hall, for the jar did not come down again.

'Will that do for your guests, O King of the Sun?' he asked, his piping voice taking on the faintest edge of insolence.

Garroch heard that note in his voice and flushed, for he too had been drinking heavily and his anger always lay close to the surface at such times.

'Where is the magic in that, Hornman?' he asked, sneering. 'It would be a poor man who could not throw a mead jar out by the chimney hole, which is wide enough for a herd of cows to go through!'

The Hornman smiled a strange little smile and bowed low to the King, in mock homage. The folk in the hall fell silent with fear.

'I stand ashamed, O Great One,' he said. 'I must do better than that, I can see, if I am to escape the keen sight of such an eagle.'

Then he sang a curious little melody of three notes, that no man had heard before and no man remembered afterwards, though it haunted their dreams for ever. And suddenly the mead jar fell down out of the smoke, into Garroch's lap, splashing his feast robes with the sticky fluid.

He stared angrily at the Hornman, but the creature's head had been bowed all the while he sang. He had not thrown it.

Garroch could see that he must take this in good part, for this trick had astounded the folk, who now gazed at the Hornman in fearful respect again, especially the golden ones who had known Barduca.

Then the Priest raised his painted head and smiled into Garroch's eyes across the room. 'was that well done, O King?' he asked.

Garroch made himself smile. 'Yes, that was well done, Hornman,' he said. 'That asks a reward! Fill up his jar again, for, as you see, he gave the last of his mead to me!'

The folk in the hall began to laugh with good humour again.

A slave woman held out another mead-cup to the Hornman, but his eyes were still on the King and his hands were making little movements, going round and round, from the King towards himself.

Then suddenly there was a great gasp in the hall, for the folk saw Garroch clap his hands to his forehead, and at the same time, they saw the glint of gold through the firelight. And then the bright crown was in the Hornman's hands, and he was looking down at it as though he had never seen it before, but smiling his strange thin smile, a wicked smile.

One warrior, worse for drink nudged his comrade and said, 'Garroch must play a sharp game when he jests with this one. He is showing the King how easy it would be to take his power from him. One had better beware of the Hornman, however great one is.'

Asa Wolf who sat beside his brother, Kaa Fox, said quietly, 'Before long I shall have to take that one's head, I am thinking. His magic is too strong for Garroch. He is a danger to us here.'

Kaa Fox inclined his head and whispered out of the side of his mouth, 'Lead him into the forest one day, on some quest or other, and I will mistake the horns he wears for those of a red deer and put three arrows into him, by mistake, my brother!'

Suddenly the crown had appeared back on Garroch's head, just as it had been before, and the Hornman was smiling across the room at the King, and bowing his knee before him in mocking reverence.

And then, as though to drive away all anger, and to turn men's minds from such things, Isca appeared through the far door, out of the smoke, covered only by a thin cloak of brightly-squared linen. She made her way to the dancing floor that ringed the fire. The cloak slipped from her body and she stood clothed now only in the gold and copper ornaments of her throat and arms. She smiled at Garroch, bowing her head, then turned slowly round, bowing to them all, for every man to see her. And when she had done this, a tiny smile playing about her face, her heavy eyelashes drooping on to her cheeks, she gave a sign to the drummers who sat cross-legged about the fire and when their rhythms beat so insistently in the head that men began to twitch their limbs for relief, she started her dance, first sidling round the dancing floor, gesturing to the man who sat nearest, and at last working herself and the drummers into such a fury of movement that the feasters were thrown into such a state of ecstacy as they had never felt before.

Men punched each other and said, 'This is such magic as would bring down both King and Hornman, my friend! This is the first of magic!'

At last Isca reached the climax of her ritual dance, and seemed to move, her eyes wide and staring, through a violent dream of orgasm, the breath coming harshly from her working throat, her limbs jerking in spasms, in time to the hypnotic drums. And when it seemed that the watchers could stand no more of this, she fell to the pine dancing floor, her body shining with sweat, her muscles twitching beyond her control.

Garroch gave a sharp cry and ran forward, flinging her cloak over her. Then he turned to the slaves and said harshly, 'Carry the Queen to her bed, and do not wake her from her sleep. She has feasted enough tonight.'

Then, raising his hands above his head, he said, 'My friends, the dawn will soon be here. We have warmed this new house together to the glory of the Sun, and we have eaten our fill. Go now to your places of rest, the feast is over. There is no more to say.'

His voice was harsh and men who were still in the dance that

Isca had performed for them looked at each other in anger at the King's tones.

Asa took Garroch by the arm and said quietly. 'Do not be angry with the woman, Garroch. She danced for *you* tonight, and not for *us*.'

The King stared at him, not understanding. Asa Wolf said, 'There are those among the feasters who would have followed wherever the Hornman led tonight, but Isca the Queen flung the dream of her body before their eyes and blinded them to all other magic. Have no fear, my brother, she danced for your crown tonight and won it back for you without your knowing. Little fool, Garroch! Oh, little fool!'

Then Asa went out smiling with his brother, Kaa Fox, and the Hunters who had been guests at the great feast, to walk with them part of the way towards the forest for he had not spoken to his brother in private for many days, they had been so busy at their separate tasks.

And so they were deep in their words to each other, in the last of the night's blackness, when the Hunter who bore the torch beside them stopped and pointed, his hand shaking in excitement.

The two brothers saw that in the shadow of the trees stood many men, their faces covered by their cloaks. The torchlight flickered on their drawn swords and their polished axes. There was no doubt about their errand.

Then, like an animal, Kaa Fox turned on his brother Asa and said bitterly, 'We have no weapons! We came to your King's feast without our weapons, according to the ancient law!

But Asa only stared at the waiting men, bewildered. He could not speak for there were no words to say.

But Kaa Fox said bitterly, 'You traitor swine, my brother! You have led us to this place so that your King's hounds can tear us to pieces! No wonder you stand silent, you dog!'

Asa turned to face him, to tell him that Garroch knew nothing of this, but Kaa Fox struck him heavily with his clenched fist on the side of the head, knocking him down.

'I would to the Tree God that my hand had held an axe when I struck you, you King's dog!' he said. Then raising his voice to the clustered Hunters, he called, 'Each man for himself, my brothers. I go to raise the folk, if the Gods will let me pass through!'

As the cloaked warriors rushed forward to their work, Kaa Fox slipped into the darkness past them. The swords and axes fell, without mercy, on the heads of the mead-bemused Hunters. But Asa Wolf had rolled sideways from the skirmish and no blow fell on him. He heard his brother's feet thudding away from him and, running bent double, he followed him, no longer caring what happened behind him in the fight.

And when he was gone some distance, he called out, 'Stop, my brother! Stop! This is no work of the King's, I tell you. He loves you as dearly as he does me, I swear! Stop, my brother!'

But all he heard was Kaa's voice howling, 'Traitors! You traitors! The folk shall wipe out Craig Dun for this! They shall burn it down and leave it as though it had never been!'

And still his feet thudded on into the dusk.

Under the trees torches were now lit and the killers went from body to body, looking for the two they wanted, rolling over the still warm corpses roughly with their feet.

At length, calling to him a hangdog fellow with a cast in one eye, Cradoc said, 'We have missed the Fox and the Wolf in the darkness, but they cannot be far away. We will seek them before the dawn. Go you now, faster than you have ever run before, and tell Vedrix that the hour has come at last. Tell him to be here before the Hunters get wind of the affair if he wishes to have his own vengeance. Tell him to bring the best of his warriors, and if he comes soon, before those of Craig Dun are fully awake again, tell him that he will do well. Go, my friend, our reward is not far to seek now!'

Then he called his murderers to him and they set off in the direction from which they had heard Kaa Fox calling in his anguish.

# 30: Morning

THE TWO brothers raced, black shadows through the night, across the foot of the hill. Now Asa Wolf could hear Kaa Fox breathing heavily and groaning in his breathing, as though the burden he bore with him was greater than the mere weight of his body.

'Stop! My brother!' called Asa Wolf. 'Do not bring doom down on this village!'

Once again Kaa Fox called back through the darkness, 'This

place shall be wiped from the hill, for it is a nest of poisonous adders! It shall not kill any more good men!'

'My brother, O my brother,' sobbed Asa Wolf, 'if you will not stop, I must kill you, for I have taken the oath to serve Garroch the King. Do not put such a weight on my shoulders, my brother! We are out of one mother, my heart; do not cause me to break the ancient law!'

But Kaa Fox did not answer.

And then, as he ran over the harsh stones, Asa Wolf gave a great cry, for a sudden shaft of dawning had struck across the lonely place, lighting it up for an instant.

'Stop, stop, Kaa Fox!' he screamed. 'You are running to your death!'

But Kaa Fox swept onwards in his headlong course and did not see the great shaft of the flint mine until his feet were on its very edge. In the growing light of the dawn, his heavy body plunged forwards and down, striking the steep walls of the pit, from one side to the other, until he vanished into the darkness, where the dawn had not yet the power to light.

Asa, his brother, stood upon the brink of the place, looking downwards and weeping.

'Kaa, my brother,' he called, 'Kaa, my brother, is breath still in your body?'

About him the morning mists swirled, casting a pearly light over the foot of the dawn-pale hill. There came no voice from the pit, only a myriad tiny whisperings such as haunt empty places, the voices of all the ghosts that have ever walked there since the start of time.

Asa Wolf cried again, 'My brother, O my brother, I have killed you; as surely as though I smashed your dear head with my axe, I have killed you!'

Then looking up towards the sunlit hilltop, above the whorls of mist, Asa jumped, outwards and down, towards the purple dusk that held Kaa Fox.

Later, when the morning had truly come and the world was bright again, Cradoc and his killers looked down into the mine shaft and saw Asa Wolf lying beside his brother, his arm thrown over him, as though in a last act of protection, their heads close together, as though they held no secrets from each other now.

Cradoc smiled and said, 'There is no more for us to do, my comrades. Let us go back to our tents now and wait either for Vedrix to arrive or for the Hunter folk to come for their vengeance. We side with whoever gets here first! And either way, Garroch will tumble from his King's chair!'

Then, as they went their ways, Cradoc called lightly after them, 'Speak no word of this affair to any man, lest it gets to Garroch before the time is ready. I would wish it to strike him between the eyes like a hammer, and for it to do that, it must come as a surprise!'

Yet the killers were hardly back in their skin tents when a frightened shepherd had stumbled into Garroch's great house to stammer to the King of what he had seen lying under the trees. And hardly had he finished when a flint miner followed him, to tell the King who lay at the bottom of the shaft.

For a while, after he had heard these words, Garroch the King sat silent, his face as blank as the stone table before him. The shepherd and the flint man crept out of that place, their heads bowed in fear.

And when they were some distance from the great house, they heard his voice rising like the wind, in mourning and in fury; it was the voice of one who cannot find the words to give vent to the anguish of the heart, so that this pain spills over into mad sound, such as the trees make, and the waters make, and the stones make when they crumble and topple down the hill-side.

And Isca gazed at her husband in fear as he turned on her, his dark face writhing with loss and rage.

'You bitch,' he whispered hoarsely, 'you dung-spawn bitch!'

He dragged her naked from the warm bed and flung her upon the dancing floor.

'So this is why you would have me invite Kaa Fox and his warriors to the feast! Which assassins did you employ, you slave's thing, eh?'

Isca stared up at him, seeing the madness in his eyes, unable to answer him yet. Nor could she speak, even when he took up the greenstone axe and came towards her. It was that strange blank look on her face which halted him, even as he raised the axe above her golden head.

His voice was quieter now. 'So you killed my brother because you envied his love for me,' he said. 'You killed Asa Wolf because he would not take the paltry thing you offered him again and again! And you killed his people so that dishonour should fall on me and drag me down and your own folk prosper!'

He turned away from her and beat his fists upon his breast. 'Oh, I have been a blind man,' he groaned now. 'I have been a child in your hands. I have let you use me, use me, use me!'

He gave a great shout then, and flinging his axe from him, he took the woman by her hair and dragged her to the doorway, pointing towards the clustered roofs and tents.

'Look down there!' he yelled. 'There is the place you have ruined! So you shall pay your penalty down there, where all men may see your punishment!'

Many times Isca tried to tell Garroch of her grief at Asa's death, of her love for them both, of her pride in being Garroch's woman, of her innocence. But the madness on him shrouded his hearing, his understanding now, and he could only lash her onwards with the great bullhide whip, until she fell in the compound weeping and begging for mercy, even she, begging for mercy.

So she lay, the crowding folk about her, as the King wielded the heavy thong again and again, dragging it back, bloodsodden to raise it high above his head once more.

Cradoc watching from the door of his tent smiled to his henchman and said, 'Unless something stops the King soon, he will not leave enough of that woman for a mouse to use!'

But now Garroch's anger had exhausted him and he swayed above the woman, the tears coursing down his face, his chest rising and falling with the great effort he had made. And Isca lay, her head in her hands, no longer the proud, arrogant creature who had danced before them all the night before. Now even the hair of her head was red, her bracelets were red, red was her colour. She coughed rather than breathed.

And as the folk of Craig Dun stared at the two great ones in horror the bronze horns of Vedrix screamed outside the gates, and then the dark folk ran back before the coming of the great stallions of the prince.

So Vedrix came to Craig Dun at last, sitting proudly on his high sheepskin saddle, his copper throat ring and the gold brooches at his shoulders glinting in the morning sunlight. A gust of wind swept across the village, lifting his long coloured cloak about him, making him seem for an instant almost as great a man as his dead father, the King Barduca. And close beside him rode Gwenna, dressed in a sky-blue linen gown, a snow-white bearskin over her shoulders, her baby asleep at her breast. Her face was that of a great Queen.

And behind them, the warriors, the hungry dogs who had long waited, slavering, for a kingdom to rule, a bone to gnaw in their jaws.

# 31: Child

NOW GARROCH woke from his awful dream and looked about him like a man who has come alive from the grave to see the bright world again. He stared at Vedrix who towered above him on the white stallion, his thin lips tight, his fair head thrown back with all the dignity at his command.

'Who is this man?' said Garroch, turning round to the folk who gazed at the strangers. 'Ask him his business, you!'

He spoke towards a group of golden warriors, who stood waiting, their swords already unsheathed and in their hands. They stared back at Garroch, their eyes narrow, their lips tightly pressed together. But they did not move.

Then the Hornman broke through the crowds and ran across the compound towards Vedrix, flinging himself with a scurry of tattered hides before the white stallion and raising his clay-daubed hands.

'The People of the Hill praise you, O Vedrix, King of the Sun! They welcome their new King, O Vedrix! Hail, Hail, O King!'

The Priest's thin voice soared above the massed folk like a questing hawk in search of the easiest prey.

Vedrix looked down on him, unmoved, a tiny smile flickering about his thin lips. Gwenna turned her head from the creature and snorted as though his smell was too rank for her nostrils.

Then Garroch gave a roar, seeing that he was encircled by his enemies, his betrayers. With a sudden violent movement, he swung the great rawhide whip about his head and brought it down on the neck of the white stallion. The creature screamed with the sharp agony and reared, shooting forth its forelegs in its whinnying fury. The Hornman fell before it, his head crushed as though by the biggest axe that the Gods had ever quarried. His red blood splashed the stallion's white chest, and then his tattered body slipped sideways and tumbled at Garroch's feet.

Now all was movement, all confusion.

Garroch howled, 'To me, the dark ones! We are betrayed!'

But the little men of Craig Dun, the dark-eyed ones, the users of flint, had seen enough. Now they knew at last that their day was over, that the great golden ones must inherit the earth! And where they could, on every side, they slipped away, through

he gates, over the stockade, under the earth tunnels, to find
what shelter they could away from these laughing conquerors
to whom the Sun God had given his precious metals.

And those few who remained, hacking about them with their
short flint knives, their clumsy axes, in their attempt to get to
their Old Man, Garroch, he who had for too long neglected
them and Earth Mother—they soon fell, before they had gone
many paces across the red earth of the compound. Short flint
was weak against the keen edge of copper.

And so, even before the morning sun had unchilled the air
about the village, Vedrix had conquered Garroch and his few,
had come into the kingdom that his father Barduca had set out
to gain—for himself.

And still Garroch stood, wielding his rawhide whip, his
clothes ripped from his body, his legs astraddle over Isca, the
only thing he had left, the woman he loved, and hated at the
same time.

And again and again the horsemen came at him, spattering
him with foam, the terrible hooves seeming to hang before his
dust-caked face. And again and again Garroch the King swung
his sharp whip, cutting horse and rider, tearing the flesh of arm
and of muzzle, blinding all with blood who came within his
spattering stroke.

And at length, Cradoc came close to Vedrix and said, 'Order
an archer to pick him off, man!'

But Vedrix looked down at the man who had gained him a
kingdom, with hatred. He did not like the contempt in Cradoc's
voice. And he said, 'If you would earn my deathless love,
Cradoc, the King-tumbler, go in now and drag Garroch down;
then there shall be no honour withheld from you!'

And Cradoc turned, sneering, to run upon Garroch, a
copper-headed javelin in his hands. As he went forward he
shouted, 'What I gain, I hold, O Puppy of a greater Hound!'

And Vedrix heard that taunt, though Cradoc's back was
turned and the noise of battle was thick in his ears, for he had,
since his childhood, been aware of insults, even those passed on
the morning breezes. And he put the white stallion at Cradoc's
back. The savage creature bore him down, even as Garroch
struck at the javelin. Cradoc fell with a scream, his ribs stove in,
and in falling he dragged the terrible whip from Garroch's
hands.

Gwenna, who sat some paces away from the thickest of this
battle, her baby clutched to her body, smiled bitterly and said,

'Well played, Vedrix, my husband! So you may take the two birds with one sling-shot! I must watch you, my little fox!'

Now Garroch stood unarmed and sobbing for lack of breath, his upper body naked, the scars of old wounds showing livid against his brown skin. The bone pins had fallen from his hair in his fighting; he flung back the heavy waves of hair and swung round, stepping carefully over Isca. His eyes searched for a friend among the crowds that pressed about him, but all his friends were gone. They had escaped from this place of death, or were dead.

Then Vedrix taunted him in a high voice. 'Little headman, they tell me you have called yourself the Sun King? Is that so, my small one?'

The golden ones in the compound heard this taunt and laughed, not so much that it belittled Garroch, as that the timid Vedrix should have dared to make it, he who had never challenged a man in his life, and who at the last had challenged the fiercest fighter most of them had known.

Garroch paused for a moment, beaten and weary, his heart torn inside him, his world crumbling about him. He paused and sniffed the air, his eyes half-closed. Then slowly he said, 'I smell a dead dog somewhere! A little dead dog, a dead puppy, drowned when his father made water in the dark!'

Now the laughter turned against Vedrix, and even Gwenna smiled, for she was a King's daughter and knew a man when she saw one.

'By the God,' she said, 'but this one should have been born with golden hair!'

Vedrix heard those words and turned pale. Then he lashed his stallion forwards, upon the defenceless man. Garroch went down, trying to save Isca even as he fell.

Vedrix would have ridden back over them to make sure; but six of the hardest warriors of his father's tribes ran forward and took his horse by the mane, dragging it away, punching its muzzle, and even shaking their fists in the white face of Vedrix.

'You little bastard,' they said. 'At least he is a man!'

Vedrix tried to remember what they looked like, so that later he might make them pay for their words, but suddenly the game was taken out of his hands, for Isca raised her bloody head, half-conscious, to stare about her now.

And Gwenna almost let fall her baby. She rode forward and gazed down at the whipped and bloody princess.

'My *sister*,' she said, 'that bitch, my *sister*. So, she has come to this! They told me Barduca had taken her, but they did not say that this little black fighting cock had rejoiced in Barduca's leavings!'

Now Vedrix gazed at this furious woman, afraid. And he was not the only one in Craig Dun that day to be afraid. Even the most scarred of the war-men were afraid.

And Isca, the darling of Barduca, the wife of Garroch, once the Sun King, looked up slowly and smoothed the wet and matted hair from before her blue eyes. She seemed to take stock for a moment, and then, in a still cold voice, she asked, so that all the folk heard her, 'Tell this new lord of yours, my sister, whose is your baby, the golden child at your breast!'

Isca lay staring up at Gwenna now, her ravaged face smiling wickedly. Vedrix turned and looked at his wife, Gwenna, the Queen who was to rule with him over Craig Dun.

Gwenna began to kick her horse forward, anxious to put an end to this questioning, but Vedrix suddenly became a man and took the mane of her stallion, kicking his own strong beast backwards so as to drag hers with it.

'Whose is the child?' he shouted.

The folk in the compound took up that cry, 'Yes, whose is the child?'

And Isca said sweetly, the blood on her lips, 'It is the child of Barduca, my friends. Look at its nose; look at its lips; look at the tiny birthmark on its shoulder, the right shoulder, for that is where Barduca had it. It is a sun, my friends!'

Then Vedrix gave a great cry and let go the stallion of Gwenna. In her anger she rode forward and struck Isca across the face with her riding whip. Isca still gazed up at her, smiling, a new weal across what once had been a lovely face.

Then Gwenna rode sobbing into the house that had been prepared for the new King and his queen. She clutched her baby closely to her.

Vedrix stared after her a moment and then in a dead voice he said to the many folk who clustered about him now, 'My people, you hear what has been said. That is the law, the ancient law, you have a king among you—though as yet he is a little King—for he was got on a true Queen, whereas I am but the son of a herdsman's daughter.'

Those who stood nearest him saw the tears in his eyes as he spoke. They were sorry for Vedrix, though they set the little child above him now.

And Vedrix said at length, 'What is done, must rest. There is no other way, my friends. Truth is truth and no man can knock down the stone of truth.'

The folk bowed their heads before his words. He had become a new man before their eyes and for the moment held a strange cold power that they had never known before.

Then Vedrix said, 'You have a little King, my people. And I am that little King's mouthpiece, until he shall use his own mouth to rule you. Listen to me; this occasion calls for an offering!'

'An offering! An offering!' shouted the People of the Sun.

Vedrix looked down from his stallion into the bloodshot eyes of Isca, whose lips curled up at him in contempt. He nodded to her carelessly, as one who had known her well, had suffered from her taunts and wished for his revenge, cost him what it might.

'My friends,' he said, 'I speak for the safety of your little King. Take this woman for an offering. take her and her black-haired lover, another little King, in his way! A stone King, a sparrow who dreamed he was an eagle, the King of the Sun!'

Now, certain of the warriors came forward and dragged the two to their feet.

'What shall we do with them, master?' they cried, drunk with their easy victory, anxious to please the mouthpiece of the King.

And Vedrix said, 'These folk have a stone, a crude thing, away from the steading. It has belly and breasts like a woman. Drag them to that stone and hoist them there; he on the one side, she on the other. Bind them with hide thongs and let them wait the little King's pleasure. Perhaps he may be long in speaking his punishment, for he is still at the breast—but that is well; let them await his first words. I speak for him. The word is spoken.'

Then he kicked the stallion forward towards the hut to which Gwenna had gone. The warriors bent and bound the thongs about Isca and Garroch. They bound them belly to belly, part to bloody part, laughing as they pulled tight the bonds.

And at last, when the golden ones had laughed their fill, they hitched them to a team of oxen, and whipped the beasts through the stockade gates towards the Old Woman stone.

It was a painful progress, over the flinty ground, and both bare-backed. Yet Isca bore it without a groan. Garroch was still in the red sleep of loss, dreaming of Asa Wolf and Marrag and his little daughter Brach, who had seemed to walk this black earth so many centuries ago. Garroch the King did groan and the folk laughed to hear it.

'She is the braver one,' they said, as they followed the team. But Isca spat at them, through her torn lips.

'There is not one of you who dared say that to him when his eyes were in his head,' she said. But Garroch never heard her words. For him, she was still his enemy, the killer of his dearest friend.

# 32: Night

SO IN the middle morning the folk of the Sun hoisted the two up on to the leaning stone, The Old Woman, with strong thongs of bull's hide. Isca they laid, leaning back, on the flatter face of the stone; Garroch hung, his arms dragged back in the motion of flying, as though he was about to plunge forward to the ground. His eyes were still closed and his thick hair hung down about his face. He looked like one in a deep sleep from which there was no waking, beyond pain now, a dead bird hung up to scare the other crows away.

For a while some of the golden-haired ones squatted or lolled about the stone, watching the two, commenting on the woman's body, even scratching insulting symbols on the base of the monolith with lumps of chalk. Then when the sun grew in power and stood overhead, they moved away, wafting the flies from their faces, towards the shelter of their tents. The children stayed a little longer playing about the stone, and hardly bothering now to stare up at the man and woman who hung silently there; then the children ran back to the village also, hungry or thirsty, or seeking fresh amusements.

Isca lay silent for a while, and then the flies that walked over her wounds became unbearable. She twitched her shoulders and hissed at them. They left her for a little while and then returned. And when she thought she could stand the constant irritation no longer and must surely go mad, she ceased to feel them. It was as though her body had exhausted its power to record the movement of the tiny feet and had gone into a deep sleep. But her mind stayed awake.

At length she dared to say, 'Garroch, my husband, I tell you for the last time that I loved Asa Wolf and had no part in killing him. I tell you that I valued the friendship of the Hunters and did not harm them. Do you not believe me at last, my beloved?'

Garroch's head swayed now and the flies that clustered about his eyelids rose in a little swarm and hovered round him, suddenly afraid. He said, 'You bitch!' Then he was silent again and the flies came back to him, satisfied that he was harmless.

Isca said slowly, 'Then if you will not see the truth, you will not. It is late in the day for argument.'

She rested then, for talking exhausted her and the pain of the thong that bound her below the breasts was coming back, worse than ever. All her weight seemed supported on that strip of hide.

Garroch's weight hung on his arms, forcing the shoulder-blades downwards, so that he found it hard to breathe now, and kept making spasmodic jerks upwards, trying to lever himself on his feet that were lashed tightly to the stone, so as to gain enough respite to let the air come into his cramped lungs for a little space.

Now Isca's tongue became bitter, against her will, for she had already forgiven Garroch the whip. She did not know why she spoke, for she loved Garroch, as much as she could love any man.

'They were right,' she said, 'a little man, after all; a sparrow dreaming he was an eagle. A true Sun King would use his magic to untie the thongs and let us down to the ground.'

But Garroch only croaked, 'Sun King! I am no Sun King! Only a fool!'

Then Isca felt a great wave of pity run across her flesh and she said, 'My husband, we might still live. Pray to your Earth Mother and I will pray to the Sun. Let us ask for a wanderer to come this way, a shepherd, say, with a knife, who would cut us down.'

Garroch only groaned and then his senses left him again.

Late in the afternoon Vedrix came out to them with two of his henchmen. They rode round the stone and Vedrix struck Garroch's dangling body a time or two with his riding-switch, carelessly, thinking him dead.

Isca heard the thuds and shuddered, for she knew what they were.

'Strike one who is strong enough to bear your malice, little worm,' she sneered, trying to draw Vedrix away from the hoking Garroch.

Vedrix came round to her side of the stone and did as he was told, striking her carefully, cleverly, so as to cause her the most anguish. She smiled down at him as long as she could; but as he persisted, slowly and with rhythm, her smiles became grimaces of pain, and her taunts, sharp gasps, which burst from her against her will.

And when Vedrix had hurt her as much as he chose, he turned from her and said to the two who were with him, 'You saw how this woman humbled me in my youth, my friends. Would you say that I am even with her yet?'

They looked back at him in contempt, but made their mouths smile, for he had suddenly become very strong. 'Yes, Vedrix,' they said. 'She has had enough. Cut her down now, and the world will call you a man of mercy, a great one.'

One of the men already had his knife out and was turning towards the stone. One never knew, he thought, the tables were often turned in such matters, and perhaps one day Isca might help him, she was a King's daughter, after all.

But Vedrix stopped him for a moment and said, 'Let me speak with her first.'

He rode to Isca again and said, 'Your wounds will soon heal, if they are tended, and one day you might even become pleasant to look at once more. I am a forgiving man who has punished you and am now willing to forget the past. I offer you your life, now that you have been humbled. You shall come down and be my slave woman.'

After her latest torments, Isca found it difficult to speak without pain, but still she made herself say, 'I will come down and do whatever you wish, Vedrix. But you must let Garroch go free too. That is my only condition.'

Vedrix smiled and said, 'You are in no state to make conditions, woman. That dog is half dead as it is, freedom would not help him. He shall stay there and you shall come down. I fancy having you, with the stripes still on your flesh!'

The nearest lord clutched at his sword, at this, and seemed almost about to strike Vedrix down. But caution overcame him and he turned away, clenching and unclenching his angry hands.

Isca saw this and her hope died. Then she shook her head and said, 'You were always a coward, Vedrix. No, I would rather hang here than go to your bed, if Garroch is to die. Go and feed your new baby, Vedrix! Feed your father's child!'

The King gave a sharp gasp at this, for she had struck on the one thing that stood between himself and power. He was the slave of that little child, and he knew it well.

He said, 'You bitter bitch!' and struck her again, this time with the weighted end of the riding–whip. Her high scream reached the villagers in the compound, who shook their heads and said, 'That is Vedrix, you can be bound! He will not let a chance escape him now, the little snake. Later, we must draw his little fangs!'

Then Vedrix and the two lords left the stone and rode over the hill to see what lay beyond.

And Garroch shuddered himself upright a little way, so as to breathe, and then said thickly, 'I know now, my love. Forgive me, Isca. I am a fool, as I have said.'

But Isca heard nothing, for the brutality of that last deep stroke had brought the darkness down again on her.

Then, as the twilight came, a heavy shower of rain came with it, drenching them through, waking them for a while with its coldness, running down their faces and into their mouths—the first drink their parched lips had known that long day.

And Isca said, 'It is almost finished, my husband. We shall not hang here much longer. I can feel that my body wishes to be rid of its burden. It does not want to live into another day. Good-bye, my husband. Perhaps when we meet again, I shall have black hair, or you gold.'

And as Garroch struggled to answer her, trying to recall her name, wondering whether it was Rua or Brach, a white-cloaked figure came out of the dusk towards them. Isca's heart leapt, and then she saw who had come, and her head drooped once more.

Gwenna stood below her, the baby in her arms. Her voice was thick and angry in the dark.

'So, you bitch, my sister,' she said, 'you must alway spoil my life with your beauty! But that has left you now, you bitch! There's no beauty about you now!'

Isca said, 'What do you want, you sow?'

Then Gwenna almost shrieked, 'You took Barduca from me. with your witchery! You left his child without its father! And so you have forced the ancient sin on me, causing me to lie with Barduca's son, unknowing. It is your doing, you thing!'

Isca said, 'I am tired, woman. Let me sleep in peace! Go back to your litter in the straw.'

Then Gwenna gasped with fury and almost flung the baby from her, on to the ground, so as not to be encumbered. She reached up towards her sister.

'I have a keen knife here, you witch,' she snarled. 'I will make sure you never use your magic again!'

Gwenna grunted with the effort, again and again. Isca swung sideways violently in the leather thongs, as though trying to avoid the thing that came up out of the darkness. Then, without knowing it, she began to howl, high like a wolf in the moonlight.

And at last when the pains seemed to go suddenly, she said, in a voice that she did not know, 'No more! I am paid, Gwenna! If your baby is to thrive, cut Garroch down now! Do that, at least!'

Then she started to scream again, not knowing why, unable to help it, rhythmically, as the sharp blood thudded inside her like a great drum and her life gushed away into the darkness. At last she was still.

And Garroch came out of his dream to feel hands dragging at him, down, down, hands that brought agony again when he had thought all agony had died in him.

A voice said, below him, 'Yes, sister, I'll cut him down! But he shall never have that which will make a King to challenge mine!'

Then Garroch felt himself pulling upwards, and the breath coming to his chest again, almost as it had always done. He knew everything for an instant. He knew the awful weight of the woman below him.

'Cut! Cut then! And finish it!' he groaned. 'The worm is in my mouth!'

'In a moment,' he heard the voice say, 'I shall find my knife, never fear! I shall soon find it again. Yes, it is by my foot.'

Then suddenly, out of the dark, Garroch felt something icy cold and sharp about his body. That cold turned without warning to burning fire, and then he was aware of a great freedom, as though the weight had been cut away from him, a terrible freedom, a freedom that left part of himself behind in the getting.

And he fell forward on to the hard ground, sobbing and groaning, the sharp air in his chest almost choking him. He heard footsteps running away from him into the darkness, and then he lost himself again.

Some time after that when the dew lay cold on his body the distant cattle lowed, a little sense came back to him. He raised his head and sniffed the air like an animal. It was pain again, but there was danger in the air, he could smell that much.

He got on to his hands and knees, sniffing the night-air for the scent of wood, the forest, then slowly, and often falling, he began to crawl from that place.

'Asa Wolf,' he said. 'Asa Wolf, my brother. I am coming. I am coming to the forests.'

As he crawled, he left a little trail behind him, here and there.

# PART FOUR

---

## Dawn

---

# 33: Barley Dream Ends

NOW THE cold time had passed on, leaving its death behind it, and the sun had come again to warm the land, to drive away the last dark dreams of the peoples.

Across the chalk hills of the south the talking-drums sent their voices, dark folk speaking to dark folk, telling each other that life had stirred in the belly of the Earth once more, telling each other that all Winters must end, even the Winter of the Sun men.

And the birds rose into the air, startled, crying out that it was all about to begin again, the thing which unrolled each year across the land.

And in the forests oak and hornbeam put out their shoots and the thick grass seemed to stretch its arms as though awaking again to feed another generation of the four-footed creatures.

And the creatures stirred and snuffled the free air, in wonder now, for their ancient enemy had gone; men had moved away to let them live out their lives after their own fashion. And the lynx and the badger and the wild cat grunted or snuffled their message to the red deer and the wild boar and even the sleepy bear.

'The old Hunters have gone! They leave only dead scents in their caves, my brothers. They do not think to come back to trouble us! They leave their smell of sorrow behind them; they will not return. Their time is done at last, now that their Chief is dead.'

Far away beyond the great forest that lapped at the feet of the high chalk hill, there was a narrow valley, a quiet place where few feet had ever stepped, a gentle place that knew neither Earth Mother nor Sun Father.

In a narrow cave, sheltered by the thick bushes that grew before its doorway, a woman lay, nursing a baby. Its face was still red and wrinkled, its voice reedy, as though it had not long come into the world. Its hair was black and thick. It was a boy.

The woman smiled down on the child, her face pale and drawn, but lustrous with a strange contentment. Her rough hands and the tattered hides in which she was dressed gave her the aspect of one who had always been near to poverty, to suffering. But now she smiled.

Soon a young girl came to her from outside, her long black

hair plaited about her proud head, a smile on her face that wrinkled up her small aquiline nose. She held out her skirt before her, to show what she carried there.

'Look, look, Rua,' she said excitedly, 'all these eggs! I have not broken one coming up the slope! They are bedded in moss, see! They will help to make milk for the baby.'

The woman nodded and began to caress the small thing that bit angrily at her heavy breast.

'He is a true little Prince, this brother of yours,' she said. 'Look how proudly he drags at the nipple!'

The girl bent over the baby and touched him, very gently. 'I wish I had a baby like that, Rua,' she said. 'It is so warm and little. It would be someone to play with, a tiny one like that.'

The woman smiled sadly and said, 'One day, one day, Brach.'

The girl moved to the doorway of the cave and waited a moment. Then she said, 'I came past Marrag's cairn. The stones are still piled high on it. The wolves have not tumbled them down as we thought they might. He rests safely there after his long journey.'

Rua said gently, 'Marrag was a good man. He was too gentle to be the Old Man. The smell of blood had gone from his knife.'

Then she sighed and said, 'Soon, when the baby is bigger and can stand the journey, we must go back to my folk by the shore. They will have food for us and will want to see their little Chief.'

But Brach said, 'I do not think I shall come, Rua. I am afraid that they will not want us now. They might even kill the baby. Besides, our Barley women are shooting up now strongly, and I must be here to cut the good corn when it is ready. I shall stay, Rua.'

Rua bowed her head and said, 'It is as you say, little daughter. Perhaps they might harm the baby if we went back. Perhaps it is wise to stay here, where there is no one to hurt us any more. Yes, we will stay, Brach.'

Then Brach went to the woman and put her arms about her and said, 'I have never loved anyone as much as you, Rua Fish, except Marrag, and he who was once my father.'

Rua saw the tears in her eyes and patted her gently on the shoulder. 'Do not cry, little Brach,' she said. 'The days that are gone can never come back. Only a fool remembers them. We must think of the day which is here. Let us eat the eggs now and forget that there was ever anyone else to love.'

In the great house on the hill above Craig Dun Gwenna

nursed her baby. It was clothed in fine linen and wore a little golden bracelet about its neck, for it was a King. 'Gwenna fed it with barley bread soaked in warm goat's milk, for her own milk had suddenly dried up after she had run from the Old Woman stone that night, her arms splashed to the elbow.

Beside Gwenna, on a painted wooden stool, sat a great broad-shouldered man, whose long golden beard spread across his chest, almost down to his massive bronze-studded belt. He fingered the mead cup that he held and said heavily, 'They have been talking on the drums all the morning, my wife. These dark ones speak to each other from hilltop to hilltop, telling their secrets. We do not understand them and we are worried.'

Gwenna gave an impatient snort and held out her cup for more honey-ale. A brown-eyed slave woman shuffled forward and filled the Queen's cup, then backed into the shadows, afraid.

Gwenna said, 'What sort of man are you, Arthog, that you do not torture one of the dark workers until he tells you what the drums are saying? I should have thought that would be clear, even to a great dolt like you!'

But though her words were sharp, her lips smiled, for Gwenna loved Arthog. He was a great warrior, a man among men.

He slapped her lightly on the thigh and said, 'I have tried that with many slaves, but they will never tell, whatever one does to them—even the worst things. They say they do not understand the drums themselves. They say that only the great ones understand the drums and that the language they speak is a secret one.'

Gwenna said suddenly, 'Go and bring one of the slaves to me. I will show you how to make him tell what the drums say. I know where the places are, my fat friend!'

But Arthog shook his great head until his plaits swung before his shoulders and then back again, jingling with the metal pins that decorated them so bravely.

'I will not have any more of the slaves hurt beyond the power to work, my Queen,' he said. 'We need them all, for there is much to do soon. We must build the great temple to the Sun before the harvest month, if the corn is to prosper. We have got the blue stones from the west. They lie ready to be erected. The slaves have already dug the outer ditches, and soon, when they have put a little more flesh on their starved bones, we will hoist up the great stones.'

Gwenna said with a little gasp, 'Can you not drag up that stone which the folk here once called the Old Woman, and use it in your temple? I would like it taken far from here, so that I might never see it again.'

Arthog answered, 'You will never see it again, my Queen. Yesterday we lit fires about it until it cracked, and then we rolled it into the flint shaft, to keep down the ghosts of the two Hunters who lie there. My warriors will not dare go near that place until the ghosts are laid, for they rise up and cry out against our people. But now, with the stone on them, and covered with earth, they will lie still.'

Gwenna said, 'That is good, little husband. I fear that some-one did a great wrong in killing those two. From what I have heard, they were two proper men, not like the one who tried to profit by their death.'

Arthog rose and looked out of the window, down the hill. A man sat there, beside a small flock of sheep, a dog beside him and a staff in his hand. He tapped with the stick on the ground from time to time and his head shook, like that of an old man. When the dog barked, he listened and then rose unsteadily and felt about him with the stick, moving clumsily round the flock.

Arthog snorted and then came back to his stool. 'Barduca's bastard son!' he said with contempt. 'He should thank the Sun he has a staff and a dog to lead him, anyway! He deserved much less!'

'What do you deserve, think you!' Gwenna said, suddenly.

Then she put the baby down on the warm sheepskin couch, and the two lay beside it, their arms about each other, beside the warm fire that must never be allowed to go out. Afterwards they slept until the sun began to sink on the other side of the hill.

So that they should not be disturbed, Gwraig, the slave-woman who had once worn a crown in her dreams, had taken the child to her own breast, for her new husband believed in keeping her occupied.

And as the sun fell at last behind the western hills, Brach came running up the little slope to the cave, breathless.

'Rua, O Rua!' she said, 'there is a man coming. I saw him coming out of the wood and wading over the stream, where it is at its shallowest. It is terrible, Rua, for I saw his face! It is Marrag come back!'

Rua stared at her, afraid for a moment, then she said, 'No, it cannot be Marrag. Marrag's cairn lies behind us, away from the little river. Beside, he went in peace and promised that he

would not come back to frighten us. Marrag was a man of his
word. He would never frighten us, for we loved him and
brought him here to pass in peace, in the warm.'

But Brach stood by the door, shuddering. 'He *is* coming
here,' she said. 'He has seen me and he *is* coming here. It *is*
Marrag, Rua Fish! It is his face and white hair. It is a very old
man, it is Marrag! He walks the same, I swear!'

Then she ran back and fell on the floor by Rua, hiding her
face in the folds of Rua's torn gown.

A shadow fell into the little cave and then a man stood looking down at them, the mother with her baby and the frightened
little girl. It was a long time before Rua saw that this was
Garroch, he had so changed. Yet when she recognised him at
last, she smiled, and he smiled back at her, uncertainly, but in
friendship.

And at last Rua said, 'You have come a long journey,
Garroch.'

And the man who had been Garroch nodded and said
hoarsely, 'A long journey, Rua Fish. I have come through the
cold time and the forest. I have died many times in coming,
but at last I have arrived where my dream has led me.'

Brach uncovered her face and turned to look at him. Then
she gave a deep sob and went to him, holding him tight and
weeping all the while.

And Garroch began to weep too, until at last Brach led him
to her own bed, of dried moss and bracken in the dark part of
the cave. And there he lay down and slept, easily, like a child.

And when he was asleep, Rua said, 'Look at his body, Brach.
He has known suffering enough, by all the Gods!'

And Brach nodded and said, 'We have all suffered enough,
my mother. We must pray now that we suffer no more, then
I shall be content, for now I have a father again as well as a
mother.'

And in the morning Garroch came back from walking outside and said, 'There is a broad field of the little barley women
above this house, my daughter. Whose is it? What sacrifice
was made?'

And Brach answered, 'It is ours, my father. I planted it with
my own hands. No sacrifice was made.'

Garroch stared at her unbelieving. 'No sacrifice?' he said.
'No blood? That is not possible, my daughter.'

Brach smiled and turned from him. 'It is only the soil, the
good earth and love; the love of the rain and the sun, that makes

the corn grow my father. Next year you shall plant the seed yourself and see the truth. The corn does not need blood shed over it, Garroch.'

Garroch stared at her, stunned for a while. Then he turned to Rua and said, 'The child at your breast, whose is it, Rua Fish?'

And Rua said, 'Look at its little nose. It is an eagle's beak, like yours. I got him on you at the Corn Dance, my husband. All was not wasted, Corn King!'

Garroch fell before her and took her hands gently and put them to his lips. 'That is good, my woman,' he said. 'That is good. So the Corn King had not lost his power, as he feared. That is good, but now there will be no more children.'

Then at last he turned to Brach and said in a low voice, 'My daughter, it is still a long time to our harvest. I cannot sit with nothing to do, my love. Teach me to turn a pot on a wheel. Teach me to weave osiers, my own.'

And Brach took his thin hand. 'Yes, father,' she said. 'That would be good, my father.'

Then she began to cry, without knowing why.

And so the People of the Hill ended their days of glory, and their houses rotted and their walls decayed. Those of the dark folk who stayed in what remained of Craig Dun did so as slaves, the dogs of their golden-haired masters, to dig stones for them, to drag them over the plain, and, at last, to lie on them, under the obsidian knife, for the glory of the Sun. Earth Mother and Old Man had had their long day and now the cruel Sun had risen above the land to claim it as his own and to drive the hill-folk into the darkness.

The People of the Hill dispersed, no longer one family, but split up into small groups, living as best they could—sometimes in the forgotten caves of the Hunters, or under tumbled cairns of rock; sometimes even in what was left of the long houses that their bright-haired conquerors had tumbled into ruins. They ate roots and slugs, or small birds that could not yet fly; for now they must forget the little green Barley Women and the goat-milk cheeses of their past glorious herds.

And often they starved for lack of snails and berries, and then they remembered the old custom of eating the 'long pig' when harvests had been bad. They used their rude flints on each other's stringy flesh, but got small enjoyment from the strange feast that followed.

Yet it was not always bad. There were the good times of revenge, when they led their blue-eyed usurpers into the choking slime of the marshes, with their torches, always running on ahead between the trees until the horses floundered and the great warriors gasped out, 'The will-o'-the-wisp! We are betrayed!' Then they came out from their shadows and taunted the struggling darlings of the sun, pushing them back into the ooze as they tried to scramble up among the rushes.

And again, sometimes the little dark ones were able to run swiftly into the tent encampments during a drunken feast, and snatch up what they could—bright things of metal, swords and shields, brooches and throat-rings. And these they would take back to their new homes under the hills, to bury them deep there as charms against the sun.

But once as the dark ones entered their secret place, laden with their trophies, the sun had shone through the last fallings of the rain-showers and then a great coloured light had struck down upon them, causing them to cry out in fear.

'Aiee! Look! Look!' they said. 'The Sun has discovered our hiding-place! He has placed the end of his hunting-bow over our cave, so that all will know where we have hidden his treasures!'

Then they ran away, screaming with fear.

Yet no one came to claim their poor things of copper and rude bronze, not for many many years; though the fear remained with the little ones.

Then there were the times when the dark ones wished for their revenge to strike longer into the hearts of their conquerors, expecially in a famine when their brown-eyed babies fell sick and the pale flesh on their bones shrank to nothing.

And they would creep by night into the tents set about the grazing-lands, and take away the strongest Sun-children they could find, leaving behind their wasted transparent moth-frail changelings, to bear witness of their vengeance.

Sometimes, later, when they were prowling about the encampments, unseen in their craft, they would see their own children again, made fat and laughing now by good care, and they would envy the golden-ones their bargain and would wish that the little black-haired child was running with them free over the hills again, free even to starve once more, if the creatures became scarce and the streams dried in the heat of summer.

But there were places where the Sun-men grew kind, as time went on and their flocks flourished. It was towards such settlements that the dark ones moved when they were hungry. And by night they would come down to the tents, sniffing like wild cats, to find what had been left out for them—a bowl of broken barley bread, a dish of skimmed milk, a partly-gnawed beef-bone. And there, between the tents they would make their little feast, starting, quick as ferrets, if a strange sound came to their ears, a scent to their noses.

And always before they left, the dark ones in their pride would perform what tasks had been set them by their ironical overlords—the splicing of an unravelled hide-rope, the re-shafting of a broken axe. Then, laying the rope or the axe before the door of the tent, they would run back to their safe darkness, already cursing the strong ones who had thrust them from the land, already forgetting the kind milk that was scarcely dry upon their thin lips.

For malice stalked the hills and plains, and was spoken across the forests by night from the skin of a drum.

But Garroch did not know of this. The fires of his heart and flesh were quenched; he was contented with his family, his own little field of barley, got without blood at last.

## THE END

he notes that follow were written by Henry Treece at various mes over a fortnight as the basis for a lecture which he gave at 1e Regional College of Art, Hull, on June 1, 1966, about a week efore his death. Together they represent the last and probably 1e fullest personal account of his philosophy as a novelist.

Treece was a very careful writer, who dated every scrap of .anuscript. By no means all the passages that he wrote for his cture were actually incorporated in the script he took with him Hull and from which he delivered that lecture. Antony Kamm as selected in their entirety passages from the notes and from 1e lecture which seem to be particularly relevant to this mono-aph, and they are presented here, from Treece's own manu-cript, in the order in which they occurred to him and in which 1ey were written down.

# Notes on Perception and Vision

## BY HENRY TREECE

**1AY 17, 1966**

o explain perception in writing is to attempt the ineffable. ne's vision is more than the words on the page, more even 1an the images described. One's writing sometimes exists 1 its own right, apart from the print, even apart from the nages and characters and speech. One can close the eyes nd *sense it*—not as words and pictures, but as a unity in the 1ind, with kinetic quality and mass. A scene from a book, ven a whole book, can be so felt in the mind, as though it had 1ctile and sonic qualities. As though it were rough as granite, r smooth as a pebble; loud as a drum or soft as an insect 1oving across a leaf.

Only when I get this three-dimensional feeling coming off piece of writing do I feel that I have truly created, brought 1to being what had not been there before, (or rediscovered omething that had been there once, but had got itself hidden).

The act of writing a novel is, for me, the slow, and lonely, nd infinitely tiring process of finding how to make magic appen. One can learn it up to a point but, once this learning eaches a certain stage one becomes automatic, a conjuror, nd the thing one creates lacks organic life. It lies stark on 1e page, has no warmth, no dimension, no capability of moving 1e, when I think about it again.

If writing creatively were simply a matter of acquiring an enormous vocabulary, and of learning grammar, syntax and the parts of speech, any intelligent person, with time to spare, could become a writer—a poet or a novelist.

To be, say, a critic, requires that one should be a grammarian, a scientist, a mathematician. But to be the writer of a novel requires one to have perhaps another set of qualities —or the same qualities in other admixtures—and certainly to have an extra sense *beyond* and out in space, in orbit, perhaps never coming fully to rest.

For certain sorts of writing are out in orbit monstrous, in the sense that one must be obsessed beyond normality even to set the words and the concepts on to the page. One must be dedicated, called, driven, by one's peculiar god, by the creation of one's curious magic. But this art is not entirely conscious, nor is the language in which it is expressed. The driven creator goes into action almost like a man under drugs or hypnosis, using words as they present themselves to give form to the world that is revealing itself to his inner-eye. Later, in cold blood, if he has learned his trade through the earlier stages of linguistic competence, he will find that the words, in the main, came to him right. The right words: the right sentences: the right paragraphs.

What then is this *monstrous quality* that has such power to drive the writer into his act of creation? What is *the force* which makes him sit down before five hundred virgin sheets of paper, knowing that once he has started, and this white anonymous mass has stirred into life, he must live with the growing incubus for perhaps two years?

Obviously, he is telling a story of some sort, and this will sustain him, will hold his mind together: obviously in his book there will be people who talk and perform characteristic actions. These too will help to keep the novelist going—he may even get his amusement, his personal and private kicks, out of letting these people look and talk and act outrageously. From such mechanisms, the novelist may gain relief in the bearing of his ·load.

But if a novel were only a story and a group of variously interesting people, acting entertainingly—*that would hardly be enough,* even though the narrative and its human units conveyed in the end a message, a moral, a philosophic answer to some dilemma posed by the book's theme. Such a book would hardly compensate the author, in the deepest sense, for the deprivations he had suffered in giving up two years of his life bringing it into being.

What then is the monstrous force that drives him forward, compensates him—and exhausts him at the same time? What is this frightful orgasm to which he submits, again and again, hating its requirements, but unable to reject them?

I see the creative writer on two levels at least. In one of his functions he is the crippled god—the maker who in his non-literary life is, or feels himself to be, somehow incomplete, inadequate. Yet, being a creator, he has pride, and a stubborn (if despairing) courage: so, he writes for himself a world in which the blind man sees all, and the cripple leaps over mountains.

On another more important of his levels, the creative writer is not the lame god, but the integrated observant man, man using all his senses and his sense, to understand and to set down archetypal patterns. Now this man will have only one essential tale to tell: and it will be the story of the seasons in their progression through the year—from the Sun's first awakening after Winter, to the burning of the stubble after the harvest. His vision will be directed to this ritual—dance of the months, the crops, the heroes; to their coming, their fruition and their death.

It is a primitive pattern, but it contains everything—the gentle colours of primroses and the sound of roaring thunder. It is a pattern over which a greater god (or goddess) than the writer, presides, and is acknowledged by him: and once this writer—who is the messenger of the god—has perceived this pattern, has surrendered himself to this vision—then he will know, without doubt, that all years are one year, all pleasures one pleasure, all disasters trivial, and all heroes expendable.

## MAY 17, 1966

It is next to impossible for the writer to see an object objectively—that is, showing it for what it is to the camera-eye and for nothing else. A writer must use words and these words attract themselves to his mind and hand because of his part personality. When he uses them, he expresses his personality perforce. He sees a white stone column in the desert: if he says that, that is as far as he dare go towards an absolute.

If he says that the colour or material or shape of the column reminds him of anything, so much does he depart from the column and reveal himself.

Now the nature of creative man is to invest each object seen with his full sense of it, his perception, his impression, his vision. And the more the writer allows his sensing mechanism to work, the less column we get and the more autobiography.

So, in the end, the writer with the richest and most diverse senses (and the least control on his surgical knife) will not expose that column, but will hide it. Not recreate it, but destroy it. That is the dilemma, the dichotomy, as I see it.

Perception is essential if writing is to have bite, freshness, individuality: yet, as the balance sinks under the cumulative comparisons, likenesses, relationships to the allied world of that column, so does perception smother itself.

Or, to put it another way: perceptions must be so inhibited, if the column is to emerge as anything like a column, that almost before he starts work the writer must prepare himself to put on blinkers. That is, as his pen touches the paper, he must already be prepared to withdraw (if he is to write of the column and not of himself-as-column). Consequently, the original first-sight glimpse of that column, the innocent view, is only remotely likely to come through since, close behind this view, is a secondary one which must be limited and even withdrawn to give the column a chance to declare itself: and awareness of what is already in store may tend to throw forward the writer's self-known necessity to prune, so that even the first words come under the knife.

MAY 18, 1966

Perception is the act, or state, of knowing the nature of anything through the senses, but in such a deep, sensitive, sympathetic way that this thing takes on an extra dimension and becomes for a while at least more than it had been before.

When the writer is so attuned that he can relate a number of such supra-things into a cosmology, or imaginative system, so as to form an entire and self-sufficient environment for his writing —that is his vision. But it is more than mere dream and imagination: it is such a co-ordinated pattern that, once it is explained, other human creatures can also move in it, if they too are in tune. Or, if they cannot actually share it, they can respect it as being valid for someone whose processes are not of their own sort. Sometimes the writer, catering for this divergence, writes closely alongside the thing so as to share it with others, perceiving the inner nature of the thing now in a related but more generalised term, and this we call a symbol. This, too, is his vision.

MAY 20, 1966

There is another point I would like to grope towards: it is this, that perception and vision in a writer—a prose-writer at least—do not operate 24 hours a day. For much of the day they are switched-off, and the writer is a very ordinary moron, moving about rather blindly, unaware of significances, just another animal eating and drinking and enjoying the sun—when there is any.

But there are times in that careless day when his perceptions suddenly go into action and his total vision accrues something more towards its completeness. These times are when the outside touches the writer's basic and personal theme—that central thesis of his life which makes him slightly different from other writers. I think that every writer, at some time or other in his evolution towards maturity, finds himself a thesis or theme (or has it found for him by outside circumstances). Often, he is not conscious of this and realises it, or wakes up to it, only a long time after it has been in operation in his work. Then he suddenly understands that he has been writing one book, all the time. Or has been rehearsing various versions of one book, unconsciously directed towards a perfection of his statement.

I was first made dimly aware of this about twenty-five years ago when, in an article in *Horizon,* Stephen Spender, writing about an exhibition of the work of Cecil Collins, the painter, said: 'Like Treece, Collins is obsessed by the concept of the Sacred Fool.'

Looking back, I think he was right at that time—though one's hard-core theme twists and turns and takes on accretions as the years go on. And, only very recently, I became sharply aware that for the past fifteen years or so the two principal themes in my writing had been the Father seeking the Son (or the Son the Father) *and* the theme of the Distracted Woman, the woman drawn away from gentleness and mercy into other, perhaps more sinister paths; the Maenad, the Bacchante.

I do not know (and do not wish to enquire) why these themes should now lie at the deep heart of my work. But what I do know is that my perceptions of the outer world, and the cohesion of those perceptions in my head (which form my vision and life) are directed towards developing and making clear in words—where one can ever clear—these two obsessive and compulsive themes.

Out of one's struggle to set down such themes grows one's personal manner of writing—one's *style* as it is called. Buffon

said, 'Le style, c'est l'homme même.' Style is the man himself—
that is, the man trying to record his struggle to make clear his
essential and obsessive theme, the theory which makes him tick.

Yet there is a strong case for believing that the writer out-
grows his own style as his vision develops. Looking back, the
writer is dissatisfied with what he said, not because it was bad
*in its day*, but because if he did it now, he would do it differently
—because his perception has developed and the old words no
longer represent his present development or change.

The writer is probably fighting a losing battle all his life, for
his perception is perhaps always one jump ahead of his technique,
his ability to set down the inner turmoil and its resolution.

## MAY 26, 1966

There are some things that a writer senses or observes objectively
—that is, as objects outside himself, and equally available to
all, and having a roughly equal shape, dimension and nature for
all.

There are other things that a writer senses subjectively. That
is, as an extension of himself, he being the subject. It is as though
he takes such things within himself as part of his own organic
functioning. When later he externalises his subjectively-perceived
images, it is possible that others may not recognise the original
object of sensing, since their own perceptions may be of a
different sort or quality, the parallels they draw of a different
dimension.

In effect I am saying that the subjective writer is much like
the oyster which takes in the irritant grain of sand and round it,
for his own reasons and in his own dark and special ways,
coats this sharp grain and converts it to a pearl, of whatever
size, quality and colour.

If a writer says: 'A poorly-dressed old man came in and sat,
half-blind, at the oak table near the fire. After a time he began
to scratch at the table top.'—this is objective writing. But writing
subjectively, he might say: 'He stumbled in from outside, from
nowhere, crook-backed as a hawthorn on which dirty scraps of
rag fluttered, blown by a long-dead wind. Like a moving tree
seeking companionship of other wood, he sat at the oak table.
The dry thorns of his fingers travelled across the golden grain,
envying its smoothness, its youth—its prosperity, trying to
wound it. Withered thorn against young oak. "Take care," said
the fingers, "be you not proud. The little fire that purrs in its
iron cage will eat us both in time. Then, of our mingled ashes,

who shall say: this was an oak tree, this was a thorn?" '

I am not trying to say that the second is better than the first —or that either is good: I am pointing out a difference in the two statements. What the first writer says would be observed by all who saw the old man come into the room. What the second writer says has an extra dimension which depends on the writer having recognised a similarity between the old man and a thorn-tree. All that follows, after this initial recognition, this simile or parallel, leans towards an almost mythic moral—that we must all die and be equal in death.

This is the *vision* which grows out of the writer's *perception* of the old man. It may not be true for anyone else who sees the old man, but it is valid for the writer: it is a part of the cosmos, the regulated complex of impressions which goes to make his world different from that of the man standing next to him.

Or, to put it another way a number of writers, seeing the old man come in, might each be struck by his similarity to a thorn-tree—but having done that, each would develop this recognition differently, according to his own personal temperament, experience, background: each would create his own myth, his own ultimate vision of the subjective world of which the old man had become a part.

## MAY 28, 1966

Sometimes I feel the need to put sunlight, and dried earth or sand, or vegetation, or salt water into my books because I often write about Greece and the Mediterranean. I feel the need for these elements not merely as background to the human characters, but almost as characters themselves. Often the scene seems to induce action or thought or feeling in the people of that scene.

As a writer of this sort of thing I tend to push my perception to its limits. I not only want to feel the sun's heat but to smell it—to smell what it does to rocks and flowers and water. Just as I feel the need to *see* heat coming off a rock or a man's face or a girl's hair.

This is not the surrealist dislocation of the senses: it is something deep at the core of a tradition. Sometimes I get so carried away by this that I go into a sort of trance of absorption in which I am *part* of the scene, the sun on rock, the rock suffering sun or frost, the leaf suffering rain, the boughs in the wind, and the wind itself. Sometimes my prose *is* the wind beating at boughs, or blowing blind over empty spaces.

When my writing turns into this, it does not, can not, tell a story; cannot push the narrative or characterisation on; it is just itself then. It *says* nothing, it just *is*.

Often editors—and especially American editors—try to cut these bits out, and sometimes they succeed if I am too tired to fight them. But I would rather have them in—because such fugal passages, such flights, occur only too rarely in a story—and more rarely still as one grows older.

They are not flights of unfundamental lyricism, not *pure* poetry: they are part of the organic movement of the piece, of the story: without them the story loses a dimension, a limit, is partly emasculated.

To an objective editor these passages seem to have no relevance: to a writer who *feels* with his body as well as his emotions (and even with his mind, his intelligence), they are essential—in that they are the *essence*, the Being, of what he feels he needs to put down at that sparking-off point of his book.

Such writing is not cerebral, not easy, not dependent on sheer thought. It comes from low down out of the pit of the stomach and the pit of life's experience. And when it comes, the writer *knows* he has to put it down, or he is being false to his book, to his being, to his talent. This is the deep part of his creation, his fusion of perceptions: this is what his vision *is*. This is what makes him tick, what his story is about, and what he is about.

Any trained literate can write a story, a novel of sheer action: but to achieve more than that needs the writer to be a poet, a recording sensitive, willing to be obedient, to put himself into the condition of the static stone, or the sea shore pebble, and to let the sun's heat and the salt tide's fury play on him—even destroy him.

In medicine there is what is called a Sympathetic Pain, or a Referred Pain. I mention this because it is in line with my own psycho-physical concept of perception in writing.

If you have a Sympathetic or Referred Pain, it means that the limb, or the tooth, in which you feel the pain is not the one which is suffering dis-ease (or disease), but that it is twanging in sympathy to that one; or is receiving pain *referred*, or sent on, by that one.

It is my contention that this 'formula' applies to all we do, in that elevated column we call our body. That a pain in my right arm might be referred from my left leg or that if I run a thorn

to my little finger I shall feel the pain in my neck. Or that if I
see the sun, I may *smell* Seville oranges.

I see the column which we call our body as being an intricate
computer—like a complex which no one—not even Freud, Jung
or Ernest Jones—has been able to chart and to make a blueprint
of.

When we talk of a writer's *perceptions,* we are up against this
complex, this unexplored labyrinth (with no Ariadne to give us
a ball of wool to find the way out): we are in it *alone:* for
writing is *the* loneliest trade, and will permit no observer in its
operation.

The writer who is *in-key* with his complex (though without
being able to communicate what this in-keyness *is*) will suffer
and enjoy, and tolerate) certain Sympathies between his senses,
certain Referred Pains: so that he may at last perceive the scent
of blue, the touch of sound, and the taste of music.

The sympathies, or *pains,* of each sense will be referred to the
other senses. But to the reader who is not a writer, is not in
some degree alive to this complexity; the reader who judges
everything by its rational content, its ability to make instant
read-meaning this reader will say that the writer has abused the
truth, has not made sense.

Of course, I too believe that certain writers do not make
sense: but I have been in the trade long enough to tell myself,
at least, *why* they do not make sense. Broadly speaking, if they
are honest craftsmen and creators, the two reasons are these:

(a) Words got the better of them—honest as the writers were.

(b) The writers used words because, like typewriting apes,
they had learned how to put them down, but not how to *feel*
them.

As a student, I was most impressed when a lecturer told me
that three chimpanzees, typing for a million years, would end
up (by the law of averages, or permutations and combinations)
with writing *Hamlet.* Or it may have been *King Lear,* I forget
which. And I am not greatly bothered which. Psychological-
statisticians can prove anything—like the Chancellor can prove
that the cost of living has gone up by one per cent.

It is not the artist's function *to prove:* but *to create.* And,
even if those poor apes *did* write Hamlet, they would not have
created it. They would merely have (by some mathematical
chance) *reproduced* it. If they had done that, as it were mech-
anically, one important factor would have been lacking: they
would not have *felt* what they wrote, or have *perceived* what

they wrote. To me, it is fundamental that the writer should have *feeling* about the thing he writes. He should suffer, experience and be aware of the forces that move him, and not be like one of those ancient Aeolian harps that hung on the antique mountains, vibrated by the breezes, and never hearing the music they themselves made.

I never thought to ask my lecturer about this when he first fed me the monkey-gimmick. But I would now: because it has long been an Article of Faith with me that the creative writer is born to awareness (if only partial) and to suffering (sometimes *in extremis*) just as the sparks fly upwards.

# SAVOY BOOKS LTD

279 Deansgate,
Manchester M3 4EW
England

All prices subject to alteration

# Other Henry Treece Titles
## from Savoy Books

### THE GOLDEN STRANGERS
(125mm x 193mm)

Set at a vital cross-roads in history, this
is the story of a young prince of the
dawn world — Garroch — who tries to
repel the invasion of Britain by the
Golden Strangers. It shows the triumph
of the fair-haired nomads of the north
with their savage sun-worship, over the
small dark Neolithic men of the South
— the Iberians.

224pp. £1.25 Paperback
ISBN 0 86130 018 1

## THE DARK ISLAND
(125mm x 193mm)

A further novel of Britain set during the
Roman invasion before Christianity has
asserted itself, and when the island is
torn and divided by successive raiders
from abroad. The time is ripe for
warriors and kings to prove their
heroism, and, as usual, this book is
written as though by an eye-witness of
the times, vividly evoking bye-gone
characters and settings, and told with a
narrative force and a language that is
both typically rich and masterful.

240pp £1.25 Paperback
ISBN 0 86130 021 1

## RED QUEEN, WHITE QUEEN
(125mm x 193mm)

RED QUEEN, WHITE QUEEN is set
before the collapse of Rome: Queen
Boadicea rises against the might of the
Imperial Legions to become the true,
if brief Queen of the British people. It
is a rebellion so bloody and brutal that
Rome itself is shaken, fearing the
complete overthrow of its empire by a
rash of uprisings.

£1.25 Paperback
ISBN 0 86130 020 3

# Harlan Ellison from Savoy Books

## THE GLASS TEAT
(210mm x 148mm)

THE GLASS TEAT is the first volume of Harlan Ellison's powerful television criticism. First published as a series of outspoken columns for the Los Angeles Free Press this book and its companion volume THE OTHER GLASS TEAT form a record of three years of fiery tv monitoring. But Ellison isn't content to remain *inside* the tube: tv is about the world we live in, and so is THE GLASS TEAT. His intimacy with every aspect of tv production, his strong personal response to subjects which concern him and his encompassing vision make this book entertainment and criticism of the highest order.

**224pp. £1.25. Paperback.**   ISBN 0 86130 004 1.

## PHOENIX WITHOUT ASHES
(With Edward Bryant)
A novel of the Starlost
(210mm x 148mm)

Eight centuries in mankind's future a great ark has been constructed to ferry earth's cultures to a distant star system. After several generations have elapsed an accident occurs which causes the colossal ship to alter course — and plunge towards destruction. This fine and compelling adaptation of Ellison's award-winning television script — with its optimistic ending — is treated to Savoy's arresting new "laser light" cover design.

**128pp. £1.25. Videoback.**   ISBN 0 86130 003 3.

# Jack Trevor Story from Savoy Books

## LIVE NOW, PAY LATER
(193mm x 125mm)

In the first book of the famous Albert Argyle trilogy the ace conman of the sixties and prince Tally-boy of Jack Trevor Story's provincial town catches the housewives and the reader fast in the grip of Hire Purchase, devious politics and easy payments.  144pp

£1.25 Paperback  ISBN 0 86130 029 7
£4.95 Hard Case  ISBN 0 86130 030 0

## SOMETHING FOR NOTHING
(193mm x 125mm)

The market seems to be dropping out of Hire Purchase and so Albert Argyle switches to Trading Stamps. Never without a woman, superbly, raffishly, entertainingly ruthless. But you can't get something for nothing.  176pp

£1.25 Paperback  ISBN 0 86130 031 9
£4.95 Hard Case  ISBN 0 86130 032 7

## THE URBAN DISTRICT LOVER
(193mm x 125mm)

Jack Trevor Story takes his character to meet his maker in a hilarious, incisive last book written with superb observation, sympathy and wit.  192pp

£1.25 Paperback  ISBN 0 86130 033 5
£4.95 Hard Case  ISBN 0 86130 034 3

## THE TROUBLE WITH HARRY
The classic novel filmed by Alfred Hitchcock
(125mm x 193mm)

Who's Harry?
Harry's a menace from the moment he
turns up on the Heath. For one long
hot, maddening day he invades the lives
of the inhabitants of the Sparrowswick
Bungalow Estate, terrifying young Abie,
puzzling the Captain, menacing Miss
Gravely the spinster . . .
No-one knows what to do with him.
THE TROUBLE WITH HARRY is he's
an embarrassment. The trouble with
Harry is he's dead.

£1.25 Paperback
ISBN 0 86130 035 1

## JACK ON THE BOX
(125mm x 193mm)

Jack Trevor Story, writer, eccentric and
star of his own television series, JACK
ON THE BOX, is renowned for his
idiosyncratic approach to life, his hatred
of bureaucracy and his unflagging
rejection of the obvious. In this volume
of short pieces he lures the reader into
his own eclectic and highly personal
universe, centred somewhere on the
edge of Hampstead Heath, some time in
the 1970's, and presided over by the
lovely Maggie (and her ghost). Why is
Jack falling into the river, fully clothed?
Who is Kaiser Konrad and why did he
announce his own death by telegram?
Will Maggie ever return from Belgium?
JACK ON THE BOX is fully illustrated
with photographs from the ATV series,
and is the first in Savoy's ten-book-
package-launch of Jack Trevor Story's
most famous and best-loved novels.
160pp plus 4pp art inserts. £1.25 Paperback. ISBN 0 86130 025 4

# Michael Moorcock from Savoy Books

## THE RUSSIAN INTELLIGENCE
(193mm x 125mm)

Michael Moorcock's hilarious comic detective thriller sequel to *The Chinese Agent* continues with the further half-cocked investigations of super sleuth Jerry Cornell. Cornell follows the mysterious clue given to him by "The Devil Rider", a vengeful character from one of Wayflete's comic strips, and quickly finds himself in the thick of espionage at a quiet Soviet ambassadorial residence in Notting Hill Gate. But he is more concerned about the "Tail" that has been put on him — by his wife. A new novel from the pen of Britain's best imaginative writer, introduced by novelist Jack Trevor Story.

160pp £1.25. Paperback.  ISBN 0 86130 027 0

## THE GOLDEN BARGE
210mm x 148mm)

Pursuing an impossible goal and hounded by dark dreams which drive him to cold-hearted murder, Jephraim Tallow seeks the meaning of life in a wild and intense world. Moorcock's first anti-hero predates the creation of the world-famous Elric of Melniboné by 2 months in a classic novel that combines the elements of symbolism and fantasy as masterfully as Peake or T. H. White. The high quality, 3-D Video-back" packaging of this very first Michael Moorcock novel follows Savoy's trendsetting design for PHOENIX WITHOUT ASHES by Harlan Ellison.

24pp. £1.25. Videoback.  ISBN 0 86130 002 5

## SOJAN
(125mm x 193mm)

Moorcock's first Sword & Sorcery hero now in print for the first time in 20 years, with superb new illustrations by leading fantasy artist James Cawthorn.

**160pp. £0.80 Paperback.
ISBN 0 86130 000 9.**

## STORMBRINGER
Adapted by James Cawthorn
(427mm x 305mm)

Brilliantly drawn in powerful black and white, this very large format illustrated version of Moorcock's famous fantasy novel tells how Elric, last Emperor of Melniboné, battled with the hordes of Chaos, summoning the Lords of Law to fight for Earth.

**30pp. £1.00 Paperback.
ISBN 0 7045 0226 7.**

## JEWEL IN THE SKULL
Adapted by James Cawthorn
(335mm x 244mm)

Containing Cawthorn's finest artwork, this is the first story in the famous Dorian Hawkmoon series, and tells of the warrior-duke's fight to save himself from the power of the Black Jewel.

**80pp. £2.95. Paperback
ISBN 0 86130 0068.**

# Langdon Jones from Savoy Books

## THE EYE OF THE LENS
(125mm x 193mm)

A fantastic journey through Time and Mind by one of this country's masters of speculative fiction. "The great clock" is a time-terror trip reminiscent of Poe's tale of the pendulum. "The time machine" destroys the boundaries of time as it moves its protagonists from prison, to an intense love affair, to a warped realisation of freedom. "The garden of delights" is a mingling of memory, explicit sexual love, reality and fantasy.

176pp. £1.25. Paperback.  ISBN 0 86130 022 X

## DAVID BRITTON & MICHAEL BUTTERWORTH (Eds)
## THE SAVOY BOOK
(125mm x 193mm)         Autumn 1978

A superior collection of stories and artwork from the fabulous worlds of science fiction and fantasy: Harlan Ellison, the winner of more science fiction awards than any other writer in history with his latest and best story, the prequel to "A Boy And His Dog"; leading English SF writer Brian W Aldiss and Sword & Sorcery master M. John Harrison; legendary rock star Jimi Hendrix, who conducts a wild interview from Rock n' Rolls' heaven with Lester Bangs; Paul Buck, Paul Ableman, J. Jeff Jones, Heathcote Williams, Richard Kostelanetz, Charles Partington and Jim Leon.

144pp. £0.95. Paperback.  ISBN 0 86130 001 7.

# Mike Harding from Savoy Books

## UP THE BOO AYE, SHOOTING POOKAKIES
(125mm x 193mm)

Illustrated in colour and black and
white by Roger McPhail.

Paperback £1.95.
ISBN 0 86130 039 4